FIGHTING GRAVITY

LEAH PETERSEN

FIGHTING GRAVITY

LEAH PETERSEN

DRAGON
MOON
PRESS

Acknowledgments

Writing a book ended up being harder than I thought. Many thanks to all the writers and readers who encouraged me along the way, and showed me how to make something of the pile of words I'd strung together. These include but are not limited to: Rachel, Pete, Moses, Roberto, Robert, Liz, Catherine, Joline, Missy, Nichole, Jessica, Jaimie, Brad, and a mean-spirited, sarcastic, unhelpful, and counterproductive group of bored and unhappy women. Also J.M. Frey who swooped in at the last minute and made sure I tortured Jake enough.

Special thanks go to the sadist who insists I write my best every time. Richard, all those insults were my way of telling you that I couldn't have done it without you.

And I will forever be grateful to Gabrielle for *getting* my guys and loving them as much as I do. Oh, and for being a really amazing editor, too. This book wouldn't be what it is if not for her, and I can't even begin to express how grateful I am that my journey in this industry started with her as my guide.

Dedication

For, Shane, who said "why don't you just write it?" and
for Bren and Aria, who want to be writers now because
"all you have to do is write and make money."

I was eight years old when they came for me.

I opened the door to them myself. In the hall were two men in a kind of uniform I'd never seen before. The cloth was heavy, whole, and clean. Never-been-worn clean. I think that's what scared me. I'd never seen clothes like that in my life.

"I'm Director Kagawa from the Imperial Intellectual Complex," one of the men said. "Is this the Dawes residence?"

My mouth fell open. I almost laughed, but there was something about the way he looked—the way his nose was wrinkling in slow, measured increments, and the way he seemed to be cringing away from the growing crowd of spectators—that made my hands clench into fists.

"Yeah," I answered.

"And you are Jacob Dawes?" He looked as if he might be sick.

"Yup."

"There must be some kind of mistake," he said, the wrinkles in his brow sagging in relief. "What is your citizen number, young man?"

"J174966523ES."

The other man flicked his thumb over a palm-tablet and the display blinked into view in the air above it, large enough for both men to examine at the same time. I didn't care anymore what they were there for. It was the most fantastic thing I'd ever seen.

The hopeful look on the director's face dissolved. He was starting to look green again.

My mother emerged from our only bedroom, where she'd

been patching up my sister Carrie after another playground fight. Ma's hair was lopsided, as if she'd started to cut it but forgot to finish. Her dress was faded and worn in all the expected places, and wrinkled too. It was too big, and maybe it always had been. All of our clothes were cast-offs; we couldn't exactly be choosy. We didn't always eat so well, either. And I knew that Ma went without more often than we did.

She stood there, staring at the director, her face slack and blank. He cleared his throat.

"You must know why I am here," he said to me. "Get your things. There are others waiting below."

I knew exactly what the Imperial Intellectual Complex was— though I was probably the only one for miles around who'd even heard of it—but what anyone from the Empire's own center for intellectual and scientific advancement was doing in my neighborhood, I couldn't even guess. The IIC wasn't a place for unclass kids like me. Most of the people in Abenez, our infamous slum in the human-landfill that was Mexico City, were lucky if they knew how to read.

"Get what things? Waiting for what?"

"Did you not get the notification?"

I shrugged. "No vid."

His eyebrows hit his hairline, a feat I found rather impressive. He was quiet for a moment, no doubt considering this fascinating case study of poverty.

"Mr. Dawes, you have been chosen in this Selection for the Imperial Intellectual Complex. You should be very proud of such an honor." His tone made it clear that one such as me should be particularly honored. "Your notification was sent weeks ago so that you would be ready to depart today."

The director's eyes cast about, as if there was an answer to this unfathomable situation painted somewhere on the apartment's grimy walls.

I couldn't breathe for a minute. The realization of what he'd said washed over me with the most incredible feeling of rightness;

and was dragged away in the receding tide of the next realization: I was abandoning my mother and sister.

At least my father had been taken for Resettlement two years past, so I didn't have to worry about what he'd do to them without me there to look out for them. Still, it wasn't much of a comfort. Acid-guilt and fear churned in my gut.

Then, so suddenly that I jumped, my mother screeched and flew at the director, claws extended like a maddened bird of prey. Her fingernails carving bloody runnels into his cheeks.

He yelped like a stepped-on dog, threw up his arms to protect his face, backing into the watching crowd outside. The wall of people absorbed the impact with barely a ripple, pushing him back into the apartment, and went back to watching. Like a herd of cows, curious but unconcerned.

I had been frozen in shock, but I rushed over and grabbed her. "Ma! Ma! Please! Ma, calm down! Ma!"

It made no difference. A few of her wild, indiscriminate blows landed on my face and shoulders. I fought to hold down her arms every time I caught one, but it barely slowed her. We struggled, the three of us; the director whimpering, trying to bat away her vicious attacks, and me wrestling with my mother's anger and fear-strengthened hysteria.

After forever, there was a flash of blue in my peripheral vision. A hand clamped down on my shoulder and shoved me aside. The policeman grabbed my mother's arms and jerked her so hard her neck snapped back and then forward again, and her teeth bit into her lip. She blinked in shock and was quiet for one stunned moment while blood welled in the cut. And then, shrieking, she went for the policeman with fingernails and flailing feet.

His backhanded blow made a sickening crack against her cheek. She crumpled to the floor like a dropped rag doll.

Fury rushed through me, a ringing in my ears, a necessity in my arms. I drove my fist into his kidney. My father's boot had taught me the sensitivity of that particular spot. The man staggered back with an *uphm*. He cursed and I was grabbed from behind by his partner. I struggled, but when his arms tightened around me, I quieted. I've never been stupid. I've never confused an unwillingness to be defeated with bravery.

Ma whimpered, but didn't move.

The policeman I'd punched looked at the director—a long, appraising look. "So, what's the story here?"

He sniffed. "I'm Director Kagawa of the Imperial Intellectual Complex. As a representative of His Excellence himself, I've come to collect this child. He has claimed the boy to do great things for our Empire."

The policeman looked at me like I'd just tried to explain particle physics to him.

"Huh. OK. Well, you should go on and get out of here. You're drawing a crowd down in the street, too."

"Is there not some judicial action necessary now? This young man has struck a peace officer."

The policeman holding me chuckled, and the other snorted. "Nah. He's all yours. What with the emperor claiming him and all."

Director Kagawa glowered.

I jerked my arms out of the policeman's grip and knelt beside my mother. Her eyes were closed, but she was breathing. Damp hair clung to her face and I tucked it behind her ear. "Ma?" She didn't answer. She could have been asleep.

"Get your things, then." The director threw a look at the growing audience in the hall. "We have a schedule to keep."

Swallowing on nausea and a growing feeling of loss, I stood. "I'm ready."

Not that I had any choice in the matter. Selection was Selection. The Empire had claimed me and that was not to be questioned.

But more important than that, I belonged there. I'd always known I was different. A kid in our neighborhood didn't spend what little free time he had in a library booth reading texts too advanced for the eight-year-olds or even the eighteen-year-olds of the world. He didn't spend the mindless vacuum of the school hours daydreaming in equations, or see the secrets of the universe where other kids saw bump-tag, or boomerball, or yard work for grocery money. I wanted to go, much more than I felt obligated to stay. And I hated myself for that.

"Very well, then," he said, laying a heavy hand on my shoulder and steering me toward the door.

"Wait," I said. "My sister." I cast a look over my shoulder.

She'd come out of the bedroom and was watching me with wide eyes, her thumb in her mouth.

The director either didn't hear me or didn't care. He pushed me out the door and I only caught that one last sight of Carrie; small, quiet, and abandoned.

The transport was the biggest I'd ever seen. It reminded me of pictures I'd seen of rail trains—long, sleek, and shiny—and it was much too big to travel on the old-fashioned streets in our ancient neighborhood. It had to have hover technology.

The buildings on my block—always dirty, even in the rain— slumped around the gleaming vehicle like muddied children in the face of parental displeasure. With their washed out colors, indistinguishable from one to the next, they seemed to cower away from the shining hovercraft. Everything and everyone was subdued, deferential.

It was pristine and bare, except for the IIC's symbol on the large doors—a galaxy cupped in a great hand. The colors were fresh and impossibly vivid. I stopped in the middle of the street, shocked and intimidated. I'd never seen a hover vehicle and in moments my fear turned to fascination. My mind was too busy considering the workings of the anti-gravs to remind my feet to move.

Director Kagawa stopped just outside the door of the transport and, with an impatient huff, gestured for me to get inside. I hurried forward.

I cast a look back at my home, behind me now. I'd never realized how pathetic Abenez looked, but now I hated it. My last look at the place of my origins was blurred by tears of shame and relief.

I followed the director down a short corridor. He stopped outside a set of double doors, as if steeling himself, and then opened them. I followed him into a large lounge.

A dozen or so children were already there, though there were enough couches and plush armchairs in groupings around the room to accommodate at least twice that number. The far wall was mostly one large window. Even though I already knew that Selection happened once every five years and only considered children between eight and twelve, I would have guessed one of the girls was older than that. One looked younger, too, though I doubted she was.

They were an interesting sight, even though I was under their collective scrutiny. Each of them wore what looked like new and uncomfortable clothes—some version of a jacket and tie on the boys and dresses on the girls, their hair pulled up or slicked back or styled. The entire tableau spoke of wealth and privilege, a life of comfort.

"Children," Director Kagawa said, "this is Jacob Dawes." He turned on his heel and left the room. Some of the children gaped at his retreating back and I got the impression that his introductions were usually much different.

We all stood where he had left us, evaluating and measuring each other. A small, dark-haired girl stepped forward. "My name is Kirti Sachar," she said. "Are you all right?"

I thought that was an odd way to greet someone, but what did I know about this sort of life? She raised her hand and touched my upper lip with a finger. I mimicked her gesture and my fingers came away with flakes of dried blood.

"Bathroom?" I asked.

She indicated a washroom and, mumbling my thanks, I retreated there.

The image in the mirror was worse than I'd expected. I was dirty, tousled and bloodied, and my shirt was torn. Instead of attending school that day, I'd worked in Mrs. Frann's garden— she was nice and patient, and paid well. My skin was coated with dirt, and there was a collection of it under my fingernails. I'd acquired a bloody nose in the scuffle, and a solid line of dried blood ran down to my chin and decorated my shirt. The seam at my shoulder had ripped.

I attacked the whole mess with soap, stepped back and confronted the mirror again. I was cleaner than usual. There was dirt I couldn't get out from under my fingernails, and my efforts had done little more than lighten the color of the blood on my shirt.

I was even more nervous and afraid than I had been before. I no longer looked like a tomcat fresh from defending his territory, but still, clean or not, I looked nothing like the children out in that room. I wasn't like them. I wasn't one of them.

Riding a rush of anger and fear, I rallied all my courage and left the washroom.

Kirti looked up from her chess board and smiled. She stood and approached me again with determination. I got the impression that she was shy by nature, but not allowing herself to act that way.

"So you're Jacob?" she asked.

"Yes."

She smiled again.

The eyes of all the children in the room were on me and it wasn't polite interest. Children do rejection very well; very clean and straightforward. None of the pretense adults muck it up with.

I stiffened, strode forward, and plunked down in a comfortable armchair in the middle of the room. I looked back over at Kirti, daring her to join me.

She started toward me, but a boy—nine or ten, I guessed, with night-black hair and pale skin—plopped himself down in a chair across from me before she could get there. "So, was it a good fight? Tell me it was a good fight. And you won, right? What did the other guy look like?"

This wasn't right. Almost all of the children were reacting to me as I expected them to. This boy's open and casual friendliness didn't fit, but I trusted his sincerity for some reason I couldn't name. Probably not astute character judgment on my part so much as a desire to be accepted; throwing a bone to the gnawing loneliness in my gut.

"Well, it wasn't really a fight," I shrugged. "Just stupid shit."

The other children gasped and it took a moment for me to figure out why. But I saw it on their faces, the self-righteous censure. I'd clinched it in one of the first dozen words out of my mouth. It didn't matter what I said now, nothing could win them over. I'd always be that kid, the outsider. A destabilizing force introduced into a precisely calibrated system.

The thrill of control shivered through me. Whatever I chose to show them now was what they would believe of me, so long as it was close enough to their expectations. There was power in that—the general choosing where to make his stand.

So I told them.

The boy in the chair leaned back, a huge smile spreading across his face. "I wish I'd been there to see you punch a policeman."

I'd been right about this boy. The other children were disdainful, but this boy had seen me for what I really was and accepted me anyway.

The other children melted away, talking or making rude noises. Only Kirti and the friendly boy stayed.

"I'm Wong Chuk Tsuen," he said, reaching across the space between us with his hand extended. I shook it. His grip was firm, sure. "My friends call me Chuck."

"Jacob Dawes. My friends call me Jacob."

"Good to meet you, Jake." He grinned.

The easy chatter with Chuck soon made me forget being angry or sad or afraid. He had a way about him that made me feel as if I'd known him forever, like the way he'd already assigned me a nickname.

Chuck got up and wandered off and Kirti settled into a chair at one of the chess boards near me.

I sat across from her. She watched me, though not like the other children. She seemed to be looking for things about me to like, rather than the other way around.

It wasn't that she made me feel uncomfortable, but I felt like

I had to say something, to be polite. To give her reason to stay.

"I had to leave my sister with my ma."

She didn't even look confused at that odd wording. "Is she older?"

I shook my head. "She's five."

Kirti nodded. "My sisters are older than me. Teresa's twelve and Jane's fifteen."

"You got along with them OK?"

She made a noise of agreement. The kind of noise you make when you don't want to speak because you're trying not to cry.

I picked up a rook. "I've never played real chess."

"My dad's a local champion," she said. Her face brightened, then clouded again.

"You like your dad?"

"Yeah, my dad's the best." She swallowed hard, like she was fighting back something and started to talk about her family. She spoke of her sisters and her mother, her voice warm and wistful, but there was a special something when she spoke of her father. I wondered what that would be like, a father you weren't afraid of, that you liked, who was nice, even.

After a while, a bell rang. I followed Kirti from the lounge and into a large dining room. A huge table dominated, with seats for two dozen people.

It was a polished dark wood—real wood. The chairs had tall backs and plush seats, which I thought was crazy in a dining room where food could spill on them. The table was set with gleaming silverware, crystal goblets filled with water, and heavy china plates with cloth napkins perched like birds in the center.

It seemed like a scene plucked out of earlier centuries. Nowhere in the room were any of the more practical, utilitarian plastics and metals I'd always been surrounded by. I took a seat like everyone else and watched as the director offered a blessing.

This was a new experience. Religion, even the Empire's secularized version, was foreign to me.

Everyone bowed their heads. "We remember with gratitude all that we have and can have and do because of our great Empire.

May the emperor live forever."

The children all repeated the last line and it was over. My first impulse was to laugh. Who lived forever? You'd think these people—the greatest minds of our time—wouldn't express such nonsensical ideas.

It was true, though, that we belonged to the Empire now. It was the emperor who would provide for and keep us. So while it was strange and smacked of superstition to me, I felt grateful and beholden in a way that made the blessing somehow appropriate.

I still remember the meal with perfect clarity. Serving men and women entered the room with huge dishes overflowing with foods of all kinds. I had never seen anything like it. Crusty breads slick with butter, dishes of meaty potatoes, two different kinds of vegetables and a salad, a plate of juicy beef slices and another of glazed pork. They brought milk for us children and wine for the director and the man who had been with him at my apartment— who kept casting fearful glances at me, as if I might jump him at any moment.

I forced myself to take portions no bigger than the other children did. Others were taking seconds, but I knew enough to take only a few bites more of my favorites. Eating myself sick and ruining this incredible feast was unthinkable. I savored each and every bite as if I'd never eat that way again.

That night, after we'd been sent to find our bunks, I lay awake a long time staring at the low ceiling above me. The bed was more comfortable than any I'd ever slept in and was larger than the one I'd shared with Carrie the night before.

My chest hurt when I thought of her. Carrie was brave, but she was only five. And she and Ma had been my responsibility. Who would take care of them now?

I didn't think, at the time, about how I'd only been a year older than Carrie was now, when Father was taken away and I'd assumed that responsibility for myself. Of course, in reality, I'd assumed it much earlier. The first time I'd put myself between Ma and my drunken father's fist, I couldn't have been more than four.

And it wasn't as if I'd been given a choice about leaving. Still, I felt like a traitor, abandoning them.

It had been quiet for a while, save for the occasional snore, when I heard a strange noise. Concentrating, I realized it was muffled crying. I crawled out of my bunk and stood in the aisle to listen. The sound wasn't coming from any of the nearby bunks in the boys' section.

I slid open the door to the girls' and located the sound. I looked at the indicator on the outside of the bunk and saw it was Kirti's. I tried the privacy screen and found it unlocked so I slid it open. Kirti turned with a shocked gasp, but when she saw it was me she turned her face back to the wall and continued sobbing. I crawled into the bunk and slid the screen closed behind me. Taking her in my arms, as I had done with Carrie many times, I hugged her close until she cried herself out. I stayed long enough to be certain that she was asleep before I eased myself out of the bunk and returned to my own.

In the morning when I returned from a trip to the bathroom, I found a set of clothes on my bed. I picked them up and held them against me for size. They were a bit long in the leg, too wide at the shoulders, but appeared to be new. I didn't know where they'd come from but wasn't about to turn them down no matter who had left them for me. When I rolled up the sleeves and pant legs, they fit well enough. I folded my own clothes to put them aside. I had swiped a picture on my way out of the apartment, and now I took it from the back pocket of my discarded pants. It was one Carrie had drawn, of her and me, holding hands. I was still looking at it when Chuck passed by.

"Hey, they fit!" He beamed. No condescension or superiority, just simple satisfaction in a gift appreciated.

I folded the drawing away quickly and smiled at him. "Yeah,

thanks. I really appreciate the loan."

He waved that away. "Eh, keep 'em. My parents went overboard, and I can only wear one set at a time, right?"

I was accustomed to anonymous charity, but not gifts. I felt awkward and embarrassed, though he obviously did not. I was rescued by the bell announcing breakfast.

The day passed much as the first one. And though Kirti spent plenty of time with me throughout the day, she never once alluded to the events of the night before, and so neither did I.

Around midmorning, Director Kagawa entered the lounge with a dark-haired boy at least a head taller than I was. He had to have been one of the oldest children eligible for this Selection.

"Children," Director Kagawa began, "meet your new classmate, Sasha Popovich." We chorused a greeting. At the director's prompting, Sasha proceeded to detail his various academic accomplishments and recognitions. He was very pleased with himself in a way that set my teeth on edge. If this was the normal form of introduction, no wonder the other kids looked at me like I had two heads. As if, covered in dirt and blood, I hadn't been strange enough to them already.

I managed to avoid Sasha until after lunch. Another new boy, Anwar, was brought in less than an hour after we ate. He was small and quiet, pale and thin. His voice was shaky and barely above a whisper when he spoke at the director's prompting. His list was more impressive than Sasha's, though he looked younger, and I watched Sasha make derisive faces during Anwar's recitation. I already didn't like Sasha, but this made me angry.

When the director left us, Anwar burrowed into a chair in a corner of the room. Sasha's voice, as he mocked Anwar's accomplishments to one of the two boys he'd acquired as cronies in the space of a few short hours, was meant to carry.

I've often wondered what scientific principle governs the acquisition of hangers-on in relation to a bully. It seems as predictable as any established scientific law I've yet encountered.

Anwar, red-faced, was trying to pretend he didn't hear. When

Sasha started toward the corner of the room where Anwar sat, I stood up to block his path.

"Leave him alone."

Sasha looked down at me. "Get out of my way, lepton."

I stood my ground. The other kids were watching us now. He started to move around me, pushing my shoulder to move me out of his way. I grabbed the front of his shirt and stopped him with a hard jerk. "Leave him alone."

Sasha took two fistfuls of my shirt and hauled me off my feet. "Get out of my way."

My hands were balled into fists. "You don't want to do that," Chuck offered from behind my shoulder. "Jake took out a policeman yesterday. I don't think you want to mess with him."

Sasha shot me a surprised look, but dropped me. "Who cares about that smear," he said to his buddies as he walked away. I started to follow, but Chuck had a hold of my sleeve.

"Enough," he whispered. I turned to him, wanting to shake him off, but he wasn't looking at me. He was eyeing Sasha, measuring and considering. "He's not worth it. Not yet, anyway." He met my eye and grinned.

I couldn't help but smile back. Sasha avoided me after that, and I him. I wish I could say that lasted, but it was true at least for the rest of our trip.

Lying in my bed that night, I made myself stay awake. Before long, I heard what I'd been listening for. I snuck into Kirti's bunk as I had the night before and held her while she cried, returning to my own bed only when she was asleep.

Two days passed. We picked up two more kids, one each day. At dinner, the director informed us that we would stop the next morning at a docking area where we would pick up the last three candidates who had arrived from off-planet. By early afternoon we would be at the IIC.

An excited ripple passed through the room and conversation

dimmed from exuberant to reserved and solemn. The seriousness, the finality of it all hung in the air.

When we went to bed that night I waited for the sound of Kirti's sobs. They didn't come. I slid out of my bunk anyway and peeked into hers. She was still awake and crying, quiet, halfhearted sniffs. I climbed in and sat crossed legged on the end of her bed. "Better?"

She shrugged. "I'm fine. Of course I am." She said it as if she'd always been fine, even when she'd shaken, sobbing against me. I recognized this—strength as a deliberate choice, rather than a genuine feeling. Kirti was new to it, though, and stubbornness alone was sustaining her. I took her hand. Silent tears slid down her cheeks but she neither looked at me nor spoke. As she drifted off to sleep, I tried to ignore the voice that snarled at me about a sister left behind with no one to hold her hand as she cried.

We buzzed with nervous energy the next morning. It was still early when our last three classmates followed Director Kagawa into the lounge; two boys and a girl.

The three newcomers were minor celebrities for the rest of the morning. Of the three off-worlders, two weren't human. Verishr, a too-tall, too-thin girl was Ramarian, and her pale violet-blue skin glowed faintly if she stood near the windows. Io was a Tlo, black as night with hair and eyes a shining, metallic silver. The other children were as affected as I was by the novelty—though Sasha blustered about his father being friends with the Tlosian ambassador and how he'd stayed at their house before—and the excitement helped the morning pass.

About an hour and a half after lunch, the director entered the lounge and announced that we were approaching the IIC. We rushed to the large window and watched for a first glimpse.

The transport passed into a long, level valley covered in a thick carpet of new green grass. Soggy patches of snow littered the ground at the base of the mountains. A flat, glassy lake in the center of the valley reflected the mountains in reverse; its mirrored surface creating the illusion of another world opening up just below the water.

I leaned close to the window, drinking in the sight of the water flashing by. The other children's excited murmurs made me look up and I saw a cluster of buildings coming into view. They were stark white, as white as the snow on the mountains, with no frill or ostentation; matter shaped and defined for a purpose far more important than subjective beauty. The transport circled around to the front of the main building, touching down before the public entrance to the IIC. The massive front doors were of a polished black wood that gleamed like metal. We disembarked in an overawed unison.

The director led us into the main lobby of the building. White stone, maybe even marble, covered the floors and walls. A mural was set into the wall all around, strips of metal and shiny polymers twisted among and around wood, stone, and bright splashes of color. The effect resolved into scenes of scholars poring over tablets, scientists in their labs, even the Newtonian apple falling from the tree. And one image of a lone boy staring up at a star-splashed night sky.

The director brought us to stand before a large statue in the middle of the room, carved from ebony stone.

"A representation of our great founder," he intoned. "You are the twenty-second Selection." He fixed each of us in turn with a serious look. "The process of Selection, as it is now, dates back only a hundred years. But the IIC, the idea of the IIC, is over three hundred years old."

He paused to make sure we were properly impressed.

"Thirty decades before your parents were born, in the days when the people of Earth were still being liberated from their broken, squabbling nations, still recovering from their religious wars—still being consolidated into our great Empire—the new Duke Edmund, brother of our second emperor, James II, envisioned a collection of all the best minds in the world. He proposed to his brother a home for the growth of ideas, a place to nurture the great genius scattered among humanity, and thus the Imperial Intellectual Ministry was born. At its founding, it was a voluntary grouping of scientists and thinkers. As it grew in size and scope, the first building of what was to become the Imperial Intellectual Complex was constructed; the very building in which you stand."

We all looked around again, as if the building would look different now.

"Every five years, twenty children are chosen for this great purpose. It is now your turn to join this illustrious institution; to add your genius to the greatest minds of your time. This is a privilege and a responsibility beyond measure. A responsibility you will take seriously. The work you do here is a sacred duty to the Empire."

He turned and bowed his head in reverent silence before the statue. His theatrics were entertaining, but I was already bored with them. He obviously had a high opinion of himself by way of his connection to this place.

At the conclusion of his moment of silence, he turned back to face us. "Because this place," he gestured to the area surrounding the statue, "is a vivid reminder of the august purpose of this institution, it is here that I teach you a very important lesson in the responsibilities you now bear and the expectations we have of your conduct."

He turned to me. "Mr. Dawes." He said my name as if it tasted bad in his mouth.

My heart stuttered and I felt my stomach hit my shoes.

"By rights, you should not be here. Your behavior and personality scores disqualified you from Selection. However, because of your exceptionally high academic scores, your file was given special review and it was the decision of the Committee to grant you an exception. In other words, a more deserving, more appropriate child is not here because the Committee chose to ignore what you are, and excuse your obvious failings."

My heart was pounding in my ears. I knew what it meant to be me. Nothing good came out of the unclass. We were little better than animals. Of course they'd never allow one of us in a place like this. It was as logical and inexorable as gravity, inertia, or the speed of light in a vacuum.

I knew.

But I suppose I'd thought that the IIC was different. Like

fairytales or null gravity. The old rules wouldn't apply, anything was possible.

But they did, and it wasn't.

"After that disgraceful scene in your home, I petitioned the Committee to reconsider. They did not. But I have been assured that, should your behavior continue in that vein, I may submit future incidents for consideration toward your removal and replacement. It is only a matter of time. I am confident that you are incapable of acting otherwise."

My face was hot. I was torn between paralyzing fear and an ache to punch his arrogant face.

"Your disruptive, offensive behavior will not be tolerated. I will be keeping an eye on you. The entire faculty will be informed of your unsuitability and will be charged with reducing your negative impact on the other students and members while you remain here. And to make that clear, you will not proceed one foot further into this venerable building until I have impressed that point on you and all your classmates."

The steward had left us earlier, but now he returned and handed the director a thin, flexible cane. "Bend over that table," he ordered. I burned with fury, humiliation, and the injustice of the situation. This wasn't punishment for punching the policeman, it was not discipline; it was something else entirely. He meant to shame me in front of the other children.

I had a strong urge to spit in his face, but had the sense and restraint not to. Defiance would be a waste of effort. They would just hold me down and I would cause myself that much more embarrassment, without avoiding the whipping at all.

But I had my own resources that he knew nothing about. I held his gaze just until he began to draw a deep, angry breath. Before he could say anything, I moved to the table he had indicated, and bent over.

What the director could not know, and would not be expecting, was that he couldn't win this way. I was no stranger to punishments in this manner, but far more important than that, I was a longtime veteran of my father's beatings. Father's thrashings had been much worse, more painful and terrifying, than anything Director Kagawa could ever do. They had, of necessity, been endured in silence—infinitely worse if I whimpered or shed a tear that he could see. And so, from much practice, I could hold my peace even through a vicious beating.

Kagawa brought the cane crashing down and I clamped my tongue between my teeth and made no sound. By the eighth bruising blow, I was trembling with the effort of holding back any reaction he could see, but I had succeeded. I had won.

"Stand up," he snapped.

I did, fighting the crazy urge to grin at him as triumph throbbed through me in time with the pain in my backside.

The other children were watching me, wide eyed. I slipped back into the group beside Kirti. Tears streamed down her face. I reached over and took her hand, squeezing it in reassurance. With a frustrated huff, Director Kagawa led us out of the lobby and into the great hall, stabbing the cane on the floor in time with his steps.

The great hall was enormous, the size of a football field and three stories tall. The empty space was broken at intervals by large tables covered in fresh flowers or graceful sculptures, sort of tortured and writhing, that looked like nothing at all.

There was a group of adults waiting for us, all dressed in the uniform of the IIC.

They were introduced to us as the various department heads, the teachers, and Mr. Shrik, the Head of Dormitories. We were presented to them as a group, but Director Kagawa pointed me out as an individual. He warned the assembled to be wary of me as a discipline issue, a disruptive element, and a dangerous influence on the other children. He instructed them to keep a close eye on me and to tolerate no offense whatsoever, no matter how minor.

My face was hot but I refused to bow my head or lower my eyes, instead meeting their disapproving looks with one of defiance. Looking back, I realize that wasn't a terribly intelligent response to the situation. No doubt, it only confirmed what the director had said.

Director Kagawa did me an incredible favor that day. Had he watched me and plotted in silence, he might very well have gotten the proof he needed to have me removed from the IIC. I was always stubborn and rebellious, but by setting up the expectation for me to misbehave, he gave me something to rebel against that helped rather than harmed me. So I resolved to be exemplary in word and deed, academically and personally. I vowed to myself that whatever I truly thought or felt, he would never see it and would never have opportunity to condemn me for it.

It is humbling now to realize how much I owe that man, whom I so passionately hated.

The rest of the afternoon was spent in a tour of the main buildings, and lessons in the rules and routines of our new home.

As we were walking through the building set aside for medical facilities, I was pulled aside by a young woman in a white smock.

I cast a glance at the teacher conducting the tour but he just nodded for me to go.

I followed the woman into a stark, sterile room.

"Sit there," she said, pointing to a raised table with a stepstool in front of it. I did as she said, trying not to squirm—and not just because of the stripes I was sitting on.

She joined a man on the other side of the room and they both cast a glance back at me. The man grimaced.

"You were right," the woman said, "they really did bring one."

The man scoffed. "Unbelievable. Have you seen this? No medical data on this one. None at all. If he didn't have a citID I'd have a hard time believing he was real."

"Emperor only knows what we're going to have to treat him for."

"Everything. Whatever it is he's probably got it."

"I'm going to have to order most of the inoculations. We don't even stock that stuff."

"Well we've got the STD panels, at least."

"He's probably too young to start those, isn't he?"

"An unclass? I'd be surprised if he didn't have half the diseases already. Wouldn't hurt to start the repro-control either. Can't start too early with them."

I rejoined the group an hour later, my face still burning. Kirti cast me a questioning look but I just shook my head and wouldn't look at her.

At the end we were shown to our own rooms.

The room I entered took my breath away. This couldn't be for me alone. It was huge by my standards at the time—fifteen by twenty feet, with a large window in the wall across from the door.

There was a sitting area, and past that a bed with a nightstand on each side. A full double bed.

The closet was full of clothes. There were ten complete uniforms: navy jackets, crisp white shirts, slate gray pants, two of them dress uniforms. There were casual outfits and sports suits, and on the floor of the closet were four different pairs of shoes.

In the drawers beside the closet were an unfathomable number of pairs of underwear and socks. (I blushed to imagine the embarrassing situations they must have been anticipating, to provide so many at one time.) There were even undershirts, something I couldn't begin to imagine a necessity for in this place that was surely always warm enough. Another drawer was full of sets of pajamas. It was an embarrassment of riches.

To the right of the entry door was the most incredible desk. The entire surface was one continuous vid screen. I turned it on with a touch. With only a few swipes of my fingers I was able to open at least ten different documents while leaving ample room in the middle front to input my own work. Happiness tingled in my whole body.

On top of that shock, I discovered I had a bathroom all my own. The shower was big enough to wash yourself in without ever hitting your elbows on the walls.

I wandered back over to the closet, looking down the line of crisp, new shirts. I stripped out of the borrowed clothes and, almost trembling, put on one—one of several—of my new suits of clothes. I was running my hands over the selection of socks when I heard the dinner bell. I looked up in panic. Dinner. I was supposed to be in uniform and on time.

I stumbled into socks and shoes, fought with one of the confounding neckties, grabbed a coat and dashed into the hall and the noisy press of the other boys. Chuck grabbed my arm and pulled me to a stop.

"Here," he said, "like this." With one tug my tie unraveled, and in a flurry he had it rearranged so that it looked like everyone else's.

"Thank you," I breathed.

"I'm not helping you with your fly, though," he said over his shoulder with a laugh as he rushed ahead to join the other boys. I zipped up and hurried after them.

The dining hall was as impressive as the great hall, in its way. There were long, dark tables set in parallel lines across the width of the room, enough to accommodate the more than 350 members of the IIC, from the youngest student (me, actually) to the oldest fellow, a centenarian from twenty Selections ago.

As with everything, there was a system of seating based on rank and seniority, the two roughly equivalent at the IIC. The seating wasn't so much assigned as enforced with the weight of tradition. There was a head table with seating for twenty set up on a small rise on the far side of the room. Spreading out from there were the oldest of us down to the youngest.

For the forty of us who were still full-time students, there were four tables, two for the previous group Selected and two for us. We were directed there and instructed to stand in place as the director entered.

He said the blessing, the same as on the transport. There was food in quantities and varieties that still surprised me. And succeeded in distracting me, at least for the rest of the evening, from the cold fear that had settled in my stomach the moment I realized Director Kagawa meant to be rid of me, and the humiliation of the medical exam.

Back in my room, I took Carrie's drawing out of my pocket and smoothed it onto the adhesive surface above my desk, careful not to tear or wrinkle it. I sat down to record a message. When I entered Ma's citID I got an error:

Access denied.

I stared at it in disbelief. I tried again.

Access denied.

I entered Carrie's.

Access denied.

I dashed out of my room and over to Chuck's. He came to the door in pajamas, his head cocked to the side.

"What's wrong?"

"I got access denied! For Carrie too."

He made out the meaning of that breathless jumble and gave me a sad little smile, patting my arm.

"You didn't know?"

"Know what?"

"We don't have families anymore," he said, with a calm matter-of-factness.

"*What?*"

"We've got an important job here, gotta have focus and dedication. No distractions. Once we're adults we can contact them if we want."

"But I didn't even get to say goodbye!"

His mouth twisted in good-natured sympathy.

"Yeah. That's rough."

I stumbled back to my room without another word, too stunned for anything else.

fg 4

I was awakened in the morning by the bell, and rolled out of my bed and into the shower. Having my own bathroom was a heady luxury, and later as I made my way to the dining hall with the other children I found myself feeling light and carefree in a way I didn't expect. I found Kirti and, though I didn't ask her about it, I could see that she'd had a better night.

In the school building, we were grouped by age: the eight, nine, and ten-year-olds in one class, the older children in the other. I would have a lot of catching up to do. Not only because I was the youngest, but because my education so far had been marginal at best.

Dr. Hammond made it clear I was to catch up and keep up in the expected time frame. To do otherwise would result in serious repercussions. I bit my tongue and said nothing.

In truth, I didn't need to be told to apply myself; it was my enthusiasm that got me into trouble. For the first time in my life, I had teachers who knew more than I did, teachers who could answer any question I could ask. And ask I did. For my trouble, the teachers labeled me disruptive, undisciplined, and hopelessly behind. Some managed to take insult, as if I were questioning their ability to teach.

Some of those things were true, of course. I *was* undisciplined. My questions were disruptive in their frequency and their tendency to wander off on tangents. I wasn't as far behind the other children as they believed. Oh, I was very behind, but more than once my questions were answered with much more basic information than I'd asked for. They had formed their opinions of me and my level of knowledge and didn't choose to see past that.

Dr. Frozt, the literature teacher, got fed up that first day and I got three licks of the cane from her. I kept more of my questions to myself after that, but not all of them. My craving for knowledge was far too potent to be squelched by a mere three stripes.

That night, in my room, sitting at my desk, which made my stomach flutter with happiness every time I looked at it, I gorged myself on answers to all the questions I'd come up with that day and then some. I was nodding off when I realized I hadn't completed my homework, having gone off point far too many times. I struggled through the rest of it and fell into an exhausted, blissful sleep.

I was bleary eyed in the morning, but no less eager. The second day went better than the first. I managed to better channel and focus my thoughts, and to save most of my tangents to research later.

In spite of my efforts, the teachers saw what they wanted to see. I went over the desk three times in the first five days. It was frustrating, infuriating, and of course painful. But there was nothing to be done about it except endure.

It took little effort on my part to carry out my resolve to be an exemplary student, simply because there couldn't have been a student more eager and appreciative than I was. Still they managed to see and punish every mistake I made and many I didn't.

I bit my tongue, took my stripes in silence, and moved on.

Kirti was more affected by my undeserved infamy than I was. She cried every time I was punished. I did my best to reassure her that it wasn't as bad as she thought, but it was quite some time before she was able to bear my punishments in white-faced silence.

In truth, the prejudice, my anger and resentment, were just minor annoyances. The experience of such schooling was like nothing I'd ever known. The only thing I had to compare it to was the stolen hours in a library booth, wallowing in text after text, chasing facts and ideas like butterflies in a field of wildflowers.

This was entirely different, though. Directed, focused, and challenging, with stimulating raw knowledge laid out before me, and answers to questions I hadn't even thought to ask.

My bottom became very intimate with the cane. But I wouldn't have given it up for all the universe.

If Kirti suffered for me in silence, Chuck seemed to take pride in the way I endured it. But what he accepted as unavoidable from the adults, he wouldn't stand for among us. It was this attitude that led to the first of our many fights with Sasha.

I suppose the first fight was inevitable. In light of the director's public opinion of me, Sasha set about goading me at every opportunity. He was easy to ignore at first; I was so absorbed in my experience of the place and my new education that I barely noticed him. But after a couple of weeks it came to a head.

Kirti and I were walking together to our next class when Sasha stepped in front of me and stopped me with a hand on my chest.

"You don't belong here," he said. "Why don't you leave?"

I tried to step around him, seething but highly motivated to avoid trouble. He stepped with me. "Are you deaf too, freak? Besides being stupid?"

"Drop it, Sasha," Chuck said from behind me. "Leave him alone. If you hate him so much, just avoid him. He didn't do anything to you."

Sasha laughed. "Freak's got a champion." He towered over Chuck.

Chuck's punch was too unexpected to be avoided. Sasha staggered back a step but then came barreling toward Chuck, his fist flying. Chuck dodged it but took the next punch in the gut, doubling over. As Sasha went to swing at Chuck again, I crashed my fist into his face. Dr. Laan came rushing out into the hallway and hauled us apart. He dragged Sasha and me to the director's office by the scruff of our necks, ordering Chuck to follow.

We stood before Director Kagawa's desk and endured a long, loud scolding. Even when the truth of the story came out, corroborated by Dr. Laan according to what the other children had told him, I was still singled out as the source of the trouble. So when the three of us went over the desk, pants and undershorts around our ankles, I took twice the punishment the other two did. I endured in silence as always. Chuck grunted through clenched teeth after every blow. Sasha blubbered from almost the very first. That alone made the stripes worth taking.

That was not the first of such scenes. Even when the fight stayed between Chuck and Sasha alone, I was still punished alongside them. I hated that Chuck had to defend me when I was quite capable of defending myself. But my hands were tied; my fear—not of the bully or the fight, but of giving Director Kagawa what he needed—was stronger than the guilt.

For Chuck, it was much simpler. I was his friend, He defended his friends. No more complicated than that. I tried to talk him out of it, once, after he'd yet again been caned for fighting my battle. He looked at me as if I'd insisted the atom had never been split.

The trips to the director's office after a fight weren't the only times I found myself before—or over—his desk. He requested regular reports from my teachers and when he had a large enough collection of infractions, I would be summoned to his office to be scolded for a list of things I usually hadn't even done.

"Cheating on a math test," he said from behind his desk.

"But I wasn't cheating. I don't even know why she thought I was."

"A liar as well," he said to himself, shaking his head as he looked down at his list again. I bit hard on the inside of my cheek and glared at the floor.

"Calling Sasha names during your exercise period in order to provoke him."

"But I didn't say a word to him! He called *me* names."

He scoffed.

"Late for curfew."

"That was the night we did the lab in the observatory. We didn't start until after dark. Most of us were late for curfew."

He laid his tablet down and placed his hands on the desk in

36

front of him, one over the other.

"Do you know why the unclass exist?" he said.

"No sir."

"Do you know why, in an empire that has spread peace and justice throughout the galaxy, poverty and lawlessness persist?"

I knew where this was going. "No sir."

"It is because of you. All of the unclass, each and every one. You live in poverty and squalor because you can't be bothered to work or to better yourselves. You suffer from crimes and violence because you yourselves commit them. You treat the laws of civilized society as if they were as worthless as you are."

I shoved my fists into my pockets.

"No unclass has ever been brought to the IIC. Not one in three hundred years. Your intellect may be a genetic anomaly, but it doesn't change what you are. The proof of that is clear in your sociological scores: propensity to anger and violence, no concept of self-sacrifice and the greater good. All of which is borne out in your behavior here.

"This institution is a shining beacon of all that is good in the Empire. Your presence here is an outrage. You are a stain on our perfection, poison in our well. And until the Committee agrees with me, perhaps I can beat enough wickedness out of you to mitigate your effect on the rest of us.

"Take down your shorts."

I hated the man with a passion, but each punishment only made me more determined, and more confident. If he had sufficient data to prove his hypothesis, I would already be gone. So no matter how many stripes I carried away from his office, or what insults still rang in my ears, I always left happier than when I had entered. Because I'd won again.

Three weeks after we'd arrived, I was sitting in math class. The class before had been physics. Not only were these two of my favorite subjects, but the juxtaposition was exhilarating. The concepts from each subject fed off of the other, inspiring me with questions and ideas.

I was making notes and sketches on my tablet, so lost in the equations flowing across the screen like a music score, interweaving the complex harmonies that had been running through my mind since physics class, that I didn't even hear Dr. Noh approach. The tablet disappeared from under my hand.

"What is this, Mr. Dawes?" Dr. Noh demanded.

I dropped my head. "Just an idea I had. I was making some notes."

"Are these the problems you've been given to work on?"

I wanted to protest that I *was* paying attention. That's where I'd gotten the idea to begin with! But instead I answered, "No, ma'am."

"Get up to the desk, then."

I shuffled up to her desk, took my three, and went back to my seat. But the real blow, the worst of the punishment, was that my tablet was blank when she handed it back. All my work had been wiped away. I slumped down in my seat and began the problems I'd been assigned.

Determined to do nothing else worthy of censure, I focused on my assignments that night and diverted no time to recreating the work that Dr. Noh had destroyed. Still, it played through my dreams all night and was foremost in my mind all the next day. I wouldn't allow myself to put down on tablet any of my ideas or questions, afraid of getting caught again, but I saved, collected, and catalogued ideas in my mind.

That evening, I was ordered to report to Dr. Okoro after dinner. Kirti and Chuck looked at me, but I shrugged.

Dr. Okoro was a physics fellow. I found him in his study in the physics wing.

The room only qualified as a study by the very loosest definition. It had the requisite features: a couch and two overstuffed armchairs, a desk and chair, almost none of which were being used for their intended purposes.

On the desk were several large pyrometers, with smaller ones in the chair behind. One armchair held a squat tokamak that was vibrating. The other, set at an angle to the first, was occupied by a vid showing a slide under a microscope, though the slide was empty. A blanket was crumpled up in one corner of the couch. At the other end, a large particle accelerator tilted at a precarious angle into the soft cushion.

There were two long lab tables shoved up against the far wall, covered from end to end with experiments in various stages. Dr. Okoro was seated in front of a table on a tall stool, his back to the door.

I lost several minutes just staring at his back. He was a large man, shaved bald, his head shiny and purple-black. I stood for a long time waiting to be acknowledged. As the minutes passed, I began to fidget. "Sir?" I ventured.

He held up a hand. "One minute..."

I waited. Several minutes later he turned to me with a broad smile on his face, his teeth stark white against such dark skin. "So sorry about that, young man. Delicate measurements. I'm sure you're familiar with that."

"Yes, sir," I replied, though I wasn't.

"Well, I suppose you're wondering why you're here," he continued. "But introductions first. I'm Adom Okoro." He offered his hand. I shook it, bemused.

"Jacob Dawes, sir."

"It's a pleasure to meet you." He turned back and searched around on the table behind him for something. Picking up and discarding several tablets, he—with an exclamation of "Aha!"—found the one he wanted and handed it to me.

"You recognize that, I assume?"

On the tablet I found the equations and scribbles that Dr. Noh had confiscated from me the day before. "Yes, sir," I said, hanging my head to convey the proper contrition, but inside I felt a rush of relief that they had been saved somewhere. I tried to calculate how long it would take me to send them to my desk and if that would be fast enough that he wouldn't have a chance to stop me. It was frustrating and confusing that this should be coming up yet again, and from someone I didn't even know. "I was doing this during class time instead of working on my assignment. I'm sorry, sir."

"Well, I'm not. That's interesting stuff you've got there, young man. How did you come up with this?"

I hesitated. I had no idea what was going on. "In Dr. Laan's class we were learning about the properties of light. So then in the next hour, when Dr. Noh was teaching us new equations, well, it looked like they could apply to the things I'd been thinking about since the physics lesson. I just started jotting down my ideas..."

He was grinning, and I didn't understand why. "Is this as far as you've gone with it, or do you have more elsewhere?"

"I...I just did this in class yesterday. I've been thinking about it, but haven't had the time to research any of this yet. So is it right, then? Is this how it really works?"

"Is what right?"

"This." I pointed to the tablet. "What Dr. Laan showed us about light waves, does it mean this is true? Or is it wrong?"

He stared at me for a long moment. "Are you asking me if your theory here is correct?"

"Yes, sir."

He leaned back and laughed. "I don't know. I'd like to know the answer to that, myself."

"Sir?" A moment before, I'd been sure I was here to be scolded, even punished again. Now he was laughing and asking me questions about my scribbles. I didn't understand.

"Mr. Dawes, what you've got here is a fascinating view of how light waves react. If you follow this line of reasoning, the logical end of this string of equations, well, if it pans out the way you've theorized, it would represent a major discovery in the understanding of the physics of light. I don't know if you're right. Nobody does. But I'm very interested in what you've got there. I'd like to test this theory and see where it goes."

"Yes, sir," I replied. My head was spinning and I didn't know what kind of response he was looking for, but silence seemed rude.

"Of course, there are your studies to consider. I was a student here as well, once upon a time," he winked at me, "so I know that's not an insignificant consideration. You haven't been here but a few weeks, so you'll still have quite a bit of settling in to do, perhaps still catching up on the workload. Hmmmm... We'll have to consider the timing." He almost looked disappointed.

"Why, sir?"

"I beg your pardon?"

"I don't understand. What does my schoolwork have to do with this?"

"Well, young man, no matter how fascinating your theory, I can't get you excused from your studies."

"I...still don't understand, sir."

He gave me a long, considering look. "I see. Perhaps you don't realize how seriously we take the concept of intellectual property."

I didn't know the term, so I said nothing.

"This is your work, your idea, and it belongs to you. If I were to pursue this theory myself, it would be considered stealing. No one has the right to pursue this theory now but you. I find your ideas fascinating, but I wouldn't dream of doing the experiments necessary to explore them without you."

I felt weak in the knees. It was too much to process. My scribbles, the product of only one of the many ideas that floated through my head, had been picked up by a physics fellow at the Imperial Intellectual Complex and he wanted to research them. He called my ideas fascinating. I almost couldn't breathe.

"I can do it, sir! I can get my homework done and then be here every night after dinner."

He gave me a searching look. "Are you sure about this? Because it's quite a commitment you're making. You should take some time to think about the matter—"

"I don't need time to think about it." I bit my lips together, hoping he wasn't angry, but he didn't appear to notice.

"Well, we could always give it a try and stop if it becomes too much for you." He grinned. "In that case, let's discuss how we're going to go about this. We'll need to start by hammering out our hypothesis..." He laughed. "I'm so excited I've already forgotten to be sensible. Your homework for this evening, you'll need to take care of that first."

"It's finished," I said in a rush.

He stopped and looked at me, frowning. I felt myself flushing with shame for the lie. "Mr. Dawes," he said, "if we're to work together, I need to be able to trust you. Can I expect to be able to do that?"

"Yes, sir. I'm sorry."

"All right, then," he said, patting my shoulder. "Go finish your work for the evening. Tomorrow, after your homework is done, if it isn't curfew yet, come find me and we'll see what we can accomplish."

I perked up. "Yes, sir! I'll get it all done before dinner."

He squeezed my shoulder and smiled. "Take as long as you need. If we don't have time tomorrow or even the rest of this week, there's always the weekend. Now, run along and get your work done. I'll see you tomorrow if all goes well."

"Yes, sir. Thank you, sir!" I hurried out the door and back to my room in full defiance of gravity—I'm sure my feet never touched the ground.

With the promise of uninterrupted time in the lab with Dr. Okoro as the reward for my focus and productivity, homework was no obstacle. Most days, I finished it before the dinner bell. When I hadn't, I would take my homework with me to the lab. It always got done at some point.

The very first evening we worked together, Dr. Okoro asked me about my previous experience with lab work. When I told him, he stared at me.

"Never? You've never worked in a lab before? Never done any practical or applied work in any scientific subject?"

It didn't seem so astonishing to me. I was only eight, and until a few weeks before, I had lived in a place where I couldn't even count on having electricity.

"No, sir. Never."

"Didn't your parents and teachers know about your interests, and your potential? Didn't they encourage your talents and help you pursue your education?"

I chuckled. I couldn't help it. The thought of either of my parents—or in fact, anyone from my old neighborhood—even setting foot in a lab was too absurd. "No, sir. I'm from Abenez."

He gasped. "Abenez?"

"Yes, sir."

He looked at me with pity on his face, and I turned away to hide my anger. He'd been kind to me as no other adult here had, but his reaction birthed a fear that he too would prejudge me, reject me, for something so meaningless as the place of my birth.

"Then I'm even more grateful that you're here now, Mr. Dawes."

My chest filled with happiness and I returned to my work, smiling.

$$\text{fg}6$$

At first, Dr. Okoro was scrupulous about the rules. He would set an alarm to remind me to go back to my room in time for curfew. But as our project progressed, he grew lax, sometimes ignoring the alarm or forgetting to set it altogether. When this would happen, he would record an authorization for me so that I wouldn't be penalized for missing curfew. Sometimes the Head of Dormitories wasn't in the mood to honor the authorization, but on those occasions I took my punishment without complaint and kept Dr. Okoro in the dark.

Dr. Okoro turned out to be single-minded in the pursuit of his science. I soon learned the reason for the blanket on the couch. We often worked late into the night, taking turns napping on the couch when our enthusiasm made it seem reasonable to push past the body's need for actual sleep.

One night I was already fighting my drooping eyelids when he said, "I'm not sure this is going to work. Hansen would roll over in his grave if he saw this."

"Hansen?"

Dr. Okoro looked at me as if he'd forgotten I was there. He grinned and ruffled my hair. "Hansen, Hansen's Law of Thermodynamics. If he's correct—and he's been correct for centuries—this is impossible. We'll be generating too much heat in too small an area."

I was a bit groggy at that point, so ignoring everything I should have known about thermodynamics seemed like a sensible option. "Not if we increase the conductive properties of the medium. It's easy, if you do that thing you were talking about with that Lavin theory."

He chuckled. "That was an entirely unrelated discussion. Lavin's theories have no bearing on..." he trailed off into silence, his eyes unfocused and staring off into nothing. "Lavin's...well, yes, that is...of course. Well of course!" He scooped me up in a hug. My feet dangled off the floor.

"Why that's just brilliant, Jacob. Brilliant! You're right, if you think about it..."

His words began to blend together, as they often did when he got completely absorbed in what he was thinking; he seemed to forget his mouth was even operating.

I tingled all over in the aftermath of his hug, pinging with more emotion than my body could contain. I wasn't tired anymore. I couldn't have slept then had my life depended on it.

Dr. Okoro and I worked together on the project for eight months. I devoted the majority of my spare time to our research. Only sports with Chuck and time with Kirti could lure me away. Dr. Okoro would encourage me to spend more time in recreational pursuits, but never objected when I showed up at the lab instead.

We were colleagues, comrades, partners in crime. I came to love that kind, brilliant man with all the thwarted affection I'd never given to my father.

One afternoon when he realized I was skipping one of the infrequent class trips into the nearby town, Dr. Okoro reached over and patted my cheek.

"Get out of here and go do something else for a change, son, the universe will still be here when you get back."

The Earth stopped spinning, my heart felt like it would burst out of my chest. Maybe there were other things in life more important, more significant than being called "son" by a man like Dr. Okoro, but I couldn't think of any.

Before my ninth birthday we brought the project to a close. My ideas, and the hypothesis we formed from them, had proven themselves in experiment after experiment. The resulting new theorem had led to the development of a new kind of laser device. It created more compact beams which emitted less energy as heat than any laser previously invented, by quite a significant margin.

Our discoveries and invention were to be presented to the Physics Committee. Dr. Okoro spent at least a week teaching me how to structure a presentation, and practicing his delivery.

But when we stood before the Committee and were told to begin, Dr. Okoro turned to me. "Jacob. You may proceed." I stood stock still in panic for only a second before locking my knees and launching into his prepared talk. I guess I had realized that his plan all along had been for me to present my own discoveries, but he had hidden it from me so that I wouldn't have time to be nervous.

The looks on the faces of the assembled scientists were disapproving, as if they assumed this was some sort of stunt; a waste of their time. But as I spoke, they became attentive, even interested. I know I wasn't in any way impressive in my delivery, but I've since observed that many scientists are not orators, and some are downright incomprehensible before a crowd. I did as well as many.

By the end they seemed to have forgotten my age. They posed question after question, and I could answer most of them. After the presentation, none of them could question whether I had been an equal partner in the research and development.

Next we presented to the entire membership of the IIC. The final presentation, held in one of the auditoriums in the main building, was exhilarating. Afterward, there was a reception with VIPs, where Dr. Okoro and I were congratulated and our work was celebrated. It was there that Director Kagawa asked Dr. Okoro what he planned to call his new laser device.

"The Dawes Laser," was Dr. Okoro's answer. My mouth fell

open. Director Kagawa's nearly did.

"You can't be serious," he protested. "It's not fitting to name an important new invention after a student."

Dr. Okoro bristled. "When it is *his* theory and *his* invention, then I'd say it is more than fitting to apply *his* name to it."

"But it was not his work alone!"

"It was his discovery. I merely assisted him," Dr. Okoro insisted.

I half believed that Dr. Okoro had only come up with the name in order to vex the director, and that we would call it something different in the end. I was wrong. The Dawes Theory of Stimulated Emissions and the Dawes Laser were officially recorded, and would remain my most well known accomplishments for many years to come.

My success and the resultant fame of my accomplishments improved my reputation at the IIC and therefore my treatment, though not with everyone and not as much as might be expected. Dr. Noh, who had already been neutral or better to me since Dr. Okoro showed interest in my scribbles, created some minor fame for herself as having been the one to first recognize the potential of my idea. She gushed over me, favoring me to a degree that made me wish she still disliked me.

Dr. Laan made a big deal about me because he was my physics teacher and one of his lessons had birthed my discovery. But his treatment of me was uncomfortable in a different way than Dr. Noh's. I never lost the impression that he felt slighted and resentful because I had ended up working with Dr. Okoro and not him. Interactions with him felt double-sided and almost dangerous.

My classmates were fairly evenly divided into three groups: those who now wanted to be my friends, those who decided I wasn't worth their attention one way or the other, and those who took my achievement as a personal insult and vowed revenge. There were a couple of memorable fights with Sasha, but now that my position at the IIC was no longer in question, I did my best to keep Chuck out of them. I think Chuck took *that* as a personal insult but, being Chuck, he didn't hold it against me.

As for Director Kagawa, the change was obvious and, at the same time, no change at all. He stopped threatening my place at the IIC. I was no longer a noxious element to be quarantined and removed. He changed the theme of his admonitions to me and to others about me. Now I was a valuable commodity that must be trained and tempered. I could not be allowed to develop bad habits or attitudes that could spoil my potential. In other words, he counseled my teachers and the administrators to the same course of action, but for different reasons.

My visits to him—less frequent because they were rarely instigated by others now—changed only in the text of his lecture. When there was punishment for a fight, I still acquired twice the stripes anyone else did. For my own good.

But, for the most part, my life settled into a more peaceful routine. I had time for friends now, and other pursuits.

One afternoon Chuck took my arm and pulled me with him down the hall.

"Boxing," he said.

"What?"

"Boxing. That's what we're doing this afternoon."

"You and me?"

He nodded.

"Why?"

He grinned. "Don't you think it's a good idea?"

"I guess. Good idea for what?"

"Exercise. And think of how much better we can pulverize Sasha next time with a little practice. We can get two pigs with one bird."

"Oh. Well, OK."

I had more time for Kirti too.

We spent many evenings in a practice hall where she played the piano and I listened. Sometimes I did so with my homework in my lap, sometimes I chased random thoughts on a tablet, and other times I sank into the back of a comfortable armchair, head back, eyes closed, watching the dance of the universe in her music.

I was happy. I had found myself, my place, my purpose. I had Dr. Okoro and Kirti and Chuck. I couldn't think of much more I could want out of life.

Except, perhaps, to know how my mother and Carrie were doing.

I'm sure the other kids missed their families, in fact, I knew Kirti did. But they'd all known before they came that they were leaving them behind in every way.

And none of them, no matter how much they missed their parents or brothers or sisters, had the same worries I did. I know I was the only one who suffered quiet moments of panic, wondering if they had food, or if they'd been kicked out of the apartment again, or who had hurt them, now that I was gone. I hadn't even gotten to tell Carrie how to get the best jobs before the other kids found out about them, or how to sneak extra food into the carrier after Mr. Sacks had already totaled it up.

It ate at me, and scared me more than any nightmare, when I lay alone in bed, with nothing to do but think of how I'd failed them.

The next idea came to me while still in bed one morning, about five months after the Dawes Laser, while I was in that muzzy place between asleep and awake. I was aware of very little that happened around me that day. By the end of dinner, I had pages of notes and drawings and equations to take to Dr. Okoro. The project took us ten months from beginning to end and resulted in the Dawes Theory of Intermolecular Force. The next project was birthed from that one and, a year following, the Dawes Second Theory of Intermolecular Force was recorded.

I had been four years at the IIC and made three groundbreaking discoveries. I was twelve. It was easy to see from the reactions of others that this was extraordinary; unheard of. But to me, it just was. In my head, I was doing nothing I hadn't done every day of my life before the IIC. Only now I had the resources to follow each question to its answer.

Whatever his private opinion of me, Director Kagawa now treated me as a favorite nephew. He gushed over and praised me often in public. He spoke of how he'd always known of my potential and had done his best to bring it out in me. He called me Jacob, something no other adult but Dr. Okoro ever did. It made my skin crawl. He even referred to himself as my mentor. I was quite happy to disappoint him by brushing him off and keeping quiet and to myself.

Without the need to justify my place at the IIC, I didn't have as many burning questions the next couple of years. The urgency, the need to unlock the secrets of the universe took a back seat as I experimented with just being a kid. I spent more time with Kirti and Chuck than I had before. Some of the other children extended overtures of friendship to me. It was intoxicating to be sought after by my peers, even if I never quite lost my resentment for their previous treatment of me.

That year, in biology class, we covered human reproduction.

The empirical biological and sociological information was all the education, philosophizing, or moralizing we were ever to have on the topic. Naturally, being teenagers, we had to conduct additional experiments on our own time to better explore this subject. There were rules in the dorms, about curfews and who was allowed where, but they were for safety and containment, nothing so abstract or intangible as right and wrong.

I didn't go as far or as fast as the others. Besides the fact that I was younger than all of them, I was too used to being different and separate to change so easily.

In spite of that, physics was still my main interest. Shortly after my fourteenth birthday I presented Dr. Okoro with a new theory. This one Kirti had given me. It happened in one of our lazy afternoons in the practice room.

Though she practiced her exercises and the pieces she was

assigned, she often simply played, taking the music where it wished to go. These times were my favorite. Lacking the structure of the written, polished pieces, the music evoked images that often revealed the flow of physical laws in unexpected ways. When she would change direction or tempo, whatever process I had been watching behind my eyelids would often break apart or change as well. And in those random and unexpected transitions or dissolutions I could see things in a new way, and watch as they unfolded before me in ways I'd never thought of before.

It was in one of these sessions that the Dawes First Theory of Wave Mechanics was born. And it was from many of these sessions that the Dawes Second Theory of Wave Mechanics was refined and codified.

Five major discoveries to my name in seven years. I was secure. I knew what my life was and what it would be. The ignominy of my past could never touch me again. This was it. I was home.

I was fifteen years old when he came to the IIC. At the time, I would have said I was sixteen. I nearly was; my birthday was less than a month away. But, more important than my impending birthday, even to me, was that we were expecting a visit from our new emperor, Rikhart IV.

For all that our importance to the future of the Empire was acknowledged by every emperor, Charles XVII had visited the IIC only once in his twenty year reign. Ferdinand VI, twice in fifty. So for the emperor to come so early in his reign was an incredible honor.

And he was young. As young as we were. He was exactly my age. We shared a birthday, which was as exciting as such random, abstract things can be when they involve an important person.

Such a young emperor was an oddity, but the Imperial Family had been plagued with disasters and tragedies for the past two generations. Charles XVII had been diagnosed with a previously unknown genetic condition, Meyer's Disease, in his childhood. He had died at thirty-eight years old, only six months earlier.

The entire IIC was in an uproar for the two weeks between the notification and his visit. There was to be an exhibit, the highlights of all the scientific and scholarly advancements and great works of art and music that had come out of the IIC in the recent past.

There were to be seven displays from each department, and so it surprised me when all five of my discoveries were chosen. A large chunk of the physics department helped Dr. Okoro and me to construct the displays.

They were quite impressive in my opinion, detailed, with a logical progression so that the process and its inevitable conclusion were clear. Our new emperor was known to be interested in the sciences, so we didn't skimp on the technical language and detail. The scientists who were old enough to remember the last emperor's visit were excited about this—when an explanation of a new discovery must stick only to the basics, it often misses the point.

The whole place was in a frenzy of preparation, much of which I missed, being practically cloistered in the physics department for those two weeks. It felt strange to emerge and rejoin my classmates when the morning of his visit arrived.

We had eaten breakfast and assembled afterward in the great hall wearing our dress uniforms. Mine was stiff and scratchy—from disuse, and probably an overexcited starching. We stood in groups, buzzing with whispers, where we would soon form up in rows. The teachers kept looking back and shushing us, but it didn't have much effect. They weren't willing to move from their groups to deal with us, and many of the adults were just as full of nervous murmurs as we were.

The entire membership of the IIC was assembled and organized by rank. We were in five rows of seventy people, the most senior in front. This meant that all of the students were in the last row. It wasn't a logical arrangement from a practical standpoint, with the smallest children standing behind rows of adults, but seniority is often weighted heavier than practicality. It was no great hardship for me. I'd hit a growth spurt and was already taller than many of the adults.

I was as jittery and anxious as anyone, perhaps more. After all, any minute now the emperor himself was going to see my work—was going to see *five* of my projects. Rumor had it that physics was one of his favorite sciences. I was bouncing on my toes.

After an eternity of waiting there was a flash of movement

from the area of the lobby and everyone froze, silence descending like a curtain. A palace functionary entered, spoke to Director Kagawa, and left. Kagawa turned and announced that the emperor would soon be entering. We were to get in our places, make no sound, remember the proper forms, and be on our best behavior throughout. His voice was low and promised dire consequences to anyone who stepped one foot out of line. He returned to his own position and we stood at rigid, noiseless attention.

It was probably only two minutes later, though it felt much longer, when there was movement again from the lobby. A different functionary entered the room, looking exactly the part of a herald in a uniform heavy with embroidery. He moved off to the side and announced His Excellence Emperor Rikhart IV. It seemed like the whole room took a breath at the same time, and held it.

And then he was there. He walked into the room just like any person walks into a room, on two feet. I almost laughed at myself. What had I expected?

Of course, there was much that set him apart from others; the obvious things like his clothes and jewelry, the circlet on his head, his position at the head of the group. But there was also something about the way he carried himself. It wasn't stiff-backed arrogance or affected dignity, but more a calm confidence. He knew who he was, and his place in the world—and the fact that his place was above everyone else was only a minor detail.

He was not handsome so much as interesting to look at. He had a shock of honey-colored hair, deep blue eyes, and cinnamon skin set in strong, solid features. He was followed by four guards and two servants. An older man, someone of importance, walked beside him.

As a group, we dropped into a deep, formal bow. When I straightened I could see something like a smile on his face. But not self-satisfied. No, more like genuine happiness. He said a few words of greeting, most of which I didn't really hear. But it was something about an honor and being excited and being grateful for what we did for the Empire. There was also something about our contribution being undervalued in his opinion and he hoped to see that changed in the future. There was a roar of applause at that.

When the choreographed introductions were over, the emperor was led to the first of the displays. The director and department heads followed.

At the third display, a chemistry project, the emperor turned to Dr. Warvrinosossi, the head of the chemistry department, and asked him a question. I couldn't be sure—I was only lip reading—but it seemed to me that he had addressed his question to the proper person by name without any guidance.

He spent close to ten minutes at each display. Watching him stand in one place, then move along to the next, quickly became boring. It was shocking to find his visit dull after all the sleepless nights of anticipation, but all we were doing was watching someone else look at things. We were too far away to hear anything that was going on. He may have been the most important man in the galaxy, but he was still just a man walking and talking the way any man would. What was there to look at?

He came to the first of my displays. I held my breath and watched as he examined it. I watched him ask Dr. Bartel questions, turning back again and again to study the work. And then I watched as he moved on.

I thought about crying. I wasn't sure what I was expecting, but I was expecting *something*. The emperor himself had seen my work! This was supposed to be some monumental, life changing event. Instead it was...nothing.

If I'd been bored before, now I was bored and depressed. It only worsened when my second display came around and, just like the first, he gave it thoughtful, in-depth examination, and moved on. The disappointment, as irrational as it was, was overwhelming. I wanted the whole thing to be over, but the morning dragged on.

So I didn't even notice when, near midday, the emperor came to my third display, the Dawes Laser. I was startled out of my self-pity by a voice at my side.

"Mr. Dawes?"

I jumped, whirling around to find one of the uniformed men who had been in the emperor's train standing beside me.

"Yyyyyes," I stammered.

"His Excellence asks if you would join him."

My heart stopped beating. I couldn't breathe. "OK," I squeaked, and followed.

The man stopped short of the emperor and waited for a pause in the conversation. "Your Excellence, Mr. Jacob Dawes."

The emperor turned to me and blinked. "Mr. Dawes?" he asked, looking at me, his brow creased in doubt. "Mr. Jacob Dawes of the Dawes Laser?"

I was too overawed to be angry, the way I usually was when people expressed disbelief that my work was actually mine. "Yes, Your Excellence."

A sudden smile lit his face and he chuckled. "I beg your pardon, Mr. Dawes. I should be the last person to judge someone based on their age, shouldn't I?"

I wasn't sure if agreeing or disagreeing with that was the right way to go, so I said nothing. That seemed to be fine.

"I am surprised, though, Mr. Dawes, because I have seen this laser in action. It was installed in one of our most important refineries. The head of the facility went on and on about what an exciting thing it was, all the wonderful improvements it would mean. He was quite overcome." His eyes twinkled with amusement. "But that was several years ago. You would have been much younger."

"I was eight," I answered, finding my courage again in the easy flow of his conversation. Several long seconds passed. "Your Excellence!" I added.

He smiled and waved his hand as if to dismiss the lapse.

"Eight," he mused. "But it wasn't just the invention of a new device, was it? There was a new theorem as well?"

"Yes, Your Excellence. The Dawes Theory of Stimulated Emissions."

56

He studied me for a moment. "Well," he said. "Tell me about this." He gestured toward the display.

So I moved closer and took him through the process from the original idea through the completion of the work, just as I would have in a formal presentation.

"What it means, Excellence," I concluded, "is that we can make laser devices out of more abundant and more versatile materials, so the same quality beam can be produced by a much smaller instrument. This not only improves efficiency and accuracy, it means laser technology can be implemented in areas it couldn't before, because of size limitations."

He nodded, still examining the display.

He surprised me. He was as he was rumored to be, not only interested in the sciences but well versed for a layman. He asked good questions and understood the answers. But there was also something so unpretentious about him, I almost felt like he was trying to put me at ease. That thought made me wary.

He turned to me and smiled. "I think I've already seen your name on one or two displays today, Mr. Dawes. Will there be any more?"

"Yes, Excellence. There are two more."

The look of surprise was brief and well controlled. He laughed. "Well then, I want you to join my retinue. When we come to your other two displays, we can discuss them."

I wasn't sure whether I wanted to hoot in triumph or throw up.

At lunchtime we assembled as usual and stood in silence, waiting for the emperor—it was probably the first time the dining room had been so quiet. It wasn't long before he entered the room with everyone else who was important enough to sit at the head table for the emperor's visit.

They took their places and the emperor deferred the blessing to Director Kagawa. He intoned the traditional phrases to which we chorused "May the emperor live forever," before we sat down. I watched the emperor to see how he would respond. He didn't. He acted as if nothing had been said about him at all. I didn't like that. I felt like he should have said thank you or something. It was reassuring to have some of my unflattering preconceived notions about people in high positions confirmed.

The lunch that was served outshone any meal I'd ever had. Wine was served at the head table, though it was only lunchtime. The emperor was given wine even though I—the other fifteen year old in the room—never got so much as a sniff of an alcoholic beverage. Not with permission, that is.

When lunch concluded we all stood in place as the emperor left the room and then we followed him back into the great hall. Everyone else went to re-form their rows but I hovered near the emperor's servants. One of them indicated that I should join the director and the heads of departments. I did, but hung back as much as possible.

Though I felt awkward and conspicuous, at least the afternoon wasn't boring. I was close enough to hear everything now. The emperor studied each display. He asked questions about each one—interesting, thoughtful questions on every subject. And while it was obvious he was more educated about some disciplines than others, he knew enough about all of them to be able to carry on an intelligent conversation.

About mid-afternoon we came to my fourth display. As soon as he read the name on it he gestured for me and I approached, bowing again just to be safe.

"Your Excellence." He nodded in acknowledgement.

"Tell me about this, Mr. Dawes," he said, gesturing toward the display.

So I did. As before, he asked questions. I got caught up in the science itself and found myself standing level with him. He either didn't notice or didn't mind, but I tried to slide back without drawing attention to my movement. After a couple more questions he thanked me and moved on.

Near the end of the exhibit he came to my last display. We stood side by side as I presented, explained, and answered his questions. We hadn't been at it long and he was just starting another question when the dinner bell rang. There were still two more displays to go.

"This has been very interesting Mr. Dawes, and I have more questions for you. You can sit by me at dinner to continue this discussion."

I gaped, but he was already moving on. I shuffled through the next two displays in terrified shock. *I* was going to sit at the head table with the emperor? It was one thing to present my work to him within the exhibit, and quite another to face the prospect of spending an hour right beside him. What would I say? What was I supposed to do? What was I supposed to *not* do? I was trembling by the time I followed them toward the dining room.

The servant behind me indicated I was to follow the emperor when he went into a lounge just outside the dining hall. I looked back for Chuck and Kirti. Their expressions begged for an answer.

I just shrugged.

In the lounge there were goblets of wine and hors d'oeuvres sitting out and the room was filled with fresh flowers. The emperor took at seat and began to talk with the man who had been walking with him throughout.

Unlike most of the emperor's attendants, functionaries, servants and guards, this man was not wearing some version of a uniform. He did have the Imperial crest embroidered on the sleeve of his jacket, and I guessed that he was some high ranking administrator.

I slid closer to a servant and asked who the man was. He called him Lord Sifer, the emperor's Head Minister, and told me that he was the man with the most authority in the palace after the emperor. He looked stern and uncompromising. I decided I was afraid of him.

Entering the dining hall with the emperor was a very strange experience. I was already nervous, and the room full of eyes on me was almost a physical weight. I'd stood before this exact group on more than one occasion presenting my work, but this was different. Then there had been pride of accomplishment, and confidence in what I had done, and if anyone was going to resent or judge me, it would be for something I had done by choice and through hard work.

But now, the jealousy on the faces of many in the crowd felt like a force all its own. I hadn't asked for this and, as once-in-a-lifetime an experience as it was, I would have been happy sitting in the back of the room between Kirti and Chuck. But I followed, because that was what I was supposed to do, and tried to ignore all the eyes on me.

I was led to the seat at the immediate right of the emperor and my mouth went dry. The servant just nodded reassurance, so I stood behind the chair. What else could I do? Director Kagawa, who had been sitting on the emperor's right during lunch, was now at *my* right. I looked over at him, taking pleasure, at least, in having moved him down a notch. He didn't look at me, but stood and offered the blessing.

I couldn't say the last words. Standing by the man himself, it felt ridiculous on the one hand, and frightening on the other. The emperor didn't seem to notice that anyone in the room had just wished him eternal life, let alone that I had not.

We sat, and the emperor turned to Lord Sifer on his left and continued the conversation they'd been having in the lounge. It gave me time to get my bearings. The food was brought for us and servants came along pouring wine. My goblet was filled like everyone else's. I looked over at Director Kagawa who gave me a stern, admonishing look. I grinned at him and sipped the wine. I'm sure it was a very fine vintage but it didn't taste very good to me. I didn't see what all the fuss was about.

I had just taken a large bite when the emperor turned to me and asked a question. I coughed, trying to clear my mouth in a hurry, but he seemed content to wait. We chatted for several minutes and I watched him to figure out how I should be combining eating and talking with a concern for manners that wasn't a priority among teenaged boys at the lower tables.

The emperor drew Director Kagawa into the conversation without talking over me, but I was freed from the obligation of talking and ate in silence. I tried more of the wine, hoping it would improve with time. That probably wasn't the most intelligent thing to do while sitting beside the emperor, not knowing my tolerance for alcohol.

After a while, and another conversation with Lord Sifer, the emperor turned back to me. "So Mr. Dawes, how do you come up with all these marvelous discoveries of yours?"

I shrugged. "They just come to me. The Stimulated Emissions theory came to me in math class from something we'd been studying in physics. The Intermolecular Force theorems were from one of those half-dreams you have when you're not quite awake yet. And I've been getting ideas from listening to my friend Kirti play."

He raised his eyebrows.

"She's a pianist. And we like to hang out in the practice halls. She'll play whatever occurs to her at the time, and I'll watch the interactions of different forces or systems in the music and sometimes it gives me ideas."

"What do you mean, you watch them in the music?"

No one had asked me that before. Then again, I'd never tried to explain this to anyone else. It just...was. But you don't just tell the emperor "I dunno" and move on.

"Well, when I close my eyes, the music is like a paintbrush that's creating pictures from the notes and harmonies. Listening to the music is like watching the interactions of things you can't see otherwise. It's different than clinical observation. It's more... fanciful I guess."

He kept watching me, considering, in a way that made me want to squirm. "That's one of the most interesting things I think I've ever heard, Mr. Dawes. Do you see this sort of thing often?"

"All the time. But not all the things I see make any sense, once I really think about them."

"Hmm," he replied. "Well, I'd like to try this for myself. We'll have your friend Kirti play for us."

He made a small gesture and two of the servants moved away. I stared at him in shock. Now I was very nervous in a different way. This would be a shock for Kirti.

It wasn't long before several servants were wheeling a piano into the room and setting it up in front of the head table. The room rang with whispers and the sound of people turning around to see what was going on. A servant approached from the back of the room, leading Kirti, whose face had gone white. She stopped in front of the table and offered a shaky bow and a tremulous, "Your Excellence."

"Ms. Sachar, would you play for us, please? Mr. Dawes tells me that your playing is the inspiration for some of his extraordinary insights, and I would like to be inspired myself."

If possible, Kirti went whiter. "Of course, Your Excellence. What would you like me to play?"

"Mr. Dawes says that he's inspired when you're not playing from a score. I'd like you to play like that for me."

"Yes, Your Excellence," she said in a whisper. She sat on the bench. I could see that her hands, as she held them over the keys, trembled.

Her music at first was soft, hesitant. Not the playing, but the intended music. It was easy to see it was a reflection of how she felt.

And before long I was watching a calm, soothing spring rain. Soon the music changed and I was right up among the turgid, angry clouds of an approaching storm. My mind ran away with the fascinating processes clashing in the heart of those clouds.

The music climbed and I was above the cloudbank and still rising until I broke free of the planet's gravity and was out in the void itself. I sighed. This was one of my favorite places to be. All I knew, all that was familiar and ordinary on the ground, was new and full of possibilities here. I watched, floating carefree, as the great forces of the universe gamboled in their never-ending play. Opposing forces kissed and spun away only to come back together again in the dance.

The music thundered and the dancers stumbled, wobbling to right themselves. I watched as powerful forces gave way to weaker ones, particles of almost no mass at all displaced planetary bodies, and a delicate pattern of neutrino radiation—silver-white strands of celestial silk—overlaid it all.

I was so caught up in the scene that the crash of applause made me jump. I realized I'd had my eyes closed. I caught a glimpse of the emperor when I opened them and he was watching me, the quirk of a smile on his lips.

"Thank you, Ms. Sachar," he said, "that was beautiful."

She bowed and returned to her seat. He turned to me. "Well, I confess, Mr. Dawes, while I enjoyed the music, I got no new insights into the workings of the universe. Did you?"

I shook my head, but to reorganize my thoughts, not as an answer. "Mmmmm. It makes sense if you think about it...there have to be more sources than we've detected. Just because we haven't observed it yet doesn't mean..." I looked up at him. The look of polite attentiveness slid off his face. When I slowed to a stop he lost control of the laughter he'd been trying to suppress.

"You're amazing, Mr. Dawes. You're going to have to come with me on my tour of the Empire." My heart stopped. "In two weeks I'm embarking on a year-long tour. I've had a lab constructed for myself aboard ship. Not that I'm qualified to make much use of it. I had hoped to find the time to spend the occasional day divining the secrets of the universe. It's been a lovely delusion, but I know it's nothing more than a sophisticated shrine to my self-indulgence. It would be such a tragedy to see it go to waste. But with you aboard ship, the lab won't be wasted at all."

My mouth was too dry to speak. I was going into space? For a whole year? To work in a lab built for the emperor himself? I sat in stunned silence. He seemed to be enjoying my reaction.

Director Kagawa's voice came from over my shoulder, "Mr. Dawes is no doubt overwhelmed by Your Excellence's generosity. Of course, I'm sure it's frightening as well, the prospect of leaving behind your only home for something completely foreign and no doubt quite strange for someone of his origins, at such a young age." I wondered if he missed the look on the emperor's face at that reference to my age. "And to do so alone? Perhaps someone should accompany him, both as a familiar presence and as a chaperone. As his mentor I'd be more than happy to fill that role."

Fury welled up in me. I could usually ignore Kagawa's insulting assumptions but this was too much. My hands clenched into fists in my lap. The emperor seemed surprised by the director's little speech and turned to me with a questioning look.

The heady feeling of power rushed through me. Kagawa was trying to acquire something extraordinary for himself by capitalizing on my success, and the emperor had laid the decision in my lap.

I didn't even look at Kagawa. "He's nothing to me, Excellence," I said. "Had it been up to him, I'd have been Resettled years ago."

The emperor's face went blank when he turned to regard

Kagawa, as if the director no longer existed. Somehow it was the most frightening expression I'd ever seen. The emperor looked over at Lord Sifer, who nodded acknowledgement of something that had passed unseen between them. He turned back to me and his face resumed its previous expression of polite interest.

"It's settled then. I can't wait to see the fascinating things you'll think up to do in that lab."

I was paralyzed with horror. What had I done? I forced myself to look over at Director Kagawa. Pale as death, he stared out into space, poleaxed. I dropped my head, my face hot with shame.

I spent the rest of the meal staring at my plate, my appetite gone. I couldn't look at Kagawa, nor could I look at the emperor, but looking up at the room would have been just as bad or worse. The closest tables would have heard the entire conversation, and many more would have seen the reactions. Unless Kagawa looked markedly different now than he had the last time I'd raised my head, the whole room had to know that something had happened. Something big. Something terrible. Something that was my fault.

I don't think the emperor spoke to me again. If he did, I didn't notice. When dessert was served, it was all I could do not to lose what I'd already eaten. I sat in agony until the emperor stood and made a small, closing speech. He praised our work. He promised to return every five years or so to keep himself abreast of all that we did. He spoke of how much he had enjoyed the day, how much he had learned, and how valuable we were to the Empire. He thanked us and we rose as a group and bowed as he left the room.

As soon as he was gone I catapulted out of my place and rushed after his departing retinue. I caught up to Lord Sifer and grabbed at his arm without thinking.

"Please sir, please, what's going to happen to Director Kagawa? What I said, I didn't mean it like it sounded. That is, I mean, please sir, I just said something stupid."

He looked at me without emotion. "Mr. Dawes, you may address me as Lord Sifer or 'my lord.' Please remove your hand from my arm."

I snatched my hand away. "Forgive me, my lord."

He nodded. "Mr. Dawes, what happens to Director Kagawa is not your concern."

"But sir! My lord! I didn't mean what I said. You can't do anything to him just because of what I said!"

He raised his eyebrows. "Was what you said untrue?"

I flushed. "No, my lord, but it's not what it sounds like..."

"Mr. Dawes, I'm sure you're very brilliant when it comes to the physical sciences. I would not be in the position I am in if I were not also very good at what I do. I won't presume to tell you how to conduct your work, and I expect the same courtesy in return."

My heart dropped. "Please," I begged.

"Good evening, Mr. Dawes," he said. I watched in despair, crawling with powerless desperation as he walked away.

Lord Sifer had almost disappeared down the long hall when a hand clamped around my upper arm and I was hauled into motion. It was Dr. Okoro. He didn't look at me, his gaze fixed on something ahead as he dragged me down the hallway, fury chiseled into his profile. I wanted to say something, but I was too afraid to make a sound. It took all my attention to keep up with his angry steps without tripping.

When we got to his study, he thrust me, stumbling, into the room. He walked past me to his desk without a word, digging through the top drawer in search of something. When he didn't find it there, he moved on to the cabinets on the left wall, then the ones on the right. He grunted in discovery and emerged from one of the cabinets with a cane in hand, which he leveled at me.

"I've never whipped you, boy. The thought never even crossed my mind. You've never given me the first reason to consider punishing you. But tonight—do you realize what you just did? What your spiteful, vengeful little speech there has just done to that man's life!"

I forced words past the lump in my throat.

"Yes, sir. But I swear I didn't mean it like that! I didn't think...I was just...I just didn't want him to come with me. You understand that, don't you? I didn't mean for anything else to happen! I swear it!"

"That's why you think about what you're going to say before you open your mouth, Jacob! That man is going to lose his assignment, or be Resettled, because you vented your petty childhood resentments in front of the wrong person."

"I know!" I wailed. "I'm so sorry. If I could do anything to fix it I would. I tried to talk to Lord Sifer but he wouldn't listen. I'm sorry!"

"I doubt that will bring Director Kagawa any comfort."

I stared at the floor, wishing desperately to be anywhere else.

"Get over the desk," he said, his voice hard.

I approached his desk and cleared a space on the surface. Without being told, I dropped my pants and undershorts before I bent over. It wasn't the worst beating I'd ever taken, but I sobbed all the way through it.

When it was over, the cane clattered to the desk beside me. The door opened and closed and there was silence. I pushed myself up, scrubbing the tears from my face, and eased my pants back up with a wince. I hadn't been caned in several years and had forgotten how much it hurt.

I looked around, but I didn't need the confirmation that I was alone in the room. I stood there for a long time, contemplating my miseries and trying to decide what to do. The one thing I was sure I did not want to do was walk out that door. It wasn't a well-traveled hallway but there was no way back to my room that didn't involve walking through one or two of the high traffic areas, and facing anyone else at that moment was about the worst thing I could think of. I grabbed the blanket and curled up on the couch to meditate on my sorrows.

I woke several hours later and decided it was late enough to risk the halls. The few people I came across were servants who only glared at me as I passed, and two junior history fellows who were a little worse for the drink. I entered my room with relief.

There in my room, Kirti was asleep on my bed. I was so shocked to see her that I stumbled backward against the closing door. She opened her eyes and sat up. With all that happened that evening, I hadn't even considered that I was leaving for a least a year. More? What if I had to stay for good? It was only then that I realized I might be leaving Kirti behind forever. I saw in her face that she had already reached that conclusion.

She stood and buried her head in my shoulder. I held her, laying my cheek against the top of her head. She looked up at me. Our faces were so close together, our bodies. Leaving. Maybe forever.

I don't know who initiated it, but we were kissing. The more we kissed the more urgent it became. My hands were tangled in her hair and clutching her close to my body.

My memories of the remainder of that night are hazy. Though I remember other sexual encounters since with almost perfect clarity, that one, my first, is just a jumble of impressions, emotions, sounds, and sensations. We clung to each other, frantic with our fears and needs until we slept, exhausted, in each other's arms.

fg 9

I woke up in the morning to the realization that I should be panicking. Kirti had been out of her room all night, which was one of the biggest infractions a student could commit. The repercussions were very serious. And yet lying there with her warm and soft against me, with all the other problems waiting for me just outside the door, I couldn't make myself care.

She woke not long after I did. I hadn't moved and was still wrapped around her. She looked up at me and smiled, but a crease of sadness appeared in her forehead.

"You're leaving."

I nodded. There was nothing else to say. She watched my face for a long moment then pecked a kiss on my lips and got up to get dressed. I watched her from the bed, wanting to say something but not sure what. She scrambled into her clothes and kissed me once more.

"See you at breakfast," she said, and left.

If I'd thought entering the dining hall the night before with the emperor had been uncomfortable, it was nothing compared to walking in for breakfast that morning. Four steps into the room, the sudden silence was palpable. It was like I had walked into a thick, sticky gunk that became more and more viscous with every step.

I made it to my table and found Chuck there, but no Kirti. I took my usual spot beside him. I tried to ignore my tablemates but I didn't miss the glares Chuck was giving out, daring them to say or do anything to me.

The conversation in the room resumed, though at my table there was a horrid, stifling quiet. Kirti soon entered and sat beside me. She acted normal; normal as anything was that morning. No one looked at her any more than usual and I wondered if anyone knew she hadn't slept in her room last night. Of course, whether our classmates did or didn't realize wasn't the problem. The dorm head wouldn't have missed it and he was the one that mattered.

She gave me a sad smile and watched as the members of the head table entered the room. Director Kagawa, of course, was not there. When crushing disappointment settled in my chest, I realized I had been holding out hope that he would be among them; that nothing would have changed. The administrators took their places, leaving the director's chair empty. Mr. Harris, to the immediate right, spoke.

"As you are all aware, Director Kagawa is no longer with us. I will be filling in for him until a permanent replacement can be selected." He offered the blessing and we sat.

When I thought about it later I concluded that Chuck must have threatened our tablemates before I'd arrived. No one said a word to me, contenting themselves with withering glares. I did my best to pretend I couldn't see them.

At the conclusion of breakfast I was summoned to the director's office. I felt an irrational stab of panic, but reminded myself that the director's office no longer belonged to Kagawa, which made me feel worse. I went, dragging my feet, and reported to the functionary outside the office. She looked daggers at me but sent me in.

I opened the door with sweaty hands, more afraid to enter that office than I had ever been. Mr. Harris looked up from behind the big desk. "Come in, Mr. Dawes." I took my place before the desk and waited. "You may have a seat if you'd like."

I stared at him, thrown off balance.

"You're not here for discipline, Mr. Dawes. Have a seat. We have a lot to talk about."

I dropped into the chair, stunned. He smiled. I was baffled.

I knew very little about Mr. Harris. He had been the second highest administrator at the IIC, under Kagawa. He was very young for such a high position at such an important facility. I had almost no previous experience with him, but I'd never had any reason to think ill of him. Of course, I'd never had any reason to think of him at all.

He watched me for a moment, maybe to let me get my bearings. Taking the opportunity offered by his silence I blurted out, "Mr. Harris, I'm very sorry for what happened last night with Director Kagawa. I promise, sir, I didn't mean for that to happen. I didn't."

"I know you didn't."

"You do?" It felt like we weren't speaking the same language. That whatever he was replying to couldn't be what I'd said.

He smiled again. "Jacob—may I call you Jacob?" I nodded dumbly. "Jacob, I was assigned here not long after you arrived. I've seen what happened between you and Kagawa, and I've heard more. I've heard things that you didn't, things that Kagawa would say behind closed doors. I never agreed with his treatment of you and I said so on many occasions. He did you a great wrong, and could have deprived the Empire of your talent. I respected and liked the man for many reasons but his treatment of you was unconscionable. It's not your fault that he is now suffering the consequences of his own errors of judgment."

I was speechless. "No one blames you for what happened," he said. I tried to examine his face without staring. I couldn't decide if he was trying to tease me in some way, or maybe trick me. "OK, *I* don't blame you for what happened." That still seemed unlikely, but a bit more believable. I didn't know what to say.

"I received your reassignment documents this morning," he told me, and chuckled when I straightened in surprise. "Yes, very efficient, aren't they? I'm envious."

"Reassignment, sir? But isn't it a temporary assignment?"

"No," he said. "You've been reassigned to the palace as a Scientist in Residence."

It was a rare thing, but it did happen. Almost always, it was an artist who was reassigned to the palace, sometimes a talented medical doctor or historian. Never a physicist. And it was always a very senior fellow, in any case.

"But, sir, I haven't even finished my basic education yet." There wasn't as much power behind my objection as I'd intended. I already felt defeated; run over and crushed and discarded.

"Arrangements have been made for your long-distance studies. There is also, of course, lab work which you'll have the facilities for. Tutors will be provided if necessary. By keeping to the schedule of assigned work, you will keep pace with your classmates and graduate from your basic education when they do."

"And my secondary education?"

"No specific provisions have been made yet, but I have no doubt that matter will be addressed when the time comes."

I sat there feeling helpless, as every objection I could think of withered and died.

Only hours before, I'd have insisted that, at fifteen, I was a man. But now I wanted to protest that I was too young for this, that they couldn't send me away forever. Though I couldn't blame them for wanting to. Not after last night. But it was all a big mistake, I hadn't meant to do it. My life, my work was here. Kirti and Chuck and Dr. Okoro were here. A year in a lab in space sounded like an impossible dream come true, but I would have handed it all back if it meant I could stay at the IIC for life. Within a day, everything had been turned upside down. I wished the emperor had never come.

It was hard to fight back tears.

"If you don't have any questions, Jacob, you may go if you'd like. We can talk more later."

I stood. "I've been reassigned?" He nodded. "So do I still go to class now?"

He shook his head. "You can, but there's no requirement for you to do so. You've already been released from your assignment here. Your status is that of a guest."

I was beyond shock. One misery piled on top of the next.

"How much longer am I here?" I managed in a strangled whisper.

"A transport will be arriving for you in nine days."

I felt like I'd been punched in the gut. I nodded. "Thank you, sir."

I moved toward the door. "Jacob, one more thing." I stopped. "If you would do me a small favor? Your friend, Kirti Sachar, if you could give her a message for me? There was a malfunction in her door sensor that made it appear as if she didn't return to her room last night. Please let her know that we're aware of the error and that it's been taken care of."

I froze. "Yes, sir."

"Of course, you wouldn't have had to worry about that had it been you," he continued. "No curfew worries when you're a guest. Why, if you didn't sleep in your own room for the remainder of your stay, there'd be no issue at all."

I turned back to him in astonishment, certain he couldn't be saying what he seemed to be saying.

"You'll pass on the message for me?"

"Yes...yes, sir." Stupefied, I left the room.

I wandered around the building for a long time. All my classmates—former classmates—were at their studies. I could have gone to class, but I couldn't bear the thought of their censure.

I was angry. At myself, at the world, at the emperor. It really was all his fault. If he hadn't come, none of this would have happened. If he hadn't tricked me into saying that about Kagawa. If he hadn't snatched me out of my life without so much as a by-your-leave. Everything had gone wrong. Everything. I had lost everything. I wanted nothing to do with that horrible lab on that hateful ship. And there was no way in hell I was ever saying "May the emperor live forever" again. I wished he'd die.

I shivered and looked around, even though I hadn't said that near-blasphemy aloud.

After a time, I found myself standing before Dr. Okoro's door. I hesitated there, not sure whether I was trying to encounter or avoid him. I wanted to see him, to talk to him, to pour out all my fears and anguish. But I dreaded finding him still angry, turning me away. I dreaded his disappointment.

I must have stood in front of the door for a full fifteen minutes. Rallying my courage, I entered the study.

It was empty. It looked like no one had been there since I'd left in the wee hours of the morning. The blanket lay where I had tossed it over the arm of the couch. The cane was on the desk. I wanted to put it away, to hide that reminder of the night before, but I didn't. I didn't feel I had the right. Instead I folded the blanket and draped it over the back of the couch. It looked odd that way, so I shook it back out, balled it up, and shoved it against one of the arms of the couch like a throw pillow.

I looked around the room as if seeing it for the first time. I remembered the eight-year-old boy who hadn't known why he was here, scared, confused. Who didn't know that everything would change the moment he entered the room. I looked at the jumble of experiments and tools that lay in disarray over the tables.

I stood in front of our current project, examining the precisely designed and calibrated experiment; such a contrast to the haphazardness of the room behind. Each instrument and tool set in a spot convenient for its use. With an unfamiliar hesitation, I activated the central heat pad, reaching for the pyrometer as if afraid of being caught doing something I shouldn't. But before long I'd lost myself in the work.

The door opened and closed behind me. I couldn't move. My shoulders tightened. I could hear him move to the desk and pick up the cane. My breath caught. The drawer opened, something clattered, it closed.

His hand settled on my shoulder. I flinched in spite of myself. "Jacob," he said, "Jacob, look at me."

I obeyed. He examined my face and laid his hand against my cheek. "I've been a fool as well," he said. "Many times. Are we all right?"

"Yes, sir." He patted my cheek with a wan smile, and dropped his hand and his gaze to the work in front of me.

We worked together for the remainder of the day, eating lunch in the study. I didn't want to leave when dinnertime came, but he insisted.

"Hiding from your problems wouldn't make them go away," he said.

We walked together to the dining hall. I hesitated in the doorway. There was no place for me here anymore. Not really. They weren't going to make me sit at the head table, like a guest, were they?

No one stopped me or said anything about seating, so I went to my normal table and dropped into my seat.

"You weren't in class today," Chuck said.

I shook my head, looking down at my plate. "No."

"So that's it?"

I didn't want to answer. I didn't want to say it, make it real. "Yes." I looked up at him. "That's it. I've been reassigned. I'm just a guest here now."

The table fell silent. Kirti gasped.

"So move," Sasha said. "You don't belong here anymore."

I glared at him.

"Why are you still here?" he pressed.

"Where would you have me eat?"

He shrugged. "Not here. You're ruining people's food."

I was already halfway to my feet when Chuck's hand clamped onto my arm and dragged me back down.

"Don't," he hissed.

I wondered if guests could be punished for fighting. But Chuck was right, and I was fed up with creating problems for myself. I was sure I didn't want to have to appear before Mr. Harris for making a disturbance. Not because I was afraid of him, but because I didn't want to lose his good opinion. I didn't have many left.

I stayed in my seat and ignored Sasha as well as I could.

When the meal was over, Kirti slipped her hand into mine. "Walk by the lake?" she suggested. I nodded.

Hand in hand we exited the building into the cold, late winter night; our breath silvery clouds in the light of the near-full moon. In silence we walked down to the water's edge. The most ambitious waves lapped against my shoes and dampness crept through my socks. Still we said nothing.

"It's not a temporary assignment?" she asked.

"No." I couldn't bear to look at her. I tipped my head back, staring at the field of stars. All of a sudden I remembered the boy in the mural in the lobby and I shivered.

"Why?" Her voice was anguished.

I squeezed her hand tighter. "I don't know."

We walked past the stream we often sat beside in the spring, now covered with a layer of ice. The tumble of pebbles on the beach looked odd, threatening in the dark.

She turned to face me. "What are we going to do?"

I couldn't meet her eye. "I'm going to go away. And you're going to stay here. That's what we're going to do. There's nothing else to do. We don't have a choice."

I heard the sob catch in her throat. I pulled her close and crushed her against me. We stood a long time in the moonlight before we made our way back to her room. There, we made love—for its own sake, but also as a way to hide from the future for a while.

The days passed. I spent the school days in the lab with Dr. Okoro. The afternoons I spent with Chuck, the evenings with Kirti. The nights were spent in her room, trying to fight off the inevitable with passion.

But the inevitable would not be denied. Eight days passed. On my last evening at the IIC there was a going-away celebration. I think most people were celebrating the fact that I would be gone. After that dinner, there was a party for the VIPs of the IIC, my teachers, Dr. Okoro, and me. I endured it as long as necessary and then excused myself to the genuine enjoyment of Kirti's bed.

The morning came, punctual and heartless.

I finished packing my things, and went to meet the transport with Kirti at my side. Mr. Harris, Dr. Okoro, and Chuck were all waiting there.

The transport was not as long as the one that had brought the group of us to the IIC, though it was newer and still very big. A man in an Imperial uniform was waiting at the open door.

I stopped several feet away and turned to Mr. Harris.

"Thank you, sir, for everything."

"Anytime, Jacob. Good luck to you."

He shook my hand, nodded, and reentered the building. Chuck stepped up next and clapped his hand hard against my arm. He pulled me into a rough embrace.

"Stay out of trouble. Then again," he grinned, "don't. Have fun. We'll miss you."

"Thanks. I'll miss you too." He smiled, smacked me once more on the back, and walked away. It was such a Chuck-like thing to do. No lingering or prolonging the moment. Just get it done and move on. I watched his retreating back and my throat tightened.

Dr. Okoro gathered me up in a hug. "Take care of yourself and work hard. I know you will." I could hear the tears in his voice and my vision blurred. "You've always made me proud of you."

It was a moment before I could answer. "Yes, sir. Thank you. Thank you for everything." I hugged him hard. I didn't know how to say what I wanted him to know. He pulled back, smiled, and hurried away.

Kirti and I were alone. Tears brimmed in her eyes. I wrapped my arms around her. "I love you," I whispered into her hair.

She choked on a sob, nodding her head. I squeezed her once more, bent to kiss her, and hurried toward the transport.

The man waiting there stepped forward.

"Mr. Dawes, my name is Jonathan. I've been assigned to serve you."

I nodded. He took my bag and led me onto the transport. He turned down the corridor but I stood at the big window by the door and watched as we moved away. I watched until Kirti was too small to see anymore. And still I stood and watched as my life faded into the distance.

When there was nothing of the IIC left to see, I turned away from the window. Jonathan waited nearby. He actually *looked* quiet, somehow fading into the background in spite of his distinctive uniform.

"Yes?" I asked.

"Sir?"

No one had ever called me sir before. It sounded strange. "Did you want something?" I asked.

"That's supposed to be my question," he said, not quite smiling. "I'm waiting, sir, for you to have need of me."

"My name's Jacob Dawes," I said, so he'd stop calling me sir.

"Yes, sir," he replied. I examined him, wondering if he was simple. He wasn't that much older than me, which made "sir" even weirder.

I didn't feel like dealing with him, or anything just then.

"Could you just tell me where the lounge is?" I asked.

"This way, sir," he said, turning to the right.

He led me down a long, bright corridor, full of windows, to a large lounge filled with plush couches, low tables scattered with tablets, and a large vid screen on one wall. "Are there other passengers, yet?" I asked him.

"No, sir, there will be no other passengers."

"No other passengers? You mean they sent this thing just for me?"

"Yes, sir." His mouth twitched. "If it makes you feel better, this is the smallest type of transport maintained by the palace."

"Oh."

It made me nervous having the whole thing to myself. As if someone was going to discover the mistake and I'd be in trouble for it.

Jonathan took up a position at the wall behind me. He just stood there. I squirmed.

"Is there something you're waiting for?"

"For whatever you need, sir."

"That's it? You're just going to stand there until I think of something I want you to do?"

"That is the plan, yes. Though I can leave if you'd like."

I wasn't sure if I'd be insulting him or making myself look stupid by asking him to leave. "No, that's fine. Just, sit down or something."

"If you don't mind, sir, I'd rather not, it wouldn't be appropriate."

I tried not to sigh. "Fine then, but call me Jacob."

"That wouldn't be appropriate, sir."

I was starting to hate this guy. I didn't like feeling out of my element, or like an idiot, and he made me feel both. I didn't know how to fix it except by ignoring him, but I couldn't forget that he was standing there.

I spent most of the trip gazing out the window, trying to find something else to think about. I hadn't traveled since I'd been brought to the IIC as a child and it was easy to lose myself in all there was to see.

We passed through plains areas and hilly terrain and cities. We floated by fields in cultivation, undulating with tall silky grains, or dotted with heads of leafy vegetables, or furred with delicate herbs.

I saw the softer, gentle faces of mountain ranges much older than the sharp, uncompromising giants I was used to. We crossed hills so subtle that I was sure they weren't hills at all until we crested a rise and dipped into the hollow below.

And, at the last, there was the ocean. I had already seen many incredible things in my life; things that no man had observed before, and things that few others ever would. Those moments were intimate, made me feel a part of something infinite and eternal. The experience of seeing the ocean for the first time was nothing like that. It felt somehow vaster than infinity, and greater than any other phenomenon. Sitting there I realized just how small and unimportant I really was.

But even that—as the effect of my first look wore off—didn't eliminate the ever-present jittery feeling, the amorphous, unformed fears that had taken up residence in my stomach. As I watched the countryside slip by, I couldn't think of anything but how alone I was.

fg 10

I should remember my first experience of the palace, but I don't. Not with any real clarity.

I suppose I do remember high walls like a swell of the sand-dunes that rolled into them like waves. And windows that reflected the blue-gray of the ocean and looked like little pools of seawater climbing a vertical beach.

I remember people. So many, many people. And huge imposing doorways and hallways—like being inside a whale—that still managed to feel crowded.

I remember feeling nervous when Jonathan told me that the rooms I'd assumed must be for several guests were for me alone.

I remember those things the way you sometimes remember dreams—never quite certain if the memory is real or if you decided it was so.

What I do remember are the books.

There in the sitting room that was just for me. Real books. Paper and ink books. Pages and pages, bound together with fabric-wrapped stiff paper backings and glue. They were stacked on one of the end tables, as if they were everyday things and not something out of a bygone era.

I picked one up and felt the heft of it in my hand. I opened it to look at the creamy white pages with thick black ink stamped on them. It smelled woody, with the tang of chemicals and glue. It was a text by a famous twentieth century physicist.

I sank into a nearby chair and began to read. There was

something so different about reading a book in this form versus watching the words scroll by on a tablet. It felt like I'd just cracked it open when Jonathan interrupted to tell me that dinner would be served soon. I was shocked. And almost a hundred pages into the book.

"This is incredible," I said holding up the book. "Does everyone here have these?"

"His Excellence collects books. They're provided to all guests of the palace at his order. There's also a very large library that I can show you if you'd like. But right now it's time to dress for dinner."

I looked down at myself. I was dressed.

"At the palace, everyone dresses up for dinner," he said.

I frowned. "This is my dress uniform. It's the best thing I have."

"Suitable clothing has been provided for you." He gestured toward the bedroom and the closet there. Surprised and curious, I followed.

Hanging in the closet were my uniforms, but in addition to those were six complete suits of clothes, three much fancier than the others. Even the "casual" ones were too rich and opulent for me. Just looking at them was intimidating. I tried to protest, but Jonathan insisted that even my dress uniform would not be suitable for dinner in the grand dining hall.

I had no choice but to relent. When I was dressed, Jonathan brought out a small case. Inside was a thick platinum ring with an imperial crest in the center.

"No, thanks. I don't wear jewelry."

"The ring is a gift from the emperor. It's a longstanding tradition that the emperor's appointees receive a token from His Excellence. It's also a symbol of status. To have one at all puts you in an exclusive group. If you have a token from a previous emperor, the bracelet from Charles XVII or even the pendant from Ferdinand VI, it's a symbol of seniority. Rikhart IV's ring is still quite rare. You are one of only eight who have it."

I wasn't sure what to say.

"Well that's fascinating," I answered. "And I'm honored.

But I don't want to wear a ring, so let's just leave it here." While interesting as a story, what he'd told me made me no more inclined to wear the ring than I had been before. Rank and seniority were all well and good if you wanted them, but I was much more interested in going unnoticed. On top of that, I was still unhappy about the appointment. I had no desire to wear a symbol of it.

He stared at me. "Mr. Dawes, this is a gift from the emperor."

"I didn't notice him giving me anything. He probably doesn't know I'm here, much less what someone put in the closet for me. I can't believe he'll care."

"But sir..."

"It's time for dinner, isn't it? I don't want to be late."

He shook his head in bewilderment and led me out of the room.

Jonathan led me through such a confusing set of hallways that I was sure I'd never be able to find my way back to my room without help. But finding the dining hall was easy. We moved along with a steady stream of elegant people all heading in the same direction.

As uncomfortable as I'd felt in the fancy clothes while in my room, I was grateful for them now. Everyone else was wearing things as nice, or nicer. I would have been horribly conspicuous in my uniform.

We entered a room that the word grand didn't even begin to encompass. It was huge. The ceiling was six stories above us. The western wall was a series of windows that framed the sun as it set over the ocean, resplendent in orange and red.

I stood by the seat Jonathan directed me to and waited, watching the people flow about me. They were a loud, gaudy, sparkling sea of importance and wealth.

The emperor entered the room with a group of men and women who exuded power like an odious smell.

The occupants of the head table took their places and the emperor himself offered the blessing. It wasn't at all what I'd expected. He said, "May we as the people of our great Empire, give all we have in service of each other, and of the greater good. Long live the Empire!"

I automatically echoed the last along with everyone else and sat down, still pondering the strange blessing. The only blessings I'd ever heard before had focused on the emperor and what we could do for him. Now he spoke of what we could do for each other. Maybe even what *he* could do for *us*. It was unexpected and unsettling. I didn't know how to mesh that with what I thought of him, of the thoughtless way he'd rearranged my life for his own benefit.

"Good evening," the woman on my right said. "I'm Dr. Sonja Henriksen, the emperor's physician." She wasn't all that old, which surprised me, considering her position. No gray hair, at least, nor many wrinkles.

"I'm Jacob Dawes. I just arrived this afternoon."

"And what brings you here, Jacob?"

"I've been reassigned here," I said, attempting to sound calm and detached about it. "I came from the Intellectual Complex."

Her eyes widened. "From the IIC?" I nodded. "But...you're Jacob Dawes? *The* Jacob Dawes of the Dawes Laser?"

I flushed. She wasn't skeptical like people usually were. She was impressed.

"Yes, ma'am."

She smiled. "No kidding? Mr. Dawes, that's incredible. I've been using your laser in my practice for several years now. In fact, I used it in one of the last procedures I did on our late emperor. You're quite talented. And at such a young age. You don't look much older than eighteen."

Her over-estimate of my age helped soothe away some of my embarrassment. "I'm almost sixteen," I answered.

Her eyebrows climbed higher. "Incredible. That's a nice bit of work you did there, Mr. Dawes. It really is an amazing improvement over the options we had before. My, my, just imagine the things you'll do."

She was almost crowing over me like a proud relative. I liked her, though. She took me at face value and hadn't once made any insulting assumptions. She was neither trying to use me nor tear me down. I wasn't used to that.

When dinner concluded, Jonathan reappeared and I asked him to show me back to my room. Once there, I buried myself again in Dr. Hawking's work until I was dozing in my chair. I was about to collapse into bed when I realized I hadn't sent Kirti or anyone else a message to let them know I'd arrived. I hand-wrote a note on a tablet in the room and sent it off. I didn't say much more than that I was there, and safe, and promised to write more later. Still I felt guilty for having managed to put them out of my mind so quickly, caught up in the experience of this place I was determined to hate.

I spent my one full day at the palace wandering, trying to see nothing while looking at everything. I was very conflicted. I didn't want to like it or be impressed, but surrounded by the best of everything, it was impossible not to catch my breath in wonder from time to time.

As an antidote, I spent the afternoon on the beach. Even the palace was no competition for the vast presence of the ocean.

When I was dressing for dinner that evening, Jonathan offered me the ring again, and again I declined. The conversation with Dr. Henriksen was as enjoyable as it had been the night before, and she asked me about what I'd seen and done so far.

At the conclusion of dinner a servant came to inform me that I was summoned to the emperor. Surprised, I followed him; Jonathan came with me. We were brought to where the emperor was chatting with some nobles in a hallway. He looked very different than I remembered him. This man was stiff and serious. Fancier too. Almost everything on him glittered in some way.

He dismissed the men he was speaking to and turned to me. As he did, his whole posture softened and all at once he was a different man; the relaxed, casual one I remembered. I bowed, trying to process the change.

"Good evening, Mr. Dawes. I'm glad to see that you've arrived in time for our departure tomorrow. You've had a chance to see a little of the palace?"

"Yes, Your Excellence. A little. It's impressive. Overwhelming, really."

The compliment didn't seem that important to him. "And your rooms are adequate?"

"They're much more than I need."

"Good." He smiled.

"In fact, with those books there, I haven't paid much attention to the rest."

His face brightened. "You like those, do you?" His expression was eager, almost childlike, and I realized I was smiling back at him.

"Of course. They're such a complete experience, the smell, the feel, the sound. And I never would have thought to look up *The Large Scale Structure of Spacetime*. It's fascinating to see through the eyes of a fellow scientist all the things they didn't know back then."

"I'm very happy to hear that someone else understands my interest in books. Most people think they're worthless." He studied me for a moment and then turned to Jonathan.

"Jonathan, isn't it?"

"Yes, Your Excellence."

He nodded. "Jonathan, why was Mr. Dawes not given an Imperial ring?"

"He gave me one," I interrupted. They both looked at me wide-eyed. "Your Excellence," I tacked on. He took a long look at my hands. "I told him I didn't want to wear it." I shrugged uncomfortably. "I just…didn't want to." My face was hot.

He looked up at me, eyebrows high. A smile teased the corner of his mouth. "Oh? Well, I'm sorry we weren't able to choose something that met with your approval."

If I didn't know better, I would have sworn he was teasing me. That scared me. I didn't want to attract his attention any more than necessary. I'd already learned that it was never safe to be on the radar of those in authority.

"I didn't mean any disrespect, Excellence. I didn't realize it was important."

"It's not," he said. "At least, it doesn't need to be. Most people place a great deal of importance on it, but if you don't, then you don't." He seemed to be sincere, but I didn't trust it. Why bring it up if it wasn't important?

And yet, the fact that we were even discussing the ring made me even less inclined to wear it, just to be contrary.

"Thank you, Excellence."

"I'm glad you're enjoying your stay, Mr. Dawes. I'm sure I'll see you aboard ship," he said, and I knew he was dismissing me. I bowed and walked away, and Jonathan followed, looking at me sideways.

"What?" I asked. He just shook his head, a slight smile on his face.

I returned to my room and picked up my book again, but I was full of nervous anticipation and still uncomfortable about the conversation with the emperor.

"Jonathan, may I ask you something?"

"Of course."

"Do you like your job?"

"Of course, sir."

"Don't say what you think I want to hear, and I'm not talking about me, anyway. Do you like serving people like you do?"

"Yes," he answered, "I do. There are many worse jobs. I'm always warm and comfortable, and in much better circumstances and places and company than I would be on my own. And to work at the palace is an incredible achievement, even if you're just a toilet scrubber."

I snorted. "They use robots to do that sort of thing."

"I know," he said, his mouth quirking.

"But didn't you want to do something else when you were growing up? I mean, this wasn't what you dreamed of doing, is it?"

He hesitated. "My dreams weren't realistic. This is. In fact, I am very lucky to be here. I'm from a mining colony on Dessas. Everyone I grew up with is working in the mines now. It almost defies belief that I have this position. Yes, I'm very happy about my job."

I thought about that. "I shouldn't be here either," I said. He looked at me, waiting. "I'm an unclass from the worst part of Mexico City. We don't get jobs at the palace."

"But you were chosen for the Intellectual Complex," he countered. "People like *that* do indeed end up at the palace."

"But that's not the life I was born to."

"Of course it is. What got you chosen for the IIC, if not the abilities you were born with?"

"Well then, your abilities are what got you here too."

"No," he smiled. "No, I'm here because of my connections. My uncle's employer got promoted to a job here on Earth and when I came of age, he helped me get here and find employment."

"Well, maybe things will keep going well for you and you'll get a better placement soon."

"There are few better placements than to a permanent appointee of the emperor." I grimaced at his reference to my permanent status, but he misunderstood. "If you are unhappy with me, Mr. Dawes, you need only speak to the Head Steward and someone else will be assigned to you."

"No, no, I'm not unhappy with you. I kind of like you. It's just...Never mind, it's nothing."

His eyebrow twitched but he said nothing. In a rush of loneliness, I burst out, "I don't want to be here, myself. It's nothing to do with you."

He raised his eyebrows but didn't ask. I wasn't sure if that was because he was being polite or because he didn't want to know. But I pushed ahead. "I don't belong here. I'm supposed to be at the IIC."

"Isn't this a more prestigious assignment than the IIC?"

"What do I care about prestige?" I countered. "I don't know anyone here. My life and my work are at the IIC. I'd do better work there with Dr. Okoro than I will here all alone. I don't belong here. I don't want to be here."

"I miss my family and my home as well, no matter how happy I am to be here." His expression was sympathetic, but that made it worse.

"I'm tired," I said. I didn't want to make a fool of myself by snapping at him, when I'd already made myself look like a whiny baby. "I'm just going to go to sleep before long. You can go. You don't need to wait around for me."

He nodded, his expression neutral. "Goodnight, Mr. Dawes."

I scowled at his back as he left the room.

I had only those two days at the palace before it came time to board the ship and embark on the year-long tour. Jonathan led me into a new area of the palace, in the Eastern Quarter. We emerged from the building onto a huge open lawn and there, on what must have been a temporary landing platform, was an enormous spaceship.

The ship was spectacular to look at, long and sleek and gleaming. Jonathan and I boarded in the belly of the ship and maneuvered through lifts and hallways. The room I'd been assigned was large and comfortable, not at all what I'd expected, and I felt guilty taking up so much space in a way I hadn't at the massive palace. Once again, there were books in the sitting room, and I thought it was odd I should find that comforting.

It was an interior room, so no window, though I think I would have been embarrassed to have one. Where a window might have been there was a tall, thin glass piece, filled with liquids of different colors and viscosities floating up or down or streaming sideways, combining or separating in response to some stimuli.

"What's this?" I asked.

"This is a replica of a piece of art that was designed for the emperor, when he commissioned the lab on the ship. The emperor asked for another to be made for you, as well."

I was baffled. "Why?"

"He thought you would appreciate it even more than he could."

I did, but that still didn't explain why he'd commissioned one for me—why it had even occurred to him to do so.

The instructions came to secure ourselves for liftoff. Jonathan showed me how to activate the localized grav/anti-grav unit on each chair in the sitting area, so that the effect of liftoff and gravity changes on the passengers could be blunted. I was crestfallen. I don't know what I'd expected but I wanted to be able to feel the liftoff, not the diluted-for-your-comfort experience. I stood there, disappointed and seriously considering not getting in the chair at all.

Jonathan was watching me and, after a moment he added, "As an alternative, or in case of unit failure, there are also safety restraints built into each chair," Jonathan said.

I grinned at him and his expression softened just a bit into what I was beginning to think was his on-duty version of a smile. He showed me where to access them and how to strap myself in, and then started to leave the room.

"Wait. Where are you going?"

"To my own quarters."

"Oh," I said, feeling foolish for asking.

"Unless you'd prefer company?"

"Not if you don't want. I mean, I was just, I was just wondering."

He hesitated a moment. "Mr. Dawes, if it's all right with you, I'd like to stay." I almost asked him if he really meant it or if he was just humoring me, but I didn't. I was glad for the company.

We talked while we waited. I learned that he was twenty-three and had two brothers and a sister, all younger, who still lived on his home colony. I told him as little of myself as I could without being obvious about it. I think he realized what I was doing, though, and skirted away from my history when I did.

I felt the change before I heard it. A low thrumming I felt in my feet on the floor and seeping up through my whole body as the engines built up energy. I caught my breath as the buildup became audible even through the sound dampeners.

The sensations of that experience, of leaving Earth for the first time, washed over me and I felt, saw, heard nothing else for several long minutes as the ship was released and energy became force, force drove velocity. I closed my eyes to better see the way the physical forces were harnessed and mastered. We conquered the powerful drag of planetary gravity against our insignificant mass and hurtled into the void.

My weight pressed against the soft cushions of the chair and I felt as if I were being pulled into it, merged with it, until Earth's gravity field was behind us and the micro-gravity of space took hold. The sensation lasted for only a moment before the ship's artificial gravity kicked in and pulled back. I sank back into the chair, having barely lifted out of it. I wanted to cry. Couldn't I have had just another moment or two?

Jonathan hadn't spoken for some time. I blushed, feeling rude for having asked him to stay but then ignoring him, but he didn't seem to mind.

After dinner, a servant summoned me to the emperor. This was now twice in as many nights. Was it about something I'd said the night before? That stupid ring?

I was led to where the emperor was talking with the ship's captain in one of the hallways.

"Good evening, Mr. Dawes. I see you survived the lift-off." He walked as he spoke, gesturing for me to accompany him.

"It was an incredible experience, Excellence. This is a nice ship you have."

"Thank you. It's not a new ship, there was no time for that. But many things were upgraded, the engines included. They're the best of the best, I'm told. I thought about you during the lift-off. I wondered what you'd make of it."

"You did?" I asked, stunned.

"Is there something wrong with that?" he asked, his mouth twisted in what looked like amusement but was probably something more dangerous to me.

"No, sir. I guess not..."

"Does it bother you?" He seemed to be teasing me again.

"Some," I answered.

He stopped. "Why?"

"Because I'm afraid of you."

He laughed, and started down the hallway again. But after a sideways glance at my face, he quieted. "You really mean that?"

"Yes."

"Oh." His answer was soft, subdued, even. I got the distinct impression that I'd hurt his feelings.

"You must get that all the time."

"I do," he answered, but didn't look at me. I was more and more sure that I'd offended him somehow.

"So why should it matter, then, Excellence?"

He thought for a moment. "I don't know. I should be used to it. Of course, no one ever comes out and says it in so many words. It's a bit of a shock to hear it confirmed like that."

He stopped again, facing me, a slight furrow between his eyes that I would have called uncertainty, even vulnerability, if I hadn't known who he was. "Why are you afraid of me?"

"Who wouldn't be afraid? You can do anything you want with my life and there's not a damn thing I can do about it."

The furrow deepened and he waited, as if I hadn't explained myself at all.

"You uprooted my life a couple of weeks ago, who knows what you might do tomorrow?"

"You mean, you didn't want this assignment?" he asked.

Apparently I wasn't frightened enough to keep my mouth shut. "I want to be here," I pointed to the ship around us, "but I didn't want to be reassigned, no."

"Mr. Dawes..." He hesitated. "I had no idea. I'm sorry."

I shrugged but didn't look at him.

"Would you like to be assigned back to the IIC?"

"Yes, Excellence."

"Then you will be." He started walking again, gesturing to me to accompany him. My stomach was jittery. I couldn't believe what I'd just said. But he wasn't reacting like an angry sovereign. He was acting like just another guy whose feelings were hurt.

"I'm sorry if I offended you," I tried.

He turned to me. "Actually, you have no idea how much I appreciate your honesty."

There was no reason for me to believe he was lying or just

being diplomatic—and I couldn't imagine why he would try to spare my feelings—but that didn't make me feel much better. I was still on edge, certain I'd said far too much.

We walked along in silence for a while longer before I asked, "Are we going somewhere in particular?"

"Yes," he answered still looking straight ahead. But after a moment he glanced at me sideways with an almost-mischievous smile.

I was still trying to process that when we came to a door. He slid his finger over the scan pad and, when the door opened, he entered.

I caught a glimpse inside. My knees locked and I stopped. For several long moments I forgot to breathe.

It was the lab. Except, it was the most fabulous thing I'd ever seen. Calling it simply a lab was almost a slur. The far wall and a good portion of the left wall were one large window. The smooth, slate gray floor seemed to flow into the void itself. My heart climbed into my throat—the first glance at the room made it appear as if it were open to space.

Lab tables lined the other walls. On every surface was a succession of instruments, devices, and other equipment, laid out like a feast. Everything was new, unused, and they gleamed and sparkled like scattered diamonds.

Near the window were a couple of couches, set facing the universe.

I stepped into the room. Turning to the table on the right, I ran my hand reverently over the first, pristine piece of equipment there. Without lifting my hand, I walked along, letting my fingers flow over each table and everything on it.

As I followed the right wall, I couldn't help but cast a look, from time to time, away from the man-made objects and out the vast window into the expanse beyond. When my casual inventory brought me to the transparent wall I let my hand trail across it, to the very middle point. I stood so close I could feel the chill on my nose and cheeks. I put my hands at the level of my face and leaned even closer, so that all I could see was the void beyond and my own hands in my peripheral vision. It was like having nothing between me and the universe itself.

I don't know how long I'd been standing there when a sound from behind brought me back to myself. I spun around and felt all the blood drain from my face. I'd just turned my back on the emperor.

Turned my back on him and ignored him for no less than ten minutes. The fear I'd felt before was nothing to the terror I felt now. I closed the distance and dropped to a knee in front of him, bowing my head. "Please forgive me, Excellence, I forgot myself."

He laughed. I looked up at him in shock. He reached down and with a hand around my upper arm started tugging me to my feet with short, quick pulls. "Get up, please. Please," he repeated through his laughter, and finally I rose.

"Mr. Dawes, I've given and received many gifts in my life but I have never seen anyone appreciate one quite as much as you seem to."

"Gift?"

"Your lab," he said, gesturing around the room.

"*My* lab?"

He laughed again. "Who else's would it be?"

"Yours," I said, trying not to sound as if I was explaining something elementary to a child.

"Oh, it's all mine, isn't it? Who cares about that? This is your lab. I have no use for it. I do hope, though, that you'll let me visit from time to time to observe, even to assist if I promise not to get in the way or mess anything up."

"Of course you can come as often as you like." He nodded as if I'd just granted permission rather than stated the obvious.

"Well I'd love to stay but I'm afraid I don't have the time tonight. Thank you, Mr. Dawes, for your time and your frank conversation. I look forward to speaking with you again."

"Thank you, Your Excellence," I said, as he left.

I turned to Jonathan, who was watching me. "Everything I do or say when I'm around him is idiotic and brainless. How long do you think it's going to be before he has me put out an airlock?"

Jonathan laughed. "While I wouldn't disagree with your assessment, I suspect the emperor likes you. Or at least finds you entertaining."

I didn't like the sound of that. Entertaining. As if I were a trained monkey. But I couldn't deny that I sounded and acted about as intelligent as one when I spoke to him.

fg 12

I spent the rest of the night in the lab. My head was brimming over with ideas for projects to start, but the equipment in the lab had been arranged with an eye for aesthetics rather than any knowledge of the function and use of the various items. My first task, with Jonathan's help, was to rearrange the room.

It was like redecorating a dream. Every piece of equipment I laid my hands on spawned dozens of ideas. I was lost in visions of the truths I would reveal. I worked until I couldn't keep my eyes open. And then I only dismissed Jonathan and sat down on one of the couches facing the great window, lost in the universe itself.

I woke there, hours later, and dragged myself to bed.

I spent the next day organizing my ideas. I had the lab arranged in an efficient, useful setup, now to do the same for all the ideas percolating in my head. I forced myself to walk away from the beautiful equipment and sit down on one of the couches, tablet in hand, and formulate a plan for my next few days.

By the afternoon I began to set out and arrange things for the projects I'd decided to pursue first. I was still at it when Jonathan informed me that it was time to dress for dinner. I told him I wouldn't be going, but he reminded me that it was the first formal dinner aboard ship and that my absence would be noted. I wasn't sure who it would be noted by and didn't believe him, but I wasn't confident enough to argue with him, either. I was still uneasy about the way I seemed to vomit words every time I was around the emperor. I didn't want to make any more trouble for myself.

There were more outfits in my closet than there had been before. Jonathan explained that it was only routine to make sure I was well supplied. Even worse, he told me that in my new position I would receive a salary. I couldn't help but think, with a painful lump in my throat, what that salary would have done for my mother and Carrie.

Before I went to bed that night I sat down to record a message to Kirti. I'd had a mail a day from her since I left, every one a long vid-mail that ended with her asking me to vid-call as soon as I could, but I couldn't seem to remember to contact her when she would be awake and available. I finally decided just to record messages to her when I could, and send them on. I told her in detail about my trip to the palace, the two days there, the ship, and my incredible lab. I skipped over embarrassing details like having my own servant and most of my conversations with the emperor, though I did tell her that he'd said I would be assigned to the IIC again after the trip. I went to bed that night with the guilt of my neglect of Kirti off my shoulders.

My days fell into a predictable pattern. I woke early, ate breakfast as I dressed, and went to the lab. I remained there, eating lunch as I worked, until it was time to dress for dinner. After, I'd return to the lab, where I would stay until I was falling asleep on my stool.

That wasn't enough lab time for me. I'd have gone without sleep if I could have. There were too many fascinating things to do and too much equipment to leave so much of it unused. By the time a week had passed I had five different experiments in progress.

The emperor visited the lab, as he'd promised, one evening after dinner. I stood and bowed to him.

"Good evening, Mr. Dawes," he said. As he looked around the room his smile grew wider. "I see you've found something to do with your time."

"It's an incredible lab, Excellence. How could I not?"

He joined me at the table. "What's this?"

"Plorium. Did you know you had a sample of it here?"

He frowned at the glass tube containing what looked like no more than simple water vapor.

"This is Plorium? The new element they discovered after the Lores Event?"

"Mhmm." I nodded. "This is its plasma state."

He reached out to touch the glass but stopped, his hand still in the air, and looked at me. "May I?"

"Yes, it's safe."

He touched the outside of the container and held his fingers there for a moment before turning to me with a slight blush on his cheekbones that I wanted to call embarrassment. "I don't know why I expected it to feel different."

I shrugged. "It still happens to me. You get so excited about something new. Well," I flushed, feeling presumptuous, "At least, I do."

"Being a research scientist must be exciting," he said, turning back to the sample.

"Not always. Sometimes it's frustrating, or downright boring. I mean...to me it can be...not that...not that I'm contradicting you or anything."

He was still watching the subtle, swirling patterns form and dissolve in the Plorium, but from his profile I could see a small smile tug at his mouth. "It's all right," he said. "I hardly ever have someone executed for contradicting me the first time."

My heart thumped hard in my chest and I stared at him, not at all sure what to make of that.

"So, what are you doing with this now?" he asked, turning to me with what looked a lot like a wicked smile on his face.

"Just some radiation measurements," I said, my voice steadier than I expected. "I'm going to use them as a baseline for an experiment. I'll show you how this works." My confidence came back all in a rush, here in my own element. "Would you hand me the radiometer, please?"

"This one?" he asked, indicating an instrument lying near him.
"Yes."

He handed it to me with a strange look on his face; amusement, perhaps.

"Do you get in the lab much?" I asked as I began to take the measurement.

"Never," he answered. "I haven't done actual lab work myself. Only what I did in my studies with my tutors."

I looked at him, surprised, but then I chuckled.

"What?" he asked.

"I never got to work in the lab either, before the IIC. I'm just surprised that someone like you, with the access and resources you have, wouldn't have done more, if you're interested in it."

"Time. I have the other resources, but I lack the time," he explained.

I nodded without looking at him. "There's another instrument over there. Why don't you take the measurement in the far chamber while I get this one?"

He smiled that same, funny smile as before, but did as I'd asked. He watched me to see what he should be doing, and accepted the corrections I offered.

"Why didn't you have access?" he asked a few minutes later.

"To what?"

"To a lab, before the IIC."

I shook my head. "I grew up in Mexico City, in Abenez."

He was silent for so long I looked up at him. He was focused on what he was doing, as if he hadn't heard me. Or he hadn't been surprised, because he'd known. Of course he'd know. But he hadn't acted like he knew. He hadn't treated me as he should have, if he had known.

After a while he said, his voice quiet, "I'm sorry if I'm prying."

It was a very odd thing for *him* to say. "Oh, I don't mind." I shrugged. "Or at least, I'm used to everyone knowing that about me. And they never seem to forget something like that, no matter what you end up doing or becoming." I picked up the radiometer again. "It's not the first thing about my life that's unconventional, and I doubt it will be the last."

"I agree," he said. I looked up at him but he had turned back to his measurements.

We worked well together. In my own element, I was relaxed and competent. I didn't blurt out ridiculous comments or do stupid things. I worked and he worked with me.

He wasn't quite a colleague, due to lack of practical knowledge and experience, but he was a competent, diligent, and bright assistant. And he seemed to enjoy the work.

We chatted about many things and at times worked in a companionable silence. He did, from time to time, look at me with that same expression, some combination of bemusement and happiness. It wasn't until he yawned that I realized how late it had gotten.

"Oh, I'm sorry," I said. "I tend to stay in here until I fall asleep on the floor. I didn't realize it was so late."

"Don't apologize," he smiled, "I'm having fun. I hadn't realized how late it was. Though the yawns I've been fighting for the last hour ought to have given me a clue," he said, his face wry. "I think I'd better go, though. I have an early day tomorrow."

"This is a good place to stop anyway."

"Thank you for letting me join you tonight, Mr. Dawes. I had fun."

"Me too. Come whenever you want."

He was smiling when he left.

"Happy birthday, by the way," I said one evening almost a week later as he accompanied me from the dining hall to the lab.

"Thank you," he replied. "To you as well."

"How did you know it was my birthday?"

"Oh, there's not much I don't know if I choose to," he said with a smile.

"OK, I should have known that. I suppose I mean, *why* do you know?"

"In my position, I've found curiosity to be an asset. I don't believe there is such a thing as knowing too much."

That wasn't a comfortable thought. How much he could know. How much he *knew*.

"I'm older," he added after a long silence. I raised my eyebrows. "Only about six hours, but it counts."

I had to laugh. "You're one of the most powerful men in the galaxy and it matters to you whether or not you're older than me?"

He shrugged. "Wouldn't it matter to you?"

"That's not the same thing. There's a huge power differential between us. At least age would be something I'd have over you."

"I get the feeling that power doesn't mean that much to you."

"Unless you mean as a function of energy." I grinned at him. "No. I have no need for it. It would get in the way of my work."

"What did you do for your birthday?" he said after a pause.

"Radiation measurements."

He laughed. "No party?"

"With whom?"

"Haven't you made any friends aboard ship? I know it's only been three weeks, but you don't seem to be the kind of person who would have trouble making friends."

"Maybe you don't know me very well. In my experience, there aren't many people who are interested in being friends with me."

"Maybe it's *they* who don't know you very well."

I frowned, puzzled. When I looked at him again he was watching me. "And what have you concluded?" he asked.

"About what?"

"You look like you're trying to decide something. My guess is you're trying to figure me out."

I thought about that before I replied. "You're confusing," I conceded.

He grinned. Reaching into his pocket, he produced something and handed it to me. "Here. Happy birthday."

He'd given me a small box. I looked at him, surprised, but when he said nothing further I opened it. Inside was a pair of platinum cuff links with a raised imperial crest on them. "I thought they might be less objectionable than a ring."

I frowned. "I didn't get you anything."

"I assure you, I don't need anything."

"Neither do I. That's not the point."

He shrugged. "It's the thought that counts. We'll just say you gave me something."

"I'm sure you can say whatever you want, but I never thought of giving you anything."

He stared at me in shock and then started laughing so hard he had to stop walking. We stood in the middle of the hallway and I watched both directions as I waited for him to get control of himself. If someone came along and saw him like this, it wouldn't go well for me. When he caught his breath he said, "You never thought of giving me anything." He repeated it as if it was the punch line to a good joke. "Not even just now, when I gave you something?"

"No," I said. "I can't imagine what I would get *you*."

"Well, whether you realize it or not, you've been giving me a gift for the last ten minutes," he said.

I grimaced. "You're not going to say something weird like 'the gift of your company,' are you?"

He doubled over with laughter again. "No," he answered when he'd composed himself. "No, I was going to say that we've been talking for more than ten minutes and you haven't called me 'Excellence' once."

I startled. "I'm sorry." It occurred to me that I should have said "Excellence" just then.

He was grinning. "Don't be. Isn't that what I just said? No one's ever done that to me before. It's very disrespectful. I like it. Tell me, what do you see when you look at me?"

"The emperor."

He shook his head. "I don't believe that."

I pursed my lips, considering. I nodded, "You may be right. Maybe I don't think of you that way. Not once we start talking, at least. You don't act much like an emperor."

"Known many of those, have you?"

"All right, you don't act like I expected an emperor to act."

He smiled. "Well, you may have something there. I've only known one other emperor, but I know I don't act anything like he did."

There was a surprising bitterness in his voice.

"Is that why you act the way you do? So you'll be nothing like him?" I'd already blurted it out before I realized it was stupid to have asked. He didn't answer, but he looked pensive.

I was about to apologize when he said, "You may be right about that too; though I don't know if there's much trying involved. My father wouldn't have had a conversation like this because he never paid attention to people, and I can't imagine being like that. His disease was his life, his family, and friend. Everything else was just an obligation to the Empire. Even me. I was just another thing that could be delegated when he wasn't feeling well, which was always. His counselors saw more of him than I did."

I didn't know what to say.

"Have I surprised you?" he asked. "I'm used to that being common knowledge. It is at the palace." When I didn't answer, he continued, "So, what about your family?"

"My father paid a lot of attention to me. When you're hitting someone, you have to pay attention to them or you'll miss."

My breath caught in my throat. I never talked about my father, if I could help it. Everyone at the IIC knew that he'd been Resettled, but nothing more. Dr. Okoro and Chuck knew he'd been a drunk. Only Kirti knew about the beatings. And now I'd just volunteered that information to the emperor himself. I couldn't look at him.

He was quiet. "I'm sorry," he said finally.

"It was a long time ago."

He changed the subject. I don't remember what we talked about then, I was too preoccupied with the shock. Not just because I'd confided in him, but because I wasn't sorry I'd done it.

A week later he came again.

I enjoyed his company. I hadn't expected to, before that first evening. But he wasn't at all pretentious or self-important. He was easy to talk to and the silences were never awkward. He was bright and quick and easily extrapolated additional information and skills from what I showed him. He was eager and willing and never shrank from work, even when what I asked of him was unimportant or monotonous. He never tried to take over or direct matters.

In other words, he was again nothing like I expected an emperor to be.

He asked me a great deal about myself. I could see that it was genuine interest and I thought that was a very good thing in a man who possessed such power over the lives of so many.

"What do you do with your time when you're not in the lab?" he asked one night.

"Eat and sleep," I answered with a grin.

"That's all?"

I nodded. "Too much to do here."

"I didn't realize I had the reputation of being a slave driver. But you haven't been shackled to the table, as far as I know."

"I know. I like the work. I'd rather be doing this than anything else."

"Do you know how much trouble was taken to make sure there were adequate facilities for the residents of this ship to enjoy themselves for an entire year's journey? I think some engineers and designers would be wounded to hear that you don't appreciate their work."

I laughed. "I'm sure plenty of people appreciate it. I don't think one person makes a difference."

"Oh, you'd be surprised." He chuckled. "Do you play any sports?"

"When I take the time to. My friend Chuck made sure I did. He dragged me out all the time. He didn't approve of my obsession with the lab." My smile was weak as I thought of my friend and how far away he was.

"Well, as Chuck is not here, I see that office falls to me. I play twice weekly with some of the noblemen. You should join us."

I made a face. "Is that an Imperial order?"

"Never." The worried wrinkle appeared between his eyes.

"Then I'll come."

He laughed. "I'll hold you to that," he said, and looked at me with a thoughtful grin. "I'd like it if you called me Peter."

Emperor Rikhart wanted me to call him Peter?

"Oh, it's buried in my list of names, I know," he said, "but it's what my family calls me."

"Peter, then." I smiled. "My friends call me Jake."

"Jake," he nodded solemnly, acting for all the world like I'd just given him a gift.

The next game was two days later. I showed up at the playing field Peter had indicated. There were several men there already, many of whom I recognized from the head table. As soon as I entered, one of them noticed me and approached.

"This field has been reserved for the emperor and his guests at this hour," he said.

"Thank you," I answered, and continued toward the field.

He caught up and moved in front of me, putting his hand on my chest. "Spectators are not invited; this is a private game."

I chose to ignore his hand. It wouldn't do to get in a fight here and I tagged him as someone who wouldn't back down. "Good."

I tried to go around him.

"What that means, young man," he said, moving to block me again, "is that you're unwelcome here and need to leave."

He had turned very red by the time Peter entered the room. "Mr. Dawes!" he called out. "I'm so glad you decided to come."

The antagonistic lord dropped his hand.

"I told you I would be here," I replied.

"You will address the emperor as 'Your Excellence,'" my new friend commanded.

I looked over at Peter. He gave me an apologetic look when the lord wasn't looking, and didn't contradict what had been said.

"Forgive me, Your Excellence," I said. "I'm still new here. I hope I haven't given offense."

"It's of no consequence," he said, but I got the message. There couldn't be the informality in public that there was in private. "I see you've already met Duke Blaine." A smile played at his mouth.

I gave the barest of nods in Duke Blaine's direction. "Here, let me introduce you to the others," Peter continued as he led me away. Duke Blaine gave me a scathing look, as if it was my fault he'd made a fool of himself. I smirked at him and followed Peter.

He introduced me to the assembled lords on the field, and later to others as they came in. It was comical, really, how they all made every effort to appear welcoming—as much as was necessary, but no more—when Peter was watching, and shunned me when he wasn't. I was no stranger to being the unwelcome outsider, and with these people, I cared even less than usual.

I ignored them as thoroughly as they ignored me; more, really, because I made no attempt to be friendlier when Peter was looking.

In spite of this, the game was enjoyable, both for the sport and for the time spent with Peter. It was amusing and gratifying the way he was able to make me feel as though we were alone together even though we were surrounded by a hostile crowd. I didn't miss the fact that he kept me at a distance, that he spoke to me no more, really much less, than to any of the others.

In spite of this, the quick, almost imperceptible looks he would throw me, the quirk of a smile in my direction, made it feel like we carried on a constant, furtive conversation. His reactions to certain things, while they could be perceived the polite, responsible way, I knew from things he had said, really meant something else, and I could see behind his careful mask the hints of the real reactions.

In many ways I came to know him better from seeing this public side of him. He didn't act at all like he did in the lab. He was still the same person, but the public face was a very locked-down, well camouflaged version of the private one. He didn't say or do anything in the presence of others that he wouldn't say or do in the lab, but the reverse wasn't true. Here, most of what I'd come to know as the real man was hidden away.

Even if I was beneath the notice of my teammates when the game was over, I enjoyed the games. The players were competent and some even talented. The type of game rotated around so that no one game ever got old. I was glad Peter had invited me and even began to look forward to them as the weeks passed.

He came to the lab at predictable intervals after that. I was always happy to see him and found over time that I thought of him between his visits.

"The captain's in a snit because I asked him to orbit in the wrong direction," he said as he strolled in one evening.

"Why would you do that?"

"So you could see the planet from your window. I told you I'd make sure you didn't miss the orange skies of Orellia."

It was something I'd always remember: The tangerine haze of the atmosphere that made the continents a coppery color and the seas purple. And the realization that the emperor had moved spaceships in orbit, just so I could see it.

On one occasion, as we were working up a new experiment—I'd saved this project for several days so that he could be a part of it from the very beginning—we were joking and laughing and I called him "Pete." His whole face lit up and I stopped calling him Peter after that.

Through all this, I tried to keep in regular contact with Kirti. She sent me vid and text mails often, but I was less interested in who Cynthia was dating this month, and Dr. Gunnarsen being promoted in Dr. Aitken's place, than I meant to be. I was surprised by how much of an effort that was. I'd expected to think of her all the time, for our separation to be painful. I'd expected to talk to her or send messages to her every day.

Not only was it nothing like that, but as the weeks rolled by, I thought of her less and less. Every time I sat down to send a mail, I resolved to do so more often, but it never worked.

About a month later, he came to the lab with news. The ship's course to the next stop would take us within four days of a planetary nebula. He'd given orders to detour and spend a week stopped in proximity; he'd cleared his schedule so that he and I could study it.

I didn't think of anything else for ten days. It was all I talked about. Jonathan stopped asking me anything and just started to make all my mundane choices for me. At dinner my neighbors stopped talking to me at all. It took me a few days to notice. When I stopped Pete in the middle of a game of rugby to tell him about a new idea for an experiment, he laughed.

"Honestly, Jake," he said, "I'm starting to think this is too much for you. Maybe we shouldn't make the stop, to preserve your sanity."

Then he laughed again when my mouth fell open, and I realized he was joking.

There is nothing more beautiful in all the universe than a nebula. Standing at the lab's window and watching our approach was like running toward an explosion in slow motion. A galactic paint-spill, color and light splashed across the backdrop of stars.

We spent a feverish seven days in the lab, almost non-stop. A few nights, we took turns napping on the couch rather than return to our beds and lose any of our limited observation time. The only exception was dinner each night. Pete insisted that we both go. I didn't see what difference it made for me. He said I needed to get out of the lab for at least an hour every day. I suspected he didn't want me to be there if he couldn't be.

But for the most part, we dedicated all our time and energies to studying the nebula. It was thrilling, and it gave rise to some of my most celebrated later work.

As all-consuming as the work was, there was a notable distraction: Pete. Or maybe it would be more accurate to say, me. The concentrated time together made obvious something that had been only teasing my attention before.

I found myself standing closer to him than was necessary. And then I'd want to be closer still. I realized I was looking for excuses to touch him; a hand on his arm, a playful shove.

We had always joked and goofed around, but I found myself doing so even more just to initiate physical contact.

His reactions, too, had me in a muddle. When I made myself stand farther away than I wanted, he closed the distance. I wasn't the only one initiating contact.

It couldn't be happening. I couldn't be attracted to Pete. There was no way he was attracted to me. Even if we were, how could that be anything but awful? We were already doing the impossible—a friendship between someone like him and someone like me. Trying to have anything more would be a disaster. It would ruin everything we did have.

Mercifully, the work was interesting and demanding enough that I didn't have time to worry about it.

The week passed and Pete went back to his own work. The lab felt too big, too empty, hollow. All the pieces were there, but something was missing. Everything seemed to take too long to accomplish with only one pair of hands. My work had never felt so much like work before.

I missed him. I cursed myself for being a moody baby and tried to focus on the work at hand; that was what I was there for after all. Time with Pete was just a side benefit. A temporary one. In a few months I would be returning to the IIC.

The thought made me ache.

After Pete had diverted so much of his time to the lab for a full week, I thought it would be longer than usual before I would see him again. When he strolled in only five days later I was shocked.

"What are you doing here?"

"What?" He grinned. "I'm not allowed to come anymore? Have I overstayed my welcome?"

"Of course not. I'm just so surprised to see you. I didn't think you'd have time for me, for the lab I mean, for weeks."

He shrugged. "I got used to being a part of this. I've wanted to come every night for the last four nights. I like being here better than anywhere else."

A thrill of excitement ran through me at those words. He frowned.

"What?" He approached and I told myself I was imagining that his hand twitched as if he wanted to reach out and touch me but hadn't let himself.

"Nothing," I said. "Nothing at all."

He looked like he wanted to say something but with a frustrated expression he turned to the experiment I'd been working on.

"How's this going?" he asked.

"Well, actually, I was concerned with how we'd been neglecting it last week but it seems to be no worse for the wear."

"Hmmm," he murmured, examining the data on the tablet in front of him.

The nearness of him crackled against my side like too much electricity. I tried not to think about it and I couldn't think about anything else. I was vividly, stupidly aware of him. It was exhilarating, I wanted to laugh, I wanted to panic. He was so close it was overwhelming. I couldn't bear it. I turned away, an agonized noise bubbling in my throat.

He moved with me, pulled me against him, and kissed me. The kiss was hurried, intense, and fearful, as if he expected to be shoved away.

My head screamed to do just that—to run, but my hands were tangled in his hair. My body yearned toward him, closing what distance remained between us. I groaned.

His shirt was coming off and I knew that it was my hands undressing him, but they felt like they belonged to someone else. I turned us around and pushed until he was backed into the table behind us, and I pressed myself against him.

It was frantic, his rough caresses, his kisses like bites on my neck and shoulders.

I pulled his face back to mine and we kissed, violence and fear and lust. He moaned and pressed against me.

I would remember all of this much later with clarity and definition. In the moment, I wasn't connected to the brain that drove the body; that would only store these memories now, to later relish and regret them at leisure. His back was to me and I had a vague awareness of having been responsible for that. I put my mouth to his neck and he leaned his head back into the sensation.

I felt my hands unclasping his pants. Something that was still aware in me was alarmed by this, but was lost in a fog of lust. My pants were gone now, too. I had no idea who had removed them and I was long past caring.

I pushed him down over the table and leaned over him. My mouth was so close to the back of his neck that I could feel my own breath warm against my face.

"If we cross this line, there's no going back." My voice was a husky whisper.

"I know," he answered, gruff and intense.

So I crossed it.

When it was over and we were still and silent but for the sound of our ragged breathing, I stood, letting my hand trail down his back. He shivered. He didn't turn around. Instead he bent to reclaim his pants. As he began to dress himself, he kept his back to me.

Icy panic twisted my guts. It had all been so sudden, unthinking. He wouldn't look at me.

I was trembling. When at last he reached down and retrieved his coat, he turned to me as he shrugged into it. The side of his mouth lifted in a half-smile. He closed the distance between us, and taking my face in his hands, he brushed his lips against mine. Then, without a word, he left the room.

I slumped down on the couch facing the window wall and stared out at the stars. My emotions were a helpless jumble that tied my stomach into knots.

I thought he'd wanted me to. Hadn't he kissed me? Hadn't he all but given permission? He never asked me to stop. He'd reached back for my hand and held on to it.

But I knew he regretted it, from the way he'd left without a word. Whether I'd read him wrong from the beginning, or whether he was just was sorry for it now that it was over, didn't matter. The result was the same.

Now he would hate me. Our friendship had become the thing that made my life make sense, and I'd destroyed it.

A couple of hours later I woke and dragged myself from the couch, returning to my own bed. There I dreamed.

In the dreams, Pete looked at me with regret in his face. He stopped coming to the lab; he asked me not to come to the games anymore. And one day, along with all my other mails, I found my reassignment to the IIC—just as he'd promised, that day in the hallway—and he never spoke to me again.

It was early and I was bleary eyed, but there was no point trying to sleep any more. I dressed myself without sending for Jonathan and went to the lab. Jonathan found me there later and brought me breakfast, which I didn't have the stomach for. He looked concerned when I met his eyes, but he didn't ask.

That day lasted forever. I was ready to believe we'd passed into some time-dilatation phenomenon. I couldn't make myself concentrate on the task at hand. My gut was in knots. I couldn't stop thinking of the way he'd kept his back to me as we'd dressed, the way he'd left without a word. That kiss could have been a kiss goodbye. It probably was.

I felt ill, but when Jonathan reminded me it was time, I went to dinner anyway.

Pete would be there.

I watched as he entered the room and took his seat. He didn't look at me. That wasn't unusual, but in light of what had passed and what I had concluded, it was confirmation. I sank down into my seat. I spoke little and ate less, and left before dessert.

I went back to the lab out of habit more than anything else. I didn't imagine that I'd be any more capable of working than I had been earlier, especially now that I knew.

I sat at the table, *the* table, and stared at the experiment we'd abandoned the night before. I don't know how long I'd been sitting there when the door opened, startling me. Pete stood just inside the doorway. I froze. His gaze was locked with mine but I couldn't decipher the look on his face. He approached and, standing not too close to me, he examined the experiment in front of us. My throat tightened and I looked away from him to the experiment, as well.

"We didn't adjust the pressure settings last night, did we?"

"No." A strangled whisper was the best I could do.

The silence stretched between us. He picked up a pressure gauge and took a reading. I forced myself to join him. If I could salvage some kind of friendship with him out of this, even something less than what we'd had before, I'd take it.

We worked in excruciating silence for a long time. Finally he put down his instrument and turned to face me. "Jake," he began.

My heart clenched. I didn't look up or answer, but I put my

instrument down as well.

"Jake," he began again, "I'm...I am so sorry for what happened last night. I hope you know, please understand, you...that is..." His voice trailed off into a groan. "I hope you know, that you *knew*, that you don't have to do anything you don't want to do just because of what I am. You're under no obligation, you don't owe me anything. I'm just Pete when I'm with you. I'm not the emperor, not here, not when we're alone. I would never want to be with you if it wasn't something you wanted, too. If you didn't understand that before, I sincerely, sincerely apologize for what happened and I hope you can forgive me. And maybe, if you want, we could still be friends and no more than that. If that's the way you want it, just say so. I promise I'll never put you in that position again. It will be like it never happened."

I was looking at him now, stunned. "You think I was with you only because I thought I had to?"

"Yes," he answered, holding my gaze. There was real fear in his eyes.

I took his face in both hands and kissed him hard. All the anxiety and anguish that had built up through the long night and day flowed away as he melted against me. He tasted like nutmeg and happiness.

His arms went around me, a hand behind my head, holding me to him. I broke away but only to pull him with me to the couch. I pushed him down onto it and lay down on top of him. We kissed for a long time, our ragged breathing the only sound.

Much later we lay together, both sated, languid. I lay with my head against his chest, his arms around me. I felt a deep peace, all the more poignant in the wake of the grief over my imagined loss.

"I don't suppose you're still worried about my interest?" I said.

He laughed, "No, I don't suppose I am." But then his face became thoughtful. "I was very worried though, last night. I hadn't thought that through—you know, planned it. I didn't think you felt the same way about me that I did about you. But then it happened. I almost didn't realize I was going to kiss you until I was already doing it."

He shifted so that his face was closer to mine and he kissed me. "I'm not used to making impulsive decisions. I have to make the right decision every time. I'm always very careful about what I do or say. Last night I was sure I'd made the wrong decision, because I hadn't given it enough thought."

"You should have known I don't give a rat's ass about what you are."

His laugh was easy, carefree.

"And anyway, I wasn't exactly a passive participant. How could you not figure out that I wanted it?"

He was looking up at the ceiling. "Jake, you have no idea how most people respond to me. You never have. That's one of the first things I liked about you. Most people will do whatever they think I want them to do, without regard for their own feelings. They're usually trying to get something from me or curry favor, or they're just afraid. But they'll do what it takes to get what they want. I could kiss anyone on this ship and they likely would do the same as you did."

I stared at him in shock. His expression was sad, but when he looked back at me, he made a wry face. "See why you surprised me so much, in the beginning? You didn't even wear my ring, just because you don't like jewelry." He chuckled. "It was very nice, to be treated like a person. It's been a long time since anyone did that to me, long before I became emperor."

He sat up, pulling me with him, and slid behind me, wrapping his arms around me, his chin on my shoulder. "Let's go back to my room."

I stiffened.

He moved his head off my shoulder. "What?"

"I don't think we should. That's a bad idea."

"Why? I'm not being impulsive now. I haven't thought about anything else since I left here last night."

"Pete, there's no way I could go and come from your room without everyone on the ship knowing about it within a day."

"That's a generous estimate." He grinned. "I bet they'd all know by breakfast. Is that a problem? Are you ashamed?"

"No." I shook my head. "Not ashamed, it's just...not safe. Or, I don't know, it's...well we can't let people know. You're the emperor and I'm...not."

His face screwed up.

"I don't mean I don't want to be with you, Pete. It's just a bad idea to make people notice you. I mean me, it's a bad idea for me to... Things can work out sometimes if you keep your head down, but if you make people remember you're there..."

His face was pensive. "But, Jake, people will always notice with me. I'll always be the emperor."

"We've managed to keep a friendship secret all these months. Why can't we keep doing that?"

"Oh." His voice was quiet. "So, you want it to stay like this? I can't keep coming here every night. And even if I could, people would know something was up. What you're asking is for nothing to change."

"Not *nothing*. This is new," I gestured between us.

His smile was wan. "So just once a week or so, we get together on the couch between experiments?"

"It doesn't sound that good to me, either. But it sounds better than the alternative."

"Does it?"

He got up and started dressing without meeting my eyes. I stood and put my hand under his chin, lifting his gaze to mine, but he swatted my hand away. He attempted a smile a moment later, but it wasn't entirely sincere. I could see the irritation he was trying to hide. I retrieved my clothes.

"Don't be angry. Please? This isn't about how I feel about you or about us."

He gave me a skeptical look.

"It isn't! Pete," I grabbed his arm as he turned away, "don't do this. Talk to me. Maybe there's another solution."

He shook his head. He wouldn't look at me. "No. No, you're right, Jake. Going public would be a terrible thing for you. And we wouldn't want *you* to be uncomfortable or inconvenienced.

It's important that *you're* happy."

"I'm not trying to make this all about me. There's got to be some middle ground. Help me out."

He shook his head, his lips drawn together in a thin line. "No. If it's so important that no one know we're together, then it has to be like this." He pushed past me. "I have to go. I didn't have the time to come here in the first place. I'll see you on the field." He started to walk out of the room, but he turned back and kissed me so hard that I thought he bit me. "Good night."

"Pete!" I called after him, but he didn't turn around.

I sank down onto the couch and dug the heels of my hands into my eyes. Pete was being unreasonable. He didn't realize what he was asking of me.

It wasn't his fault. He was classed-out before he was born. He couldn't understand what it was like to be lumped in with everyone else and then sifted to the bottom. He didn't know what it was like to be the dirt that better people stood on.

I'd spent my whole life trying to make the impossible work, fighting the gravity-well of my birth. It was one thing at the IIC, where there were mitigating factors important enough that we could all pretend we didn't know what I was. This was different.

I knew about people like this Duke Blaine. And he had a lot more at his disposal than a cane if he decided to hurt me. He would have much more efficient means of getting rid of me, too; quiet, unpleasant ends that didn't involve petitioning committees.

I was so tired of being afraid.

I tossed and turned again all that night, kept awake by a whole new set of worries.

But in the lab the next day I found it easier to concentrate and not fixate on my problems. After all, this was such a small thing in comparison to what I'd feared the day before. Pete did want to be with me. The rest was just details.

It was Pete's reaction that I was still frustrated and upset about.

I hated that he'd left angry and hurt. It made it worse that I had no access to him, no chance of seeing him or talking to him until he came to me. And it was that way because I had insisted on it.

It was a hard week. Every night at dinner I watched him, waiting for him to look over, smile maybe, something to let me know that he wasn't still angry, that he understood or at least accepted. Or beyond that, just that he was thinking about me, in spite of the rest. But he never did. All my sanguine conclusions from earlier in the week became harder to hold onto as the days passed.

The next game was three days after I'd last seen him, but he never came. When I thought about it I realized that he'd already told me the Arelian Ambassador's visit would keep him from the game. I almost left. I had no desire to play with the others there. The gathered nobles made no attempt to be nice to me, but no one had the courage to uninvite the emperor's guest.

I stuck it out, in part just to be contrary. And being able to funnel my aggression helped release some of the pent up frustrations. I got called out several times for being too rough. I did try to rein it in, but I didn't try very hard.

When my mood plummeted after that game, I realized how much I had been counting on seeing him. The rest of the week was miserable.

I went to the next game, even though the thought of the nobles there made me angry. I went because Pete should be there. It was nearly a week now and I was consumed with frustration.

When I arrived at the playing field Pete wasn't there yet. I began warming up and stretching but I ignored everyone around me.

When Pete did come in he was, if anything, interacting with me even less than normal, which wasn't much to begin with. He didn't meet my eye and only offered a quick greeting when he passed.

He named off two team captains and we began to divide up. I was selected for the team that Pete was not on. That was normal because, in spite of what they thought of me, it was obvious that I was the one person willing to play my best against Pete, ignoring his title and instead seeing the position he held on the field. So I was assigned to play opposite him.

The game for the day was soccer and the teams were well chosen. At one point, as Pete drove the ball down the field, my defense caused him to slip and go down. I took advantage, stole the ball, and turned that into a goal for my team. We did our whooping and hollering but Pete stormed over, planted his hands on my chest, and shoved me so hard that I stumbled a few feet backward.

"Watch where you're going, will you?" he spat.

I shoved him back. "What the hell is your problem?"

Silence fell over the entire group. I didn't need to look around to know that everyone was watching. Pete was staring at me, anger still boiling below his expression but overwritten for the moment by shock. I growled, glaring at him, and dropped to one knee, bowing my head. "Forgive me, Your Excellence, I forgot myself."

I waited. He made a disgusted noise. "Oh, get up." He traded positions with a lordling on the other side of the formation and demanded, "Well, play!"

The man who'd come to take Pete's position across from me regarded me with a mixture of amazement and grudging respect. "Either you've got a pair the size of an elephant's or you're the stupidest man I've ever met."

I snorted, too angry to be amused. I jerked my head in Pete's direction. "I guess we'll see, won't we."

He just shook his head.

Play resumed but no one was paying much attention. Pete's team won in the end. My teammates practically helped them. When the game was over, Pete left without a word. I wasn't far behind but in the opposite direction. Hard glares radiated against my back.

I returned to the lab after showering. I managed to be somewhat productive but I was distracted. I didn't go to dinner that night. I was angry and didn't trust myself.

Dinner had been over for at least a couple of hours when the door to the lab opened and Pete entered. He stood there without saying a word, but there was no anger or frustration in his face. If anything, he looked embarrassed. He came over to the stool where I sat, and I pulled him to me so that he was between my legs, my arms around him. "What was that, today?" I asked.

He sighed. "I'm sorry about that. I've been on edge all week."

I shrugged. "It's nothing. I've been irritable too. More than irritable really. Moody. Ask Jonathan. He's probably sick of me now." I put my forehead to his chest. "This is harder than I thought it would be," I admitted.

He put his head on mine; I felt him nod. "But you're right," he said. "I don't know what it's like to be you, just that my life is very, very different. If you say that going public would be bad for you, well, you would know."

We held each other. I wanted to disagree with him, tell him that I was being stupid and that I wanted a real relationship more than I wanted to stay out of the spotlight for all the right reasons. But I didn't.

"I just need time," I said, willing it to be true. He nodded again. I lifted my head and kissed him.

We didn't use the lab for its intended purpose that night. There was, between us, the unspoken acknowledgement that we were going to make the most of this, our only time together.

Weeks passed; months. Subtle changes crept into our public lives as I lost the fight against the pull of Pete's personal gravity. On the playing field he dropped the pretense of indifference. From time to time we'd joke around in a casual manner that earned us puzzled looks or vicious glares from the others.

He included me in the reception for the delegation from the amphibious Naxari. He explained it away as a safety precaution. Since our atmosphere was deadly to them, and vice versa, but they got claustrophobic in enviro suits, the reception was conducted on separate sides of a glass wall with accommodations made for sound to pass between the two groups.

I pointed out to him that most people knew the difference between a physicist and a biologist. He pointed out that the rooms obviously had special seals or something that I would know about. I rolled my eyes at him, but secretly I was pleased and fascinated.

Two or three times, when there was some special entertainment scheduled, he invited me to join him after dinner. That was worse than the games; while the actual programs were nice, the difference between the other guests and me was more obvious in the formal setting, and the general shunning more blatant.

Pete had trouble stomaching the treatment I received from those around him, but to defend me would have made people wonder. What little he did only made things worse anyway.

When he made an effort to talk to me or in some way emphasize the point that I was his invited guest, the others only made more of an effort when he was around and less when he wasn't.

I assured him that I didn't mind, or at least, that I was inured to it. It did bother me. I would have preferred not to go to the more formal functions, but I went. It was my concession to the much larger role Pete wanted me to play in his life.

It became easier, with time, to deal with the self-inflicted separation. Routine wore away hurt and resentment. We even did some lab work now and then.

As we got closer to our return to Earth, Pete began to hint that things would have to change. The first time we talked about it, he asked me if I still wanted to be reassigned to the IIC. I thought he was only asking in order to prove he'd learned a lesson from having reassigned me unilaterally the last time. When I saw the relief on his face when I told him I didn't want to go, I realized he hadn't been sure of me at all.

With that question out of the way, his references to our future became more circumspect. He would mention how much less time he'd have once we returned to the palace, how little he'd be able to visit my lab. He talked about how many more people would be around, how much more scrutiny he'd be under. I listened and nodded but didn't comment.

I wanted more for the two of us as much as he did, but I'd come to the uncomfortable realization that our relationship wasn't the only thing that would change. While we remained a secret, I was still Jacob Dawes the physicist. I'd worked hard for that, to get people to see *me*, not just where I was from. If I gave in to what Pete—what we both—wanted, I wouldn't be Jacob Dawes anymore. I'd be The Guy Who's Sleeping With the Emperor.

But the closer we got to Earth, the more it began to feel that he was already being taken away from me, and it became harder to remember what I was afraid of.

Still I waited. I had another reason: Kirti. I could reconcile myself to what all of this meant for me, but in the end, Kirti was going to be hurt no matter what I did. She was far too important to me to not do everything I could to salvage our friendship. She would be hurt, furious. But I owed it to her to tell her in person.

Of course, the whole Empire would know about us three point five seconds after someone figured it out. If I didn't wait until after I'd seen her to make any public appearance with Pete, it was possible that she'd hear of us the way most would: old fashioned gossip.

But the IIC, in many ways, was a world unto itself. The focus and value system of the place put little importance on the frivolous goings on of the outside world. A matter of pure social gossip, no matter how important a person it pertained to, could go unknown at the IIC for weeks. I couldn't count on her not hearing of us, but the odds were in my favor.

My gut twisted with guilt when I thought of Kirti. Still, there was no way to undo what had been done. I didn't want to, anyway.

It was little more than a week before we were to land, and I decided it was time. Pete and I were working in the lab that night, closing down one of the remaining experiments. He moved to stand behind me. Sliding his arms around my waist, he put his mouth to my ear. "Let's take a break," he murmured.

"Mmmm." I smiled, melting back into him. He took my hand and began to lead me toward the couch but I didn't move.

"What?"

I shook my head. "Let's go to your room."

He stared at me, incredulous, and then beamed.

"Really?" he whispered. He moved back to me, pulling me close, searching my eyes. "Are you sure?"

"Yes."

He grinned like a boy on his birthday and, taking my hand again, led me to the door. He dropped my hand before we left the room, but I was glad about that. Deciding to take our relationship public and shocking everyone with sudden and unexpected public displays of affection were quite different things.

We walked together, an air of electric excitement between us. Before long we entered a section I'd never been in, the area reserved for the nobility. It was still early enough in the night that we passed several individuals and couples in the hall. They all stared; their attempts to pretend otherwise ranged from impressive to pathetic. No one knew what to make of an unclass in their section with the emperor himself. We passed through a double doorway into an exclusive section of the exclusive section. "The Imperial area," Pete said. "No one comes in here unless I invite them."

"Do you invite people often?"

"Never."

That explained the open mouthed expressions on the last couple we'd passed. There was a huge set of doors just past the entrance and Pete led me through those.

And I realized that all those months I'd thought I was giving careful consideration to becoming a part of Pete's life, I hadn't even had the first concept of what Pete's life was like.

There was enough space in those rooms for twenty emperors.

There was a dining room for a dozen important people who never got invited, and a guest bathroom for those never-invited guests.

The bed looked like it would swallow us alive. The bathtub was a pond in the middle of a tile meadow.

The only place I felt I could catch my breath was a small room off the main, an old-fashioned library. There was only one chair, a lamp, and small table before a lit fireplace. Rows of books covered each wall, their colored spines like so many dropped crayons.

Pete was watching me as I wandered through the rooms, his face amused.

"It's...incredible."

He shrugged. "It's supposed to be."

He started to take off his jacket and a pair of servants stepped forward. I let one of them help me out of my jacket but I was uneasy, and Pete took on a thoughtful look as he watched me.

"Thank you, gentlemen, that will be all for tonight," he dismissed them.

I watched them leave through a door out in the sitting room. When they were gone Pete approached me and, standing closer than was necessary for the task, began to unbutton my shirt. "I thought you'd be used to having a servant by now," he said.

I thought about that. "Jonathan's never been around when I was intending to take someone to bed."

Pete's smile was suggestive. "Don't do that often?"

"Never," I answered, pulling him against me. "But I plan on doing something about that."

His grin widened. "So do I."

I woke the next morning to find Pete still asleep beside me. In defiance of the monstrous bed, we were both tangled together at one edge, my arm thrown over his chest. I lay still, reveling in the sheer peace and contentment of waking beside him. I would have kicked myself for having kept us from this for so long if I hadn't been too happy to feel anything else.

I wasn't awake for long before he stirred and opened his eyes. A slow smile spread across his face when he met mine.

"I'm sorry," I said.

The puzzled furrow appeared between his eyebrows.

"I'm sorry I took so long," I said.

He shrugged. "This is a big deal. Your life is going to change as soon as you walk out that door."

"It's worth it." I leaned over and kissed him. A long, luxurious kiss. I lay my head on his arm when we stopped for breath.

"Pete, I'd like to go back to the IIC." He drew in a sharp, quick breath, tensing. "No, no, not like that," I chuckled. "I mean, I want to visit. I'd like to take the samples and results of my work here."

"When?"

"As soon as we get back; that day or the next. I'd like to stay a couple of weeks, I think. That should be enough."

He nodded without comment and was quiet again.

"I love you," he murmured.

I smiled. "I know. I wouldn't be here if I didn't."

He pushed me over onto my back and it was us, together. Nothing else mattered. I have few memories that compare to the one of that morning.

We had breakfast in a "little" breakfast room, our table set near the window-wall looking out at the field of stars.

We were almost finished eating when he asked, "Do you want me to have your things moved here, or do you want to keep your room?"

I didn't need to think about it, I'd decided to take the plunge and halfway down was a stupid place to try to stop.

"I don't think I need my own room, do I? I've got plans for you that will keep us up pretty late. I may be too tired to go anywhere after that."

He grinned.

We left the room together but parted while we were still in the nobles' section of the ship. His office was down one of the hallways there. I was almost back to the public part of the ship when I stumbled onto Duke Blaine. He was leaving a room that I would learn belonged to a minor but lovely noblewoman. His face registered shock, then annoyance, but settled on anger.

He approached me, haughty, and full of righteous wrath. "You've wandered into a restricted section of the ship, Mr. Dawes. And whether you are here due to a poor sense of direction or because you've given yourself airs about your imagined friendship with His Excellence, let me be clear. You are not permitted here."

I smirked at him. "No? I'm surprised, Duke Blaine. For someone who does nothing with his days but play social politics, you're woefully behind in the gossip." A plump young woman in a servant's uniform came out of a nearby door carrying a breakfast tray. "Would you come here, please?" I said.

She approached, her eyes darting back and forth between us. "What is your name?" I asked.

She hesitated, looking back at the door as if for a way out. "Anna."

"Anna, would you please tell Duke Blaine why I'm in this section?"

She colored but locked eyes with him, "Mr. Dawes was the emperor's guest last night, Your Grace."

Duke Blaine stared at me in obvious confusion. I leaned toward him and in a stage whisper I said, "She means I'm fucking the emperor."

He blanched. Anna's mouth wasn't smiling but her eyes were. He opened his mouth to speak, closed it, turned very red and then made as if to push past me, but checked himself at the last minute, stepped around me, and hurried away.

I winked at Anna, who giggled, and I continued to the lab.

My day passed as normal, but for a persistent peaceful feeling. Somewhere in the back of my mind I knew I'd only had the good and there was bad to come, but I made myself ignore that and enjoy my high while it lasted.

When I left to dress for dinner I automatically turned to the right outside the lab before I stopped and, with a smile, went the other way toward Pete's—toward *our*—rooms.

Pete was already there and in the room-sized closet with Davin, his head servant. I asked Davin to leave. He looked at Pete, who nodded. The servant left and I closed the door behind him. I had Pete on the floor before another word was spoken. When, some time later, we lay side by side on our backs, panting, Pete laughed.

"It's good to see you, too."

I laughed with him. "The temptation was too much to resist." I came up on my elbow and rested my head in my hand. "This could complicate things." I grinned.

Pete stood and Davin re-entered the room at his summons, followed by Jonathan. I blinked in surprise.

"I thought you'd rather have Jonathan here than someone you don't know," Pete explained. "Then again, maybe you're sick of him and we'll just get rid of him."

"Eh," I shrugged, "let him stay. For now." I grinned at Jonathan, who ignored me.

"By the way," Pete said, after we'd been dressing for several minutes, "was it really necessary?"

I grimaced. I knew perfectly well what he was talking about. "No," I admitted, "but it was fun."

He gave me a stern look and I did my best to look shamefaced.

"I'm not saying I wouldn't have loved to see that. But Jake, you're only going to make things harder for both of us if you go around antagonizing one of the most powerful dukes."

"I know," I said, "and I did have good intentions before I walked out the door. If it had been anyone but Blaine..."

"It's going to be Blaine often. He makes it his business to stay close to me. He's very ambitious and I'm the means to what he wants."

I sighed. "I'm sorry, Pete, really I am. He caught me off guard. I wasn't expecting a confrontation so soon. Looks and gossip, but not that. I didn't think, I just reacted. He's good at getting to me."

"He tries to be."

"When he's *trying*, it's so transparent it's comical. It's when he's being himself that he gets under my skin. He's a dense, pompous blowhard, that's what he is."

He chuckled. "Just try to avoid him if you can."

"I would be very happy to."

We dressed and went to dinner. Everyone assigned to the head table was assembled in a lounge just outside the emperor's entrance to the dining room.

All conversation stopped when we entered the room. Pete acted as if it was nothing, but I knew this heavy silence wasn't the norm. I met each and every hostile, judgmental stare like a personal challenge. Pete, on the other hand, did a beautiful job of not seeing them at all.

He introduced me to all twelve occupants of the room but the ones I already knew. Duke Blaine gave me a withering glare when Pete turned away and I let my eyes float right over him as if he wasn't even there. I had the satisfaction of seeing his face go red. Pete "didn't see" this either but I could see the smile he was trying to suppress.

The experience of entering that dining room turned out to be much more intimidating and uncomfortable than I'd anticipated. I'd expected it to be like entering the dining hall of the IIC at

Pete's side. It was much worse. These people had no reason to be interested in anything about me and every reason to be unhappy about seeing me with Pete. They made sure I knew it, too.

When dinner was over and we were leaving the dining room Pete turned to me. "There's a performance by the resident string quartet tonight, Mr. Dawes. Will you be joining us?"

"No, thank you, Your Excellence. I have some things I need to finish up in the lab."

The assembled regarded me with disbelief. Pete was hiding a smile. "Maybe next time, then."

Much later, Pete found me in the lab. "I came to see if you were close to finishing up for the night."

"If you're asking me to come back to the room with you, then yes."

He grinned. "You know, you shocked everyone tonight by not coming to the concert."

"I got that impression. Doesn't anyone ever say no to you?"

"Rarely," he answered. "And among those who were there tonight, never."

I shrugged. "It's not my fault if other people don't think for themselves."

He laughed.

The following evening, as I was leaving the lab, I turned down a hallway to find Duke Blaine there, clearly waiting for me. I cast a quick look around. I could take Blaine in a one-on-one, but he might have friends nearby. He seemed to be alone.

I stopped a few feet away from him.

"Can I help you?"

"The proper form of address from one such as you is 'Your Grace.'"

I trembled with a rush of adrenaline but I didn't respond.

"I know what you're doing," he continued.

"Walking back to my room—well, the emperor's room, but, you know..."

He went red. "Whatever you hope to get from or do to our

emperor I will not permit it. Do you understand? Don't ever make the mistake of believing you're alone with him, or that no one will know. I have eyes on you you'll never even see. And don't get comfortable, either. You won't be here for long."

"Are you threatening me?"

He stepped closer but then wrinkled his nose and leaned back.

"It's shameful that I should even have to speak to you, much less threaten you. But I will and I am. You're a disgrace and an insult and I'll make sure you're dealt with. I promise you that."

"What's the matter?" Pete asked when I got back to our room. I looked at him, his eyes bright with happiness.

"Nothing," I said. "Nothing's wrong."

The rest of the week was so normal as to be unremarkable. The only real changes in my life were location. I went to dinner as I always had, but I sat in a different place. I went to bed every night, just in a different room. Of course, those changes meant everything, and they made my experience of normal things very different. And the encounter with Blaine made me twitchy about the way people looked at me now.

The third night, I joined Pete after dinner in a luxurious lounge.

The agenda for the evening was apparently socializing. I regretted my decision at once. The only thing that stopped me from bolting was the discovery of a chess tournament in progress. There had been one lord who had been left out of the competition because an odd number of players had signed up, so I was able to add myself to the roster.

He was a decent player, but I had spent my formative years at the IIC among those who took chess very seriously at an early age. We weren't allowed to be decent.

I didn't play my best, but I don't think my partner realized I was going easy on him. I figured taking that tack was politic.

Pete was not in the tournament for obvious reasons, lack of

interest not being one of them. He sat beside me for most of our game, watching.

We had an interesting public relationship. Everyone knew that I'd moved in with him, and had drawn the obvious and correct conclusion as to why. But we never alluded to our private relationship and no one else did either. Pete made no attempt to disguise his preference for my company, and yet we never touched in public. He called me Mr. Dawes and I called him Your Excellence. In my opinion, it was a ridiculous pretense, but it seemed to make it easier for the nobles to stomach our relationship.

Our private relationship was the opposite of our public one in many ways. When we were alone, we were Pete and Jake; all difference in power, all distance between us was gone.

Pete was affectionate and very loving in private. He'd never had any sort of real relationship, no one he could open up to or trust. It was daunting when I realized how completely he'd given himself to me. The need to protect him was overwhelming.

Maybe if I had been older, I would have known how to do that.

We landed on Earth in the late afternoon.

He went straight from the ship to his office and I went to our rooms. I was hoping to get my bearings in the huge palace. Jonathan led me through the grand hallways with a great deal of narration. By the time we entered the Imperial wing in the West Quarter I knew it would take me a few days to be able to find my way around. Jonathan assured me that it was well laid out and logical and not as bad as I thought.

I'd assumed that Pete's rooms on the ship would prepare me for his rooms in the palace, but I was wrong. I would realize later that the basic layout and features were the same, but it was so much grander in appearance and scale I didn't even notice. It just didn't fit to try to compare those rooms to these.

The details of the décor at that time escape me now so many years later, but I remember an overall impression of grandeur and power. The rooms looked long lived in. Not worn or tattered, of course, but older materials, gold and platinum and other things long ago mined away on Earth, and real woods, sat beside verium accents and the crystallized plasma sculptures of Vir. It exuded a sense of permanence.

There were two chairs in the reading room and I wondered if both had been there a couple weeks before.

The windows that made up most of the west wall looked out over the ocean, somewhat diminished when set against the grandeur inside. The rooms were their own continent. I was completely intimidated. What had I gotten myself into?

I settled into a chair in the reading room and attempted to lose myself in a book, but I couldn't get over the uneasy feeling that I was trespassing, or that the room itself didn't find me worthy. It was a relief when Pete arrived later. He came up from behind and slid his arms around me, his chin on my shoulder. "Hungry?"

I was, but that wasn't what I wanted at the moment. I pulled him through the rooms and we made love in the huge bed. Besides a desire for him, there was some need to "conquer" the room. It sounds ridiculous now, but I know I was thinking at the time of proving that I wasn't cowed, that I had every right to call these rooms my own because Pete wanted me there.

After a delicious lovemaking session he led me to a garden within the Imperial wing. On a flat pebbled area in the center of the garden there was dinner spread out for us. The breeze carried the tang of the ocean.

The meal, the quiet conversation, the soothing silences were the perfect antidote to my jangled nerves. Pete examined me from time to time, considering.

"Better?" he asked as we lingered over wine.

"Yes." I sighed.

"I was worried there for a while. You looked like a rabbit about to bolt."

"I admit, I considered it."

We stayed in the garden until the sunlight filtering in from above gave way to the approach of night. And we remained a bit longer, as the stars became visible through the trees. It was peaceful and perfect and I forgot everything else but that I was with Pete.

The next morning he walked with me to the transport. Pete wanted me to put off my visit to the IIC until after the return celebrations, but the whole thing sounded like an extravagant form of torture to me so I begged off. He didn't try to persuade me.

He led me to a private courtyard, and parked there was an enormous transport. The Imperial arms were on the side. Anyone who saw this would assume the emperor himself was on board.

"You have got to be kidding me," I groaned. He was grinning. "This isn't for me, is it?"

"Of course it is."

"Pete, this is one of yours."

He shrugged. "It's one of the smallest ones, if that makes you feel better." He was chuckling.

"Don't do this to me. Please?"

He leaned over, wearing his mischievous grin, and kissed me. "You'll survive."

"Thanks," I muttered. He laughed and then pulled me close in a real goodbye kiss.

I knew it didn't really matter if I rode in that thing. I was going to make a spectacle of myself at the IIC with or without it. The embarrassing transport seemed somehow appropriate; just another thing conspiring to make my life as uncomfortable as possible. Life was exacting a steep price for my relationship with Pete.

I followed Jonathan aboard the transport. He led me first to the very back and the main bedroom there; I followed, grumbling about needing a whole bedroom on a trip that would take less than a day. And, of course, I was the only passenger. He showed me a private sitting room attached to the bedroom and I opted for that over the large, empty lounge. I picked up a book and sank into a chair facing the window but I never even opened the book. Instead I brooded.

I'd never had a comfortable position at the IIC. Even after those horrible early months passed and I found my niche with my precocious scientific abilities. I didn't mind being an outsider, it left me free and unencumbered by unwritten social rules in a way that the accepted could never be. But I was discovering that passive exclusion and active rejection were two very different things.

I wanted very much for the IIC, for my home, to be a sea of calm in the midst of this storm I'd walked into; the tempestuous, dangerous game of social politics at the highest level. But I wasn't a fool to wish for foolish things. I knew I could expect resentment from those who had not been distinguished as I had, especially all of those who were older and more experienced than I—in other words, everyone.

Even more than that was the problem of Director Kagawa. Thinking of him made me squirm.

But worst of all was the thought of facing Kirti and confessing. Though she knew I was coming now only for a visit, I'd let her believe it was a step toward moving back to the IIC again. I ached for her to understand. For my choices, my happiness not to hurt her. I'm not one to delude myself either so I didn't waste time hoping for the impossible.

My thoughts drifted back to Director Kagawa, and I realized I could probably obtain access to his records now, if I asked for them. I tried to sound casual as I asked Jonathan if he could get them for me, and then to not act surprised when I had them within minutes. He hadn't even asked why I wanted them.

It was as bad as could be. He'd been Resettled. He'd spent three months in a Resettlement camp and then had been reassigned to a job in a small rural town. On a landscaping crew.

I felt sick. Nothing he had ever done to me warranted the humiliation a high class, educated man must have felt, being reduced to manual labor like that. I could recall every whipping he had ever given me, and all the ones I'd gotten at his instigation. The months and years struggling to overcome the reputation he'd set me up with, and to secure my place at the IIC that everyone else had by right. I still couldn't find justice in what had been done.

Of course, I knew that what he'd been condemned for was more than just his personal offenses against me. He'd had a prestigious Imperial position and so much that was important to the future of the Empire had been his purview. But he'd worked against the Intellectual Committee's decisions just because he was petty and let his prejudices make him shortsighted. That the Empire hadn't suffered the loss of my innovations and discoveries was in spite of his efforts, not because. It still felt like my fault.

I did a quick check and discovered that the town he'd been assigned to, Stolven, was only two hours out of the way of my planned route. I sent Jonathan to tell the driver to take us there. I had to know.

Once I'd made the decision, I wouldn't allow myself to think of what I was doing, of what I was planning to do. So I challenged Jonathan to a game of chess. I wasn't surprised to discover that he was a good player and the game kept me occupied enough that the time passed without me completely obsessing over Kagawa.

Before long we stopped and I found myself in front of a small hospital. I looked at Jonathan, puzzled.

"When I searched for your friend's address, I found that he is currently a patient here," he explained. I stifled the guilt at his assumption—that I did not correct—of Kagawa being a friend.

"What is he here for?"

"Apparently, he fell down two flights of stairs. Though, the doctor recorded that the injuries were suspicious."

"Suspicious?"

"Far more damage to the face and torso than would be expected in a fall."

"Someone beat him up."

"I didn't say that, sir."

I rolled my eyes at him and entered the hospital with him on my heels. I was about to approach the reception desk but Jonathan got there before me. He informed them that I was there to visit Mr. Oshiro Kagawa and that I'd want to talk to his doctor first. The woman at the desk looked annoyed but when she saw the Imperial crest on Jonathan's uniform, her eyes widened. "Of course, my lord, immediately."

A very few minutes later a middle aged doctor came rushing out into the lobby where we waited. "Forgive me for keeping you waiting my lord. I'm Dr. Shale."

"Mr. Dawes," I corrected. "I'm no lord."

He blinked. Taking in the scene and apparently skeptical of my denial, he replied, "Of course, Mr. Dawes. I apologize for my error."

"Forget it," I said, but I was irritated. "You're Mr. Kagawa's doctor?"

"Yes," he answered, his expression grave. There was much more in his look than an affirmative to my simple question.

"Why is he here? How is he?"

"He fell down two flights of stairs, I'm told," he hedged. "He's doing well. Recovering. But I'd like to keep him here at least another day."

"Dr. Shale," I said, in my best imitation of one of the more arrogant lords, "please tell me what it is that you think really happened. It's obvious you don't think he fell down the stairs."

He cleared his throat. "Sir, Mr. Kagawa was attacked. I have no doubt of that."

"Why?"

"His injuries are not consistent with a fall. That's a beating if I've ever seen one. And it's not the first time he's been in here with similar injuries."

"How many times before? Any why?"

"Twice before, his injuries have been bad enough to land him in the hospital. Though that doesn't mean that there haven't been other instances. As for why, of course, I couldn't say, but Kagawa isn't exactly the sort of man this town sees very often. His manners and the way he speaks, and acts...Well, he doesn't fit in with the rough, uncultured sort you find here. There is a particular man, Rohr Lieffson, who seems to take Kagawa's ways as a deliberate affront, as if Kagawa just being who he is means he is looking down on the folks here." He made a disgusted noise. "And, with him being Resettled, well Lieffson appears to be determined to put Kagawa in his place. Whatever that is."

"I'd like to see him, please."

"Of course," he answered. "Right this way."

I followed him down one hallway, then another, until he stopped in front of a generic hospital room door. He gestured inside and I nodded my thanks as he turned away. I stood outside for a long moment, rallying my determination, then stepped into the room.

He was lying in the single bed, eyes closed, and didn't appear to hear my entrance. His injuries were obvious even from the doorway. Most of his face was bruised. His left eye was swollen closed, his mouth so puffy that it was at least twice the proper size. I took a few steps farther into the room and his one good eye opened lazily. When he saw me his eyes went so wide that the swollen one cracked open.

He shot up, with a wince of pain. "Mr. Dawes."

"Please, don't get up, Dir—Mr. Kagawa. The doctor said you're still not well."

"I'm well enough," he said, but the strength of his voice and the way he went white when he tried to move gave the lie to that.

"Please," I said, moving to the side of his bed and laying a hand on his shoulder to enforce the request.

He looked up at me, half embarrassed, half afraid. There was a long, awkward silence.

"Mr. Dawes, I—"

"Who did this to you?" I interrupted.

He blanched. "I don't know what you mean. I fell down the stairs."

"Please, sir, I'd like to help. Who did this to you?"

"Why?" he asked.

"Sir?"

"Why would you help me?" he asked.

Shame washed over me.

"Sir," I hesitated. "I can't expect you to believe me, but I never intended for anything like this to happen. I didn't mean..." I was horrified to feel tears burning behind my eyes. "It was an accident. I didn't mean for it to sound so awful like it did. I can't tell you how sorry I am that you're here now, hospital or no."

His eyebrow went up. "An accident?"

I wanted to cry. Of course he'd never believe that of me. He'd only assume I was so vicious because that's what he would have done. I wanted to protest that even if he was petty and mean-spirited, I was nothing like him. I didn't.

"I'm sorry I got you Resettled, sir. I tried to stop them."

He sighed. "You didn't get me Resettled, Mr. Dawes, I did." He looked down, as if struggling with something. "It's clear that you did belong at the IIC, I should never have tried to undermine the Committee's decision. It was gross mismanagement of an important position. They weren't wrong about that. They didn't take me away because of what you said. It just made them investigate the matter. What they discovered got me Resettled."

I shook my head, not ready to forgive myself. "Well, you don't deserve this. This is too much. I'm going to get you out of here."

His eyes were wide and he winced as he tried to sit up again. "Another day or two, Mr. Dawes. That's what Dr. Shale recommends. And I assure you, I have no desire to leave just yet."

"I don't mean the hospital. I mean Stolven."

He gasped. "But, Jacob," he was so distressed that he used my name, "I've been Resettled here. I can't leave."

"Well, that might be true under normal circumstances. But I happen to have the emperor's ear," I had a lot more than that, "and I'm getting you out of here."

He was halfway out of the bed, grimacing in pain but ignoring it. "Do you mean you've spoken to the emperor about me? That he's agreed to have me reassigned?"

"Sure," I shrugged. It wasn't exactly the truth, but it would be. I would talk to Pete and he would agree to it. Probably. Hopefully.

"But where am I going?"

"We can talk about that later," I said. I was nervous now. I knew what I was doing was wrong, so I was anxious to get it over and done with before the rational side of me talked me out of it.

I sent Jonathan to arrange things and with a long, meaningful look at me he went off to do what I'd asked. He knew how stupid I was being but he was helping me anyway.

I was certain, when I allowed myself to think of it, that I was going to get my ass chewed off for this. At best. But I'd make sure I took all the blame.

After a half hour, most of which I spent alone in the hallway,

Jonathan returned, followed by the doctor, a nurse, and an orderly. The nurse and orderly helped Mr. Kagawa into a hoverchair while the doctor spoke to Jonathan and me about the arrangements and his recommendations for Mr. Kagawa's follow-up care.

The nurse would be accompanying us to the IIC. Instructions had been recorded and sent to the head medic there. I suppressed a wince. They'd know I was bringing him. My vague, unformed plan had been to keep him on the transport while he healed and while arrangements were made for a suitable reassignment. I didn't want anyone at the IIC to know he was there, and I didn't think he would, either.

Too late. I'd figure something out. We were still six hours away from the IIC because of this detour.

We left the hospital, and Mr. Kagawa was carefully loaded onto the transport and settled in one of the two unoccupied bedrooms. I went to the lounge, preferring the larger space for pacing. Jonathan watched me with a careful non-expression.

"Perhaps consulting His Excellence about your next decision might ease some of your concerns," he volunteered. I glared at him.

"No thank you, I'll work this out. No need to bother Pete."

He stared me down. I sighed and dropped into a chair. "OK, you're right, I should have talked to Pete before I did any of this. But it's done. I'll settle this whole matter and tie up the loose ends on my own. Then I can talk to Pete."

He held my gaze, unblinking. "And ask for forgiveness," I added. "And beg him not to kill me, all right? Is that what you want to hear?"

His expression softened. "I just want to make sure you realize what you're doing."

"Yes, thank you, I'm quite aware that I've dug a big hole for myself and I'm still digging. Well, I'm good at that. That's how I started this whole mess, might as well finish it that way." A smile quirked at the corner of his lips. "And thank you, by the way, for helping me anyway, and saving this lecture for afterward."

He nodded.

I sat, or stood, fidgeting and fretting through the various diversions I attempted and abandoned that afternoon.

About four hours out from Stolven, less than two hours from the IIC, I looked up at the sound of the lounge door opening. Mr. Kagawa made his slow, deliberate way into the room shadowed by an anxious nurse.

"He said he needed to talk to you, sir, and he wouldn't let me send for you," she explained. I waved away her concerns and got up to help Mr. Kagawa into the nearest chair. I sat across from him.

"Thank you," he said, his face white and chagrined.

"You shouldn't have gotten up," I said. "I'd have come."

He flinched at the suggestion that I'd come to him. I hated this drastic, embarrassing reversal of roles.

"Mr. Dawes," he began. He looked down. "I would like to ask you about our destination. And my future."

Reasonable questions. I didn't want to answer the first one, not now that I knew the head medic was aware of Kagawa's coming and that the entire IIC would learn of it soon after.

"The immediate destination isn't really important," I hedged. "As for your future, well, what would you like it to be?"

"Sir?"

"Please don't call me that," I begged.

"I'm sorry," he said. "I don't understand. Did you not have a plan for where I'm to go from here?"

I flushed, not wanting to admit how impulsive and reckless my actions had been. And unauthorized.

"Mr. Kagawa, I think an injustice has been done to you. I hoped that you could help me with what your next assignment should be as a way to rectify that."

"I'd like to be assigned to the IIC," he said.

I blinked. "Sir...I have some influence with the emperor but I don't think I have that much. I can't get you your job back."

"Oh, that's not what I meant." He looked embarrassed. "I would like, if possible, to take whatever assignment I may be allowed to have at the IIC. If that's permissible. Whatever it is, it's just that...the IIC is my home. I understand I'm in no position to request anything at all, but you asked me for my preference and there it is. Whatever the assignment, however low, I'd count myself fortunate."

I was speechless, stunned. I understood. Of course I did. For all of the unimaginable luxury and privilege of my new life, the resources and opportunities, for all that Pete lived there, the palace wasn't a home, it was a place I must be. The IIC was my home. If bringing Pete to the IIC with me were an option, I'd choose it in a heartbeat. I'd give up everything else to be able to mesh those two truths: that Pete was the most important person in my life and that I belonged at the IIC.

"Mr. Kagawa, we'll be at the IIC in less than two hours. And sir, I'll do my best to find you an assignment there. You have my word."

Tension I hadn't noticed drained out of him and he blinked back tears. I couldn't watch. I turned my head. "If you'll excuse me, please," I said, and retreated to my own room.

The time passed too quickly and before long Jonathan came to inform me that we would soon be arriving. I nodded weakly.

"I've been looking into the matter," he began. Of course he had. "And it seems that there is a position at the IIC that has been recently vacated, as a junior clerk in the history department. It's a very minor position, recordkeeping and cataloging, and some overflow research as necessary."

I gaped at him, and then I felt my whole face fill with a smile. "Jonathan, I could kiss you."

"Please don't."

I laughed. "And have you had him assigned?"

"No." He gave me a long look. "He's not eligible for that assignment, or indeed any assignment at the IIC, because of his status. Such an assignment would require a high level authorization. Typically I would submit the request to Lord Laudley, the Head of Corrections, but anyone above him would have the authority as well."

I sobered. "In other words, I have to ask Pete to approve this."

"Yes."

I grimaced. "Thank you."

"You should know that all the necessary paperwork has been completed and filed. It only requires authorization."

"Thank you for that. Really."

"It's what I do," he said. I smiled and went to sit down in front of the vid, filled with dread.

Y ou did what!"

I dropped my head, hoping the humble gesture would gain me a bit of sympathy. "Pete, the situation was just wrong in every way. He has no business being a manual laborer. And he was getting pummeled regularly just for being educated and well-spoken. You can't mean you would just have left him there."

He glared at me. "Well, I didn't have a choice one way or the other, did I, Jacob? I was never consulted."

I could feel my face getting hot. "OK, I was wrong about that. And I'm sorry. But I can't go back and undo what's already done. Taking him out of there was the right thing, Pete. It was. And the assignment at the IIC is perfect for him. It just makes sense."

"Jacob Dawes, are you out of your mind? An assignment at the IIC? After he was Resettled for gross mismanagement of the very same institution?"

"You're making it sound like something it isn't," I objected. "Gross mismanagement? Come on, Pete, I've explained it. It wasn't 'gross mismanagement,' it was being a shortsighted jerk."

"Well you would know about being shortsighted, wouldn't you?" he retorted.

I bit back an angry, *shortsighted* answer. "I deserve that. I'm sorry. I was wrong and it's all my fault, but him being there was my fault, too. If I made an ass of myself trying to fix it, well, at least I was trying to clean up my own mistakes."

He looked like he was biting his tongue, and he didn't say anything for a while.

"I'm going to approve the reassignment. I don't agree with it, but I'm going to do it anyway. You're absolutely sure that this isn't going to cause a world of problems?"

"Absolutely sure."

He sighed. He looked down at his desk and made a few notations, then looked back up at me. "It's done."

"Thank you," I said.

"We can discuss this at length when you get back."

I bit my lips together and nodded.

"And please, please don't do anymore insanely stupid things until then."

I couldn't help an impish grin. "Thank you, Pete. I promise. I'll wait until I get back." He glared at me, but then his face softened.

"You're welcome. I'll talk to you later."

The vid blanked, and I turned back to Jonathan in triumph. He gave me a stern look and did not comment.

We pulled up in front of the grand main entrance to the IIC. Through the window I could see a small group waiting to receive us: Director Harris, who had been installed as the permanent director several months back; Dr. Okoro; Dr. Roma, the Head Medic; and Dr. Bartel, the Head of the Physics Department. I suppressed a groan. If I'd had my way, we would have parked in the garage and I would have entered the IIC on my own and this entire, awkward scene would have been avoided. But when did things ever go the way I wanted?

They gaped, if in a polite, cultured way, as I exited the transport with Mr. Kagawa behind me in the hoverchair. I almost laughed to think of how I'd wanted the attention diverted from myself that very morning, to not be the focus of all the stares and whispers. I certainly wasn't the only one in the spotlight now. And yet somehow it was worse.

Director Harris approached and shook my hand. "It's good to see you again, Mr. Dawes."

"Jacob," I corrected him. He smiled. But his attention was quickly diverted to his old superior in the chair behind me, the man he'd replaced.

"Mr. Kagawa," he began. "It's good to see you again as well."

Mr. Kagawa held out his hand and shook the director's. "It's good to see you too, Les."

There was a long, heavy silence. I stepped forward and hugged Dr. Okoro.

He beamed. "Wonderful to have you back, Jacob. You're here for a few weeks?"

"Yes, at least a couple. I've brought some samples with me," I turned back toward the transport and found three servants waiting with the crates already in hand. "Oh," I flushed, "here they are."

Dr. Okoro looked startled to see the three people in attendance, not counting Jonathan, but he recovered quickly. "Well, I'm sure the various department heads will be very happy to get their hands on those," he turned to include the head of his department. "We've been reviewing the results you've been sending us. Fascinating work, Jacob, simply fascinating. I admit I've been in a constant state of envy this past year reading about all the things you've seen and done..."

Dr. Okoro was chatting away but I lost the trail of his conversation.

"Excuse me, Dr. Okoro, Dr. Bartel. May I meet you in the main lab a bit later, after I've gotten settled in?"

"Of course, my boy, of course." Dr. Okoro assured me, turning to Dr. Bartel. Indicating the crates the servants held, he began talking and gesturing as he escorted the three into the building.

I hung back to enter the building alone. I was barely out of the great hall when Kirti crashed into me.

"Jake! Jake! Jake! Oh, I'm so happy you're here!" I hugged her hard, burying my face in her hair, wanting so badly for what I had to tell her to not matter at all.

She nuzzled into my shoulder. "Mmmmmmm," she murmured. "Oh, Jake..."

I held her and said nothing, breathing in the smell of her, feeling the silk of her hair against my lips. She raised her face to mine and kissed me. I extricated myself perhaps too quickly, pulling her arms from around me with the pretense of taking her hand.

"I've missed you," I equivocated. "A year is a long time, isn't it?"

She examined my face, frowning. I wrapped my arm around her waist and pulled her with me. "Come on, you can help me find my room."

Jonathan was waiting at the end of the hall and he showed us to the guest suite I'd been assigned. I think I would have laughed, if I hadn't been so wound up, when I realized that my first impression of the room was that it was small.

In truth, it was more than three times the size of the room I would have had at the IIC if I still lived there. Kirti looked around the room, nodding. Her assessment was based on a whole different set of perceptions than mine, now.

Jonathan proceeded to my luggage, already deposited near the closet, and began to unpack my things. Kirti stared at him, wide-eyed.

"Jonathan," I cleared my throat, "that can wait. Can you go see if they need any help unloading the samples and equipment?"

Smooth as always, he betrayed no knowledge of the real purpose of his dismissal. With a quick "Yes, sir," he left us alone.

Kirti slid away from my arm and turned to me, her arms folded across her chest. Her hair was shorter. She'd always been proud of her thick, black hair and insisted on keeping it long. Now it barely brushed her shoulders. For a moment it distracted me, and I wondered what had changed so much in the year I was away that she'd cut her hair. Her expression was hard.

"Who is she?"

I felt my face go red. "What are you talking about?" I stammered. Of course I knew, but I'd had an entire speech prepared, a gentle, kind way of explaining everything to her so that maybe she would understand in the end. This wasn't starting right at all.

She advanced on me. "Jacob Dawes, who is the other girl?"

I backed up. "There is no other girl."

She scowled at me. "I am not stupid. You kissed me back there like I was your sister. You couldn't get away from me fast enough. Who is she, Jacob? Is she rich? Beautiful? Powerful? You might have mentioned her before. As a courtesy at least."

She spun away from me, but not before I saw the tears in her eyes.

"Kirti, don't—" I stopped myself. Her back was ramrod straight. I realized she was thinner. Lean. She'd joined the volleyball team. Now I remembered. She'd written to me about it.

I took her by the arms and turned her to face me. She glared. I took a deep breath.

"I'm sorry. I'm sorry. I promised myself I'd be calm about this."

Her face crumpled and she started to turn away again but I stopped her.

"I love you, Kirti. I've always loved you. But things aren't the same as they were before I left and—"

"And I'm sure she's very exotic. Or very rich? I hope she's something special, Jake. Because it sure didn't take you long to decide I wasn't worth waiting for."

The conversation was spiraling out of my control. Why didn't I remember she could be so stubborn? Why didn't I know she could even get mad like this?

"Stop it." My voice was too high. "Please, Kirti, won't you please let me explain?"

"You've slept with her, I assume?"

"There's no her!" I yelled.

Her face snapped into hard, angry lines, she spun to leave but I grabbed her arm and pulled her back.

"Pete. His name is Pete. And I'm sorry, Kirti, I'd do anything I could not to hurt you, but I'm in love with him and I can't change that."

She stared at me, wide-eyed and silent. I released her, feeling suddenly self-conscious. I'd put a couch between us before I realized I was sidling away.

"*Him?*"

"Yes," I answered, straightening.

"Is that supposed to make me feel better?" she snapped.

"No. Of course not. That's not an excuse. It doesn't even matter. I just...I just wanted...you to use the right pronoun..." I trailed off. I felt myself flush with embarrassment, but I didn't know where I was in this conversation anymore. She'd taken control of the situation and I was floundering.

"Oh," she scoffed. "Well, I wouldn't want to get something like *that* wrong. How awful. Why, that could be so annoying."

I had a retort in my mouth, but she cut me off. "You know what, Jake? I hope I'm annoying you. I hope you're so damn annoyed you can't see straight. Because then you might have some tiny, vague notion of how you've made me feel."

"I'm sorry—"

"You told me you were coming back. Was that before or after you got in bed with him?"

"It wasn't like that. I didn't even realize what was happening until it was too late. If you consider that Pete's not a girl, maybe you can at least acknowledge that I might have been slightly surprised about the turn of events myself. It's not like you think. I didn't mean for it to happen, it just did."

"How many times did you write to me? And you didn't tell me anything. I thought," her voice caught. "I thought you were coming back..."

"I didn't think it was fair to tell you in a mail."

"Now you're worried about what's fair?"

I gritted my teeth. "I wasn't trying to hurt you." I sighed. "That's the last thing I'd ever want to do. I love you, and I want you to be happy. But I love him, too. And it's different. You were always one of my best friends. If it became something else for a while, that doesn't change what I did feel, what I do feel about you."

I took a deep breath and pushed on. "But I love Pete in a different way. He's right for me, and I know I make him happy. I just wish it didn't have to hurt you."

She was pale, her face blank but her eyes were filled with pain. I reached out for her. She stepped away and turned to leave.

"Wait," I said, grabbing for her arm again. She jerked away from me, but stopped.

I'd come this far, so now I had to finish. "Look," I said, the words tumbling out of me, "this doesn't make any difference because it's not the least bit important, but everyone else thinks it is, and I came all this way because I wanted to tell you myself before you heard it from someone else."

She raised her eyebrows and waited.

"Pete's the emperor."

Kirti stared at me silently for a long, uncomfortable moment. "I see," she said. "Well that explains it, doesn't it?"

"No!" I exploded. "It doesn't explain anything!" But she turned her back on me and left the room. This time I let her.

fg21

The bell for dinner rang not long after that and, though I really did not want to go I went anyway. It would only make things worse if I hid now.

I hadn't thought about the matter of seating until I entered the hall. I was directed to the head table, as a visiting peer and guest. I groaned, but the one place in the room I wanted to be less than the head table was at one with Kirti. Unfortunately, I wasn't there to be ignored and I was required to answer questions through most of the meal.

When it finally ended I was angling to intercept Dr. Okoro when Chuck caught me by the arm and spun me to face him. "Hey there!" he exclaimed. "Were you going to say hello, or what?"

"I'm sorry, Chuck," I answered, sighing with relief to see a friendly face. "I was going to come find you. I just needed to track down Dr. Okoro too."

He looked over his shoulder, only just then noticing where my trajectory had been taking me. "You two will disappear into a black hole for the next few weeks, anyway. You'll have plenty of time to talk to him. So, tell me about your trip."

I opened my mouth but before I'd said anything, he caught sight of something and interrupted me. "Oh. I almost forgot. Look," his tone became serious, "it's none of my business what's going on between you and Kirti, but I think you should know. She's telling everyone that you two aren't together anymore because you're with the emperor."

"I am."

He grinned. "No, I mean she's saying you're lovers."

"We are."

He was on the verge of laughter. "No, I mean she's saying you and *the emperor* are lovers."

"I heard you the first time, Chuck. Did you hear me?"

The amusement melted off his face. Now he just stared at me. My stomach dropped. I didn't know what I'd do if he jumped to the same conclusions Kirti had; if he chose to think the worst of me, too.

"You're not kidding?" he asked.

"No, I'm not kidding."

A smile spread across his face. "Unbelievable. How did you pull that off?"

Tension I hadn't realized was there flowed out of my muscles. "Thanks, Chuck. Really. Thanks."

He looked puzzled. "For what?"

I just smiled. Trust him not to guess that people might be judgmental.

"So are you going to tell me anything or just stand there making no sense?"

"What do you want to know?" I asked as we left the room.

"Anything. I guess that explains the fancy clothes. I heard the transport you came in is like a palace on anti-gravs."

"Trust, me, if you'd ever seen the palace you'd know how impossible that is."

"So what kind of stuff do you get for having an in with the most powerful guy in the Empire? What's your room like?"

"I live in his rooms. And they're indescribable, Chuck. The total area of his rooms is bigger than the dining hall." His expression was avid and astonished all at the same time.

"So what, are there diamonds on the toilet seat?"

"No, they're in the tile mosaics." His mouth fell open. I couldn't help but smile. I hadn't expected the gaudy details of my good fortune to actually be well received by anyone. I'd forgotten to factor in Chuck's matter-of-fact view of life.

He started examining my clothes, pushing up my sleeves, turning me around. "What?" I asked.

"I'm looking for all the jewels."

"Oh, please. You think I'd wear that stuff? I look enough of a dandy already."

He snorted, amused. "So show me the transport, then. At least that much."

"Seriously, Chuck, it's not about that."

He looked confused at first. Comprehension dawning, he said, "Well of course not. But he's not here and that transport is. Come on, you can tell me all about him while you give me a tour."

Later that night, after I had shown an open-mouthed Chuck the transport, I went to find Dr. Okoro. He was in a lounge with several other physics fellows. When I came in he excused himself, apologizing for taking me away, and we left together. He threw an arm around my shoulders as we walked down the hall to his study.

"Jacob, my boy, it's good to see you. I hate that you're not staying. But I can't be selfish. I can't even imagine what life at the palace must be like."

"I don't really know, myself; I was only there for three days."

"True," he nodded. "But tell me what you do know, what you've seen. Tell me about traveling through space."

"Sure," I said. "But first I want to get this out of the way. Though I doubt I've beaten the news to you."

His face was neutral. He had heard. But I told him anyway because he was pretending that he didn't know for my sake. When I finished the essentials of my new situation and relationship he clapped me on the shoulder. "Congratulations," he said. "He sounds like a wonderful man and in spite of this doom and gloom you're carrying around, I think you're actually quite happy aren't you?"

He was right, I was. I sighed with relief. I'd been carrying around such a burden of guilt. Some of it had been justified, because of Kirti, but some of it had been simply for being happy.

Oh, it was more complicated than that. I felt guilty and defensive about the things that others would assume about me that were entirely wrong. But I had taken all that on because Pete made me happy. Was I going to let everyone else ruin that?

Dr. Okoro was watching me with a smile that spread across his face in direct proportion to the draining of tension from my body. I hugged him.

"Thank you, sir." He just patted my back in acknowledgement.

My two weeks at the IIC passed both too quickly and not quickly enough. On the one hand, it felt as if there wasn't enough time to spend in the lab with Dr. Okoro, or with Chuck, though I spent all of my non-lab time with him. Kirti wasn't talking to me. About me, but not to me. That hurt worse than the shunning.

Chuck invited me to a few gatherings with our classmates. I went to a couple. Not because I wanted to but because I didn't want people to conclude I thought myself too good to associate with them anymore. In both cases, when I entered, Kirti left.

Even though I spoke to Pete most nights, I still missed him more than I had expected. When the two weeks were over, I wasn't sorry to go. I didn't enjoy saying goodbye to Dr. Okoro and Chuck again, but it was an unspeakable relief to be away from the stifling weight of Kirti's pain.

On the way back to the palace it hit me: Ma and Carrie.

If I could do something to help Director Kagawa, I could do something for them too. I sent Jonathan in search of the data, my heart pounding in my throat. In spite of the trouble I'd caused with my last bout of curiosity, he didn't hesitate for a moment when I asked about my family.

Once again it took him no time at all to access data I had wanted for years.

I stared in horror at the tablet he handed me.

My mother was dead.

She had died of pneumonia, something even a dose of back-alley antibiotics could cure, if you could afford them. But she had been working double shifts already, and the wait for a doctor in Abenez could be hours, even days. By the time Carrie called the ambulance because Ma had passed out on the floor and wouldn't wake, it was too late.

Carrie had been placed with a foster family. We had no relatives to speak of. The only ones I knew were no better than my father, and I was secretly relieved that they hadn't been interested in another mouth to feed.

She was with a different foster family now. The first had been accused of fraud. Something about misusing the funds they were given for the several children in their care.

She'd been placed with a family just outside Abenez. A single family home, married couple, but she was currently one of five foster children, and that number and the makeup of the group changed many times over the months she'd been there. I scanned the data on each of her foster siblings. Most of them had arrest records. I had to admit they were the sorts of things I'd probably have been caught for already if I'd still been there. Petty theft, breaking and entering. Truancy, of all things.

One of the options that flowed along the side of the display was the data on other possible homes in the area. There were many larger homes, better neighborhoods, some without other children at present. One couple, two doctors living in one of the new, state-of-the-art residential complexes on the edge of the entertainment district, had no children placed with them at all.

I did a quick entry, filling their application with a transfer of Carrie to their care.

Error. It flashed. *Class incompatibility.*

My face burned. Oh. That was why Carrie was in a crowded home on the edge of the slums. She wasn't good enough for anything better. My breathing was too loud and I wrestled it under control. I couldn't give myself away.

Override.

Authorization?

I glanced up at Jonathan. He wasn't looking at me. I could ask him to do this for me. If he didn't have the proper authorization, he could get it. He'd managed Kagawa for me.

But he'd also seen Pete's reaction to that.

It probably wouldn't work anyway, but I could try. I entered my citID.

Confirmed.

My vision blurred and I sat back, my heart thundering, blinking back tears. My mother was dead, but Carrie would have a good home now. Real parents. Money.

A hundred Dawes Laser discoveries wouldn't have compared to that.

I never thought I'd be happy to see the palace. When I disembarked from the transport Pete stood on the platform with Lord Sifer, waiting for me. He hugged me and I stiffened, surprised that he'd touch me in front of a lord. I raised my eyebrows after he pulled away.

"Lord Sifer's already scandalized that I came to meet you, instead of requiring you to come to me."

"I said nothing of the kind, Excellence," Lord Sifer protested in his mild, calm voice.

Pete grinned at him but said nothing. "I couldn't wait to see you," he said to me. "Don't ever go away for so long again. OK?"

"That sounds good to me."

He had cleared some time for me, so we spent a few hours alone together walking barefoot on the beach, even though it was really too cold for it. We talked of nothing important, or even very interesting, and I felt the tension I'd brought back with me draining away.

He returned to his office in the afternoon. I was getting settled back in and about to go find my lab when I was summoned to appear before the emperor in his office. Baffled, I followed the servant. I was shown in and when the door closed behind me, I was berated by the emperor over the matter of Mr. Kagawa. He promised dire consequences if I ever acted on my own like that again; if I ever took advantage of my relationship with him to do things that should not be done.

I waited, barely breathing, for him to bring up Carrie as well, but he never said a word. I took a long, deep breath. I'd only done it that morning, he probably didn't even know yet. Maybe he wouldn't find out and maybe he would. But while I could accept that I deserved to be scolded for helping someone I'd never liked much anyway, no one was going to tell me it was wrong to do anything I could for my sister. Not even the emperor. Not even Pete.

I endured my chastisement in silence and gave my promise, when it was required of me, to never do such a thing again. That done, he dismissed me; I left with my ears ringing.

I only realized later why he'd waited to bring it up. Our private lives had nothing to do with his position or his responsibilities. I had done nothing that concerned us as a couple and he didn't bring it up in our private time. I had done something wrong, using my influence with the emperor as the means, so it was the emperor who reprimanded me.

That evening when he returned to our rooms to dress for dinner he acted as if nothing had happened and he never spoke of it again. Carrie never came up at all.

Before dinner that night, in the pre-dinner lounge, I was introduced to the Grand Duchess Aliana, Pete's cousin and the heir to the throne. Aliana was exotic and stunning, with creamy-chocolate skin and butter-colored hair and a prominent nose that somehow made her more beautiful rather than less. She glittered like a butterfly among caterpillars, and I didn't need the introduction to know who she was.

I liked her immensely. I think I would have liked her anyway— she was pleasant and intelligent and well spoken—but it didn't hurt that she didn't seem to care what class I wasn't.

Later that night, as I lay in bed with Pete, I said, "It was horrible, by the way."

"Telling Kirti about us?"

"Yes."

"You two were together before you left?"

"Yes."

"You couldn't have expected her to take it well."

"I didn't. But I hoped...Well, I knew she'd be angry. But I thought she knew me better than to assume that your position had anything to do with it. She not only assumed that, she told everyone as if it was a fact that I'd confirmed." I felt sick just thinking of it.

"You know," Pete said after a time, "she may not even believe that herself. Not really."

"What?"

"Rejection is easier to take if you can believe that the other person isn't worthy of you."

It made sense when he put it that way. Maybe she was just trying to make herself feel better. I could understand that. It still hurt.

"I'm sorry I cost you Kirti," he said.

"You didn't cost me Kirti. What happened between Kirti and me is between Kirti and me. It has nothing to do with you. And in any case, I have no regrets. I hate that Kirti has gotten hurt, but I'd do the same thing over again." He was quiet.

"I love you, Pete."

I'd never said that to him before. I'd been strangely reluctant, though he had said it more than once.

He pulled me on top of him. "I know." He smiled. I kissed him, a long, blissful kiss. Which led to other things, of course.

At dinner one night, several weeks after I'd returned, the conversation turned to the issue of the day, the riots on the planet of Carolis.

"Now's the time to act decisively, Your Excellence," General Mondejar said. "Show them that their new emperor is committed to keeping Carolis in the empire. Your father wasn't in a position to do that and you are an unknown to them. Make them respect and fear you and they'll quiet down."

The planet's troubles often originated in its notorious slum— ironically named Wildflower Hill—which was second only to Abenez as a miserable place to live. But while Abenez had long ago accepted its lot with docile despair, Carolis was new to the empire, and Wildflower Hill hadn't learned to accept its place in the grand scheme of things.

Pete nodded. "You make a good point, General, about giving them confidence in the Empire. But I'm not sure fear is something I'm interested in inspiring."

"Of course not," the general continued, "but it is only the unclass who are making trouble. That rabble won't understand diplomacy and soft words. They need a firm hand. Not until you've cowed them will you have any chance of teaching them to obey you."

"That's a sound piece of advice," I said, "for training an animal."

The general looked at me, his nose wrinkled in distaste. "There are distinct similarities between the behavior of a mob and a wild animal."

"There are distinct similarities between the behavior of arrogant assholes—"

"A mob is made up of people, General Mondejar," Aliana interrupted. "You cannot treat people as you would an animal and expect success."

"I'm sure any solution we settle on will involve considering the needs of the people as individuals, as well as the mob as a whole," Pete said. "A little consideration will go a long way in inspiring loyalty, which is vital to long-term stability on Carolis."

"Loyalty's not high on your priorities when you have no food," I said.

"So you agree that your unclass won't be loyal, then?" General Mondejar said.

"No, I'm saying that they're not rioting because of anything so abstract as disloyalty. You don't worry about what your actions will result in tomorrow if you're starving today."

General Mondejar looked past me at Pete. "I would caution you, again, Your Excellence, about divisive and disloyal influences kept so close to you."

"Dis—!"

"I need to hear more of this situation before I will know what I think," Aliana spoke over me.

"There's plenty of time for that tomorrow," Pete said, laying his hand on my knee under the table and squeezing. "I'd like to talk about something more pleasant with my dinner."

As I turned down the hall into the Imperial area with Pete after that dinner, I was stopped by the sudden jerk of a fistful of the hair on the back of my head.

"Ouch!" I tried to turn around but that hurt more, so I reached back to extricate myself. For my efforts I got an even harder jerk that pulled me backward.

"Stop yowling like a little cat and stop fighting me, you foolish man," Aliana's voice cut through the air behind me. I didn't need the hand trying to remove a whole patch of my hair to tell she was angry.

"Ouc— What? What did I do?"

"Aliana," Pete began.

"Go away, Peter, I am having a conversation with Jacob Dawes that you are not a part of. Go on."

I looked at Pete, pleading, but he just grimaced and cast a long, meaningful look at Aliana. She nodded in one quick jerk and then, without a word to me, he turned and walked away.

Aliana jerked me down the hall to her room and, not keen to part with all that hair, I stumbled along with her. Once we were in her room she released me with a shove and I fell against an armchair. Only a quick grab at the chair back kept me from falling.

"What was that?" I yelped.

"Is there so much physics in your head that there is no room left for thinking?"

"What are you talking about?"

"You are being an idiot, Jacob Dawes. Do you really think you can say those things at the head table?"

"I wasn't the only one talking about Carolis. I didn't even start it."

"Others may say what they think, but you cannot."

"Oh no? And why's that?" She heard the edge of anger in my voice because her eyebrow quirked.

"You know why. Because of what you are."

The hot rush of anger spread from my head down through my fingers and toes. My fists clenched. "I thought you were different than them, *Your Grace*, but I guess I was wrong. I don't get to have an opinion because I'm unclass? I should have known. You're like all the rest of them."

The crack of her hand against my cheek left my jaw throbbing and my ears ringing.

"Stupid man. Yes, it is because you are unclass, and you know I do not think less of you for it. If I did, would I be trying to protect you?"

"This is protecting me?"

"You question Peter openly in front of the nobility and you put yourself in danger because you are unclass and they hate you for it. You have as much right to your opinions as anyone, this I believe. But you cannot afford to speak them in front of people who would have you dead for daring to even look the emperor in the eye, let alone sleep in his bed."

"I'm supposed to sit there and keep my mouth shut? For how long?"

"For forever, if Peter is important to you. You have to make sacrifices to be with him, and you always knew this. Do not play the fool now. You cannot become forgetful or get comfortable. If this is something you cannot do, then spare yourself and Peter and go back to the Intellectual Complex. It is not only your happiness, or even your life at stake here. Do not hurt Peter by your carelessness or your idiocy."

I trembled with anger and adrenaline.

"Do you understand this?" She fixed me with a laser stare.

"Yes," I croaked.

Her face softened and she trailed her fingers over the burning patch on my cheek. "I should do this to you more often," she said. "You are less argumentative with my handprint on your face."

I wasn't quite sure what to make of that but she smiled softly. "Will you do this, Jacob Dawes, for me? You are good for Peter and you make him happy. I would want to keep you for that reason alone. But I find that I like you, myself. I would not see you hurt if I can help it."

I tried to smile. "Right now I'm too scared of you to do anything other than whatever you say."

Her mouth twitched at the edges. "It is not me you should be afraid of, my friend."

She left the sitting room without another word, and, stunned, I returned to my own.

She was right, but it made me angry to think about it, the

suffering of others being just a minor annoyance in otherwise civil conversation at the Imperial table. An inconvenience to me that must be pushed aside for my own welfare.

Maybe I couldn't talk about it, to save my own skin, but I could do something about it.

"I want to give my salary to Wildflower Hill," I said to Jonathan the next night.

"Anyone in particular?" he asked.

I huffed. "A charity, or something like that. You know what I mean."

"I'll draw up a list—"

"Don't complicate the issue. I just want my money to go to the kids. They're probably hungry, and cold, and afraid... It's—can you just take care of that for me?"

"Yes," he said. "I'll take care of it."

When our birthday came around, Pete took me for a long weekend, just the two of us, at the chalet in the Swiss Alps. It was so easy to forget, there, that a world outside of us existed at all, much less with problems I had to worry about.

He taught me how to ski.

When I was lying on my back for the fifth time that morning, winded and covered in snow, my skis and poles scattered across the slope, Pete stopped downslope of me.

"You know, there are very simple principles involved in this," I groused, "gravity, mass, force, friction."

Pete grinned and held out his hand to help me up.

"Yeah. But there's also you."

That night I joined him in the den where he sat in front of the fire, sipping mulled wine. As I walked past him to sit down, he grabbed my hand and pulled me into the chair with him, between his legs, pulling me back to lean against his chest. As usual, whenever he did anything like that, I tensed, counting out a deliberate few moments to let him hold me like that, then I squeezed his arms and stood, sitting down in the chair next to him.

He threw me a quick smile but it was guarded.

Guilt sloshed in my stomach. "You know, that's not about you, I mean, it's not that I don't want to sit with you, or that there's anything wrong with us."

"I know," he said, easy and effortless, forgiving.

I shrugged, my ears hot. "It's just one of those things, I suppose."

"Mmmm."

I stared down at the cup of wine in my hand. "How do you do that? How do you trust people the way you do? It's like you want to believe the best of everyone all the time. I don't understand how you can do that. With who you are and all you see, hasn't life proven to you how...how unsafe that is?"

For several minutes he didn't say anything, staring into the fire as if the answer was there.

"I think you have a hard time trusting anything in life at all, or anyone, because nothing was ever certain, and you couldn't rely on anyone. It was different for me."

He looked down at his hands.

"I don't remember my mother," he said. "I've always imagined she was everything my father wasn't. Even so, he wasn't a bad man, or even a bad emperor. He wasn't even a bad father, exactly. He never hurt me. He just wasn't a *father*."

I shifted to lean against the chair back, closing my eyes, letting his words roll over me. I loved listening him talk about his past. I'd always hated it with other people. It was so hard not to be jealous. But this was Pete.

"One thing that was good about my father was that he was patient. He was good at waiting. I think that's why I managed his coldness as a father without becoming bitter. I didn't have someone I could love and trust without reservation. But life always gave me everything I needed and most of what I wanted, so that would come too. I just had to wait."

I stared into the fire, trying in the hazy warmth of the evening, to assimilate the idea, concepts that were so foreign to me.

"Thank you," he said quietly, "for not making me wait very long."

My throat tightened and my muscles tensed, ready to stand and go to him, but my mind kicked in, that frightened, instinctive voice that told me to stay away, to run. He wanted too much, too close, too vulnerable. But I shoved it away and got up, dropping into the chair between his legs and lying back against his chest, relaxing with fixed determination. His arms went around me and he kissed the side of my face. He pressed his cheek to mine and we sat together like that for a long time. The smile I felt against my cheek never went away.

We returned to the palace and to life—to our life—there.

I was in the lab one morning when Pete came to find me.

"May I talk with you for a moment?"

"Sure."

"Somewhere else?"

I cast a look at my experiment but I didn't need to see it to know whether or not walking away at that point was OK. It was just that it made me nervous, the way he asked.

"Yeah, that's fine."

We walked without speaking through the hallways until we came to a part of the palace I didn't know. Pete led me into a small gallery there. The paintings dotting the white walls were done in soothing blues and greens but in the Tveldian style that always set my teeth on edge.

He sat down on a bench and I sat beside him. He took my hand, looking down at it, stroking the back of my hand with his thumb. But it felt like he was looking for comfort more than he was trying to give it. I stiffened.

He looked up.

"It's your sister."

I'd been afraid of a lot of possible things he might have said, but that wasn't one of them.

"Carrie?"

He nodded. "Jake..." he swiped his thumb over my hand a little too hard for comfort, "she died yesterday."

Everything in me went cold. He clutched my hand harder as if I'd tried to pull it away. Maybe I had.

"How?" I croaked.

He engulfed my hand in both of his now.

"She hanged herself," he whispered.

"She..."

He didn't answer what hadn't really been a question anyway.

"Why?"

"There was a note. It seems the man, her foster father, had been..."

"He raped her?"

"Yes. Apparently he'd been doing it for a while."

"But—" I shot up and started pacing. "But why didn't she say something?" I turned to him, he was blurry. "Why didn't she try to contact me?"

The strength went out of my legs and I thunked back down on another bench. "She thought I wouldn't care. I didn't try to contact her once I was the emperor's lover, living at the palace, just moved her around and—"

Pete rushed over and sat beside me, grabbing my arms to turn me to face him.

"No. That's not it. She thought you were dead."

I blinked. "Dead? Why?"

"Your mother told her you were. That the men who came to take you from them had killed you. Carrie never knew you went to the IIC. Maybe she wondered how she got into a home like that—" he hesitated only a moment in which I heard him decide not to address the fact that he knew what I'd done, "but she had no reason to think it would be her brother. Even with a Jacob Dawes at the palace."

I stared at him. I felt so stupid and numb and empty.

"I sent her there."

Pete sighed. "I know. But it's not your fault. That man had been cleared by the authorities to foster children. You were just trying to—"

"To assuage my conscience without ever doing anything for her. Without calling her or going to see her. Without inconveniencing myself in any way."

"Hey, it's not like that. And anyway, it would have been a delicate situation even if you had talked to me about it." There was only a hint of reproach in the words. "It's not like we could have brought her here to live down the hall."

"Why not?"

He stared at me for a minute.

"Well, because...Jake she was—"

"Unclass."

"That's not what I was going to say."

"That's what you were going to mean."

"You're not being fair."

"I wonder sometimes how you accomplish this great feat of having an unclass in your bed like there's no difference between us. It's just because you make yourself forget what I am. It would have been harder with Carrie here, wouldn't it?"

"It's not like that. There are political complexities—"

I walked out.

I dreamed of Abencz that night. I dreamed of Carrie with her new family, only they lived in the penthouse apartment in the building we'd grown up in. It was as bare and dirty as ours had been, just bigger. I found them there, Carrie, a gaunt, pale teenager, huddled in a corner. Our father stood over her, his belt raised. Thick, livid welts screamed on her bare arm. The belt cracked down again and the sound was like a world exploding.

He dropped the belt and hauled her up, shoving her against the wall. He grabbed her breast hard enough to make her cry out.

"Now, bitch, you know what I want."

Carrie looked straight at me with hollow, hopeless eyes. "Why?"

I woke up sobbing.

"What is it?" Pete asked, his hand warm and heavy on my arm. I was trembling so hard it hurt to try to hold myself together.

"Jake?"

I buried my face in the pillow and pretended I hadn't woken enough to hear him. He wrapped his arm around me and stroked my face and hair until he fell asleep again, long before I did.

He waited for me to say something first. It was five days before I had anything to say about it. I came to find him in his office.

"Are you going to kill him?"

His eyes darted back and forth for a second as if he could catch the traces of the conversation he'd missed.

"Who?"

"That man."

He knew what I was talking about then.

"No," he said. "He'll be Resettled."

"I want to kill him."

"I know. But that's not how it works."

"Why not? Make it work. You're the emperor."

He grimaced. "Believe it or not, Jake, I can't just break the rules when it pleases me, or you. If I don't abide by the laws too, the whole system falls apart."

"It's just one man."

"It's never just one man. Look, they know what he did. No one goes easy on child molesters. Not the judges or the Resettlement officials or the other inmates. And someone always manages to make sure wherever he's sent they'll know what he did. He'll pay for what he did. For the rest of his life."

"Just this once?"

He shook his head. "Not once, not ever."

There was something missing in that argument that I couldn't put my finger on, but it did prove one thing, I couldn't count on Pete for help with this.

He meant well, I knew he did. But there were some things that you couldn't talk about between an unclass and the emperor himself. And in spite of whatever else we were to each other, we were still that.

As if in some cruel cosmic joke, the months after Carrie died were some of the best I can remember. Maybe Pete was trying to make it up to me. Maybe I was trying to make it up to her, by living for both of us.

It was at an evening party Pete was holding for the Torrean ambassador when Blaine sidled up to me.

"It's a shame about Carrie."

I nearly dropped my drink. "What?"

"Your sister. I heard how she died."

I stopped myself asking him how he knew. He'd told me that already, back on the ship.

"It was one of your precious high class who did something like that to her," I hissed.

"Yes," he said. "A high class man. And he knew exactly what you'd put in his home. What else was he to do with that?"

Jonathan had come up beside me and if he wasn't in time to hear what Blaine said, he saw what I made of it. Jonathan grabbed my arm as my fist flew toward Blaine and he put all of his weight into it. I stumbled backward with the power of the counter-force applied against my fury.

"Jacob!"

I was never sure afterward if Jonathan had actually used my name or if I'd imagined it.

I straightened slowly, in the echoing hush that fell around us. Blaine smirked at me.

"Are you well, Mr. Dawes?"

Jonathan pulled hard on my arm. "His Excellence sent for you, Mr. Dawes."

I glared at Jonathan but he didn't drop my gaze.

"I believe it's rather important," he said.

I shoved Jonathan hard as I turned and stormed off.

"Blaine's an ass," was my only answer when Pete asked me that night in our rooms what had happened at the party.

"You know you can talk to me," he said, hesitantly. "If there's anything wrong. Just talk, you know." He slid his arms around me from behind and laid his cheek on my shoulder. "I love you."

"If there was anything to tell, honestly, I'd tell you. Who else do I even talk to?"

He snorted.

"Sometimes I wonder what you're doing behind this brooding exterior," he said.

"Yeah. Me too."

I may not have known how to talk to him, but I did love him, and he made me as happy as I'd ever been, more than I thought was possible.

A few weeks after our nineteenth birthday, he returned to our room in silence one evening, radiating tension.

That meant there was trouble with Wildflower Hill and he was trying not to tell me about it. After all, I was the one who wouldn't talk about it. My policy of silence on all things political had become a force all its own since the first assassinations nine months back.

"I found the problem with the fusion experiment," I said. He looked at me, pushing down his shoulders with an obvious effort. "It was a cracked tube. Just a hairline. You wouldn't see it unless you were really looking for it. That explains why the results were deteriorating over time. It's two weeks' work lost, but at least I've found it now."

He made a noise of acknowledgement, but said nothing. After a while, I picked up the tablet I'd put down when he entered. His frustration was like a raging fire against my wall of disinterest, but I pretended to read.

Finally he took a deep breath. "I'm leaving for Carolis in the morning." He hesitated. "You're welcome to come with me."

"I don't think I can leave the fusion project right now," I said. We both knew it was a diplomatic lie.

"Oh."

"How long will you be gone?" I asked.

He looked away and shrugged. "I don't know." His face was tense and he straightened, as if he'd made a decision, and met my eye. "They've taken hostages this time. A whole platoon of the additional troops we just sent in. I don't know how long I'll be gone. Until things are under control. Maybe until a workable agreement is reached." He let out a huge sigh, like draining a pressure valve, now that the news was off his chest. "I don't know."

It was more than he'd said to me about Wildflower Hill in the last year.

"Oh." I looked down at the tablet again, as if that was somehow a logical conclusion to the conversation. Even I could see how ridiculous it was. He was going to another planet to deal with an armed uprising, and I was going to see him off with nothing but polite noises?

But I didn't know what else to say. I'd spent months building a wall around the subject, between us, when it came to a part of his life that increasingly took up his attention. Now I couldn't break the wall down. I didn't know how to, and I didn't want to if it meant acknowledging the thing that Wildflower Hill had become in my head.

I was probably as frustrated with myself as he was with me. I knew he was doing his best. Even with an active and conscientious emperor, some places really did just become human dumping grounds with problems no one could fix.

Even as Pete tried to address their concerns and deal with their, usually corrupt, merry-go-round of leaders, the situation had escalated from riots to assassinations of city officials. Now they'd taken imperial troops as hostages.

With a groan, he gave up on me and any further conversation, and turned to leave the room.

I said, "You can't deal with it from here?"

He stopped. "No. Not with lives on the line like this. The time lag's too long. I need to be on the planet, at least. I won't go anywhere near the trouble zones. I'll be fine."

"Of course. I know." I stood up, unable to sit still anymore.

He was biting his lip, looking down. He lifted his head. "Jake..."

I was such a muddle of guilt, anger, grief, and fear that my face must have been a picture. He stopped and sighed again. It was becoming a fixture in our conversations.

"I'm not going to dinner tonight," he said. "Want to eat something in here with me?"

"Of course. I'll go tell Jonathan."

He nodded, gave me a tired smile, and went into the bedroom. I sank back into the chair and buried my face in my hands.

He left the next morning and I really did see him off without saying another word about where he was going or why. He was gone for three months.

I spent that time mostly hiding in either the lab or our rooms, but also trying to figure out what was wrong with me. Why I wouldn't—why I couldn't—talk to him about Wildflower Hill. Even thinking about it made my heart pound and my breaths come too fast.

I'd spent years trying to forget Abenez, and I'd done a good job of it, too. But the first time I'd seen pictures of Wildflower Hill, my palms started to sweat. It was as if I was back in the slums again. The fear and despair I felt may not have been an accurate reflection of how I'd felt as a child, but they were overwhelming.

And I knew, I knew that whatever the situation, those people were in the right. All the up-classes, all the authorities, were the cause of their problems and were the enemy. Even when I heard the reports coming in early on—when I would let Pete talk about it— even with contradictory evidence in front of me, of culpability on both sides, I couldn't change the way I felt. When Pete talked about Wildflower Hill, I hated him and everything he represented. Even after the assassinations. Even with soldiers and negotiators taken hostage. No facts changed the way I felt.

So I had to do something about it.

In addition to the salary I still collected as the emperor's appointee—and which I sent to Wildflower Hill—I had access to discretionary funds; I'd never been able to fathom what I might use them for.

But I knew now.

"Jonathan, I want to send more money to Wildflower Hill."

He raised an eyebrow.

"You're already sending your entire salary."

"Yes, I know, but there's other money I can use. I want to send that too."

He considered for a moment.

"That could be...problematic."

"Why?"

"You must understand, that is the emperor's money, not yours."

"But I'm allowed to use some, right? So then it is mine."

A smile flickered at his mouth.

"I understand it seems uncomplicated to you, but it won't appear so to anyone on the outside. On the books this will appear as the emperor sending assistance personally to a people in rebellion. You can't do it, sir."

I frowned, frustrated.

"But I could give money to you, right?"

"Why would you?"

"As a gift. You're such a great servant that I want to give you a gift on top of what Pete pays you. No one would freak out about that, would they?"

"No," he said with exaggerated care.

"So I could give you money regularly and you could send it to the Wildflower Hill charities."

Now he frowned, eyeing me from under knotted brows.

"I admire the sentiment, sir, but this sounds very foolish, and dangerous for you."

"But you'll do it?"

He sighed. "Yes. I'll do it."

When the soldiers were finally released, a few rebel ringleaders were executed, and additional field personnel were sent in to deal with the food and shelter issues underlying the whole situation, Pete returned to the palace. And still we didn't talk about it. So I suppose the outcome was inevitable.

It wasn't Pete's fault.

He knew that I tried to stay out of it, but, as close to the center of political power as I was, he didn't think it was safe for me to stay completely ignorant. So about once a month, I would attend open council sessions.

I would go when something on the agenda piqued my interest. It was one day, when one of the scheduled issues pertained to education, that the news came in.

It was less than two weeks since Pete had returned from Wildflower Hill. The rebels had captured a company of soldiers again. And this time they didn't bother holding prisoners.

Pete went pale. "How many dead?"

"Current estimates say fifty-four soldiers, Excellence."

Pete nodded. "I want the families informed as quickly as possible. We'll never beat the news to them, but I don't want them sitting around wondering about their own any longer than necessary."

General Poe, seated at the table with the other counselors, nodded to one of his men and the man left the room.

Blaine spoke up from across the table. I hadn't noticed him there. I didn't remember him being on Pete's council at all. "Surely now, Excellence, it's time to take more drastic measures."

Pete put his head down and rubbed his forehead for a minute. "Yes, I know." He was quiet only a moment before he lifted his head. "General Mondejar, start the evacuations. I want them out of there yesterday. Make sure everyone knows and has an opportunity to get out if they want to. We raze the sector in three days."

I was the only one in the audience who gasped.

"A voluntary evacuation, Your Excellence?" General Mondejar asked, but he didn't sound surprised; satisfied, more like.

Pete looked tired. "Yes. If anyone's stupid enough to play chicken with us, then they were a problem we needed to deal with anyway. They can save us the effort. But I want everyone else out and sheltered before a single building falls. General Holmes, the plans are completed?"

"Yes, Excellence. We can bring down the sector with no damage to the surrounding areas."

"Very well," Pete said. "Get it done."

"No!" I shot out of my chair. "You can't do that!"

Every head turned in my direction. Pete met my eye, his expression weary but resolute. "Mr. Dawes, this is not the time or the place for a debate. Sit down or leave the room."

I pushed past the people around me.

"How can you do that? How can you even consider it? Those are *people* Pete, not pieces on a game board. You can't just move them out of your way when you get tired of them."

"You don't know what you're talking about, Mr. Dawes. This is a last resort, but it's a well-considered and well-planned action. These people will be taken care of. We've tried everything else. I'm not putting any more of my people's lives in the hands of these rebels."

"What else have you tried?"

He stepped closer to me and said in a low voice, "If you'd talked to me about this even once in the past year, you'd know the answer to that. Calm down or get out, Jake. I can't let you do this here. Go home, we'll talk about this later."

I reared back. "Go home? Oh yes, I have a home to go to, don't I? All of you," I whirled around, "have homes to go to and you'll have them three days from now. But women and children and old people who have never done anything wrong are going to watch theirs demolished because they're inconveniencing you—"

"Stop this!" Pete cut through my rant. "Provisions have been made—"

"Provisions? Do you have the tiniest idea what their lives are like? You're not just moving them from one place to another; you're taking away everything they've made for themselves. You're not just demolishing buildings but a community, a support system. Are you going to put old women down in one town, alone, and the children who have been caring for them—and who they've been providing for—in another city altogether because there are no legal ties between them? You won't even know. They have nothing at all, and you're going to take even that away from them."

"Not here, Jake," Pete hissed. "Please. I can't let you do this."

"Some of them will die, you know. The innocent and defenseless. It's not only cocksure rebels who will stay behind. Women, children, old men will stay behind because they don't understand, or don't believe. You're going to *kill* them."

"I'm sure your origins make you sympathetic to these people," Blaine interjected, "but the Empire has larger concerns. We'll be improving their lives. Perhaps they'll be grateful. You can't possibly speak for all of the unclass of the Empire."

Black fury washed over my vision and for a moment I couldn't even see.

"I understand your concerns," Pete said, his voice calm and firm. "This is a complex situation that has been considered at length. I'm sorry that we can't make this painless for everyone, but good men and women are dying down there and still nothing changes. I won't let that happen anymore."

I could hear the logic in the words, but something inside me was eight years old and scared sick. Everything that had been building up for months finally came to a head. I rounded on him.

"You're no different than they are. Your precious soldiers are more important than tens of thousands of unclass *vermin*. You didn't even have to think about that one, did you? You make me sick."

All the color rushed from his face before the slow flush of

anger touched his cheekbones and his eyes. "That's enough!" Pete said, sitting back down. He gripped the arms of his chair until his knuckles turned white but I was probably the only one who knew that was because his hands were trembling. "Mr. Dawes, you are out of order."

"And not just here, Your Excellency," Blaine said, standing. He looked at me like a particularly pleased predator. "I've recently discovered that he's been supporting these rebels all along."

Pete's eyes found me.

"He's been sending them money to purchase weapons," Blaine continued.

The entire court took a breath. Pete went pale.

"No!" I said. "No, that's not why I send them anything!"

"But you do support them behind the emperor's back?"

"It's not behind his back." I looked straight at Pete. His face was pinched, as if he was in pain. "Not behind his back. I just never said anything to him about it. That's not the same thing."

Murmurs filled the room.

"Your Excellency," Blaine continued, "I have proof that this man has been supporting these rebels for months. He argues for them now, which would be admirable, if one was not aware of him suborning treason."

"No!" I yelled. But Pete was looking at me wide-eyed, with that look of horror you see in the old vids when the guy realizes his best friend just shot him.

"You're going to believe him? Him over me?" Fury rang in my ears. "Of course you are." I took in the room with a sweep of my arm. "Of course. Because he's one of you. Sure, Pete. Believe him. I'm just a filthy unclass. I'm one of them."

I moved closer to Pete but I saw the guards shift with me in my field of vision. That just made me angrier. That I could share his bed but I'd be the threat the moment anyone was reminded of who we all were.

I grabbed Pete by the arms. "Don't—"

He shoved me off, hard.

I didn't even have to think about it. In fact, I didn't think at all. The next thing I knew Pete was several steps away holding his nose, a line of crimson blood trickling between his fingers, which I saw from my position on the floor, on my stomach with my arms bent behind my back as if the guards holding me meant to break them.

My grunt when they twisted harder was the only sound that broke the long silence.

"Take him to a detention cell," Pete said, looking away from me. I didn't resist and didn't say a word when they dragged me out of the room, too furious and too stunned by what I'd done and the look of anguish I'd seen cross Pete's face when he gave the order.

I was shoved down the hallways and into an inter-palace transport. After a short trip I was pulled from the transport and manhandled through corridors in the South Quarter until we entered the main detention center.

It wasn't a very large place, as prisons go. Very few people were ever held at the palace itself. Sam, the captain of Pete's personal guard—a giant of a man whom I'd always been little scared of— shoved me through a door. It didn't appear to be any sort of logical admittance area. Not far down the hallway we came to a large open room that seemed to be a gathering place for off-duty guards. My stomach clenched.

The next thing I was aware of was that I was lying on the floor, my cheek throbbing against the cool tile, my head ringing. There was a rumble of voices above me that gradually resolved into words.

"...hit the emperor."

I was hauled off the floor and set on my feet. They kept hold of me, which was the only reason I was able to stay vertical. The room swam around me.

Sam put his mouth so close to my ear I could feel his breath. "Stick your cock in him one time and think we'll just let you do whatever you want, do you?" Angry murmurs rippled through the room.

His fist slammed into my gut and I doubled over, all my breath going out in a rush.

My arms were pulled tight behind me and, one after another, the guards took turns pummeling me until the room swam around me in a haze of pain and blood. When even the men holding me from behind couldn't keep me upright anymore, they dropped me to the floor and took turns kicking me.

At some point the floor started moving and I realized they were dragging me down a hallway. About halfway down, they opened a door and threw me inside.

I lay on the floor in a whimpering heap. I was only just aware of them pulling the mattress, blanket, and pillow off the bed and throwing them into the hall. The door shut and I heard the heavy thud of a real bolt slide home. A few moments later all the lights in my cell and in the hallway went off. They did something to the climate controls and soon I was shivering. Miserable, body and soul, I drifted in and out of consciousness.

I woke later in a pink-tinged gloom. The early evening sunlight, after many twists and turns, bled into my cell through a small barred window in the door. I levered myself up with a groan and lay down on the hard platform that was all that was left of the bed, hoping it would be some improvement on the floor. It wasn't. I lay as still as possible. Even breathing was painful.

The next evening I was brought a tray: two pieces of meat, mostly gristle, cold and quivering in congealed fat; a pile of mushy vegetables; and a hard, stale piece of bread. I couldn't imagine the effort it had taken to find food that awful anywhere in the palace. I ate every bite.

I was brought the same tray once a day. Otherwise I might not have existed to the guards. That was fine with me. The last time they'd noticed me had been very unpleasant. I wanted to know what was going on outside my cell, what was happening with Wildflower Hill, but I was too afraid of the guards to ask any questions.

I had terrible dreams in there. Women and children in the streets of Abenez, running from some unseen danger, calling out to me for help, but I stood behind a force-field surrounding the sector and did nothing. It was raining, hard. The streets filled with water that pulled at their ankles, slowing them, dragging them back with each laborious step. Every one of them was my mother, or Carrie.

Sudden, simultaneous explosions ripped out of each building, tearing through the women in the street, and they slid below the water in a smear of hot metal and blood. A few of them, still standing, bleeding from deep cuts and livid with burns, reached out for me, struggling against the water.

I looked down at my hands, glittering with gemstones, watched myself enter a code onto a tablet I was holding. I looked back up and met the eye of a little Carrie, only a dozen feet away. I finished entering the authorization and in an instant, dozens of iterations of my mother and sister exploded.

They came for me after five days. I was taken from my cell to the room where I'd been beaten the first day. A dozen or more guards waited there. I groaned. My arms were pinned behind me again and Sam drew himself up in front of me. "You're going to mind your manners in there, you understand?" His fist folded me in half again and the only answer he got was *umphf*. "'Cause that's what's waiting for you if you don't."

I nodded, and was hauled from the room.

I was brought before Pete in the throne room. It was full of fancy, important people, but he dominated it with no more than a circlet and a chair. I was jerked to a stop several feet away from him. He was wearing his emperor face but he had dark circles under his eyes.

My gut screamed in pain when they shoved me into a bow and jerked me upright again.

"Mr. Dawes," Pete said, "five days ago you were removed from the council chambers for your disrespectful and violent behavior toward the emperor. This is treason. But we are confident your actions were thoughtless rather than deliberate. Is that not so?"

It would have been so easy, a few simple words. But with the residue of the dreams clinging to me and the royal "we" ringing in my ears it was beyond me. "Did you go through with it?" I said.

A look of disbelief flickered on his face, and then he stiffened. "You have no right to question me."

His defensiveness was all the answer I needed. He had destroyed the lives of all those helpless people.

"You disgust me," I spat. "I have nothing to apologize for. I'm not the one who killed innocent women and children."

He stood and advanced on me. So close, I could see the faint flush of anger on his cheeks, and the crinkles of confusion around his eyes. The guards' hands were cutting off my circulation.

"This is not your decision. Even if it had been, do you think you could do better? It's easy for you to stand there with your righteous anger and yell about what I should have done, but I'm the one who has to make these choices and live with them. I'm the one with those lives in my hand and on my head. I'm responsible for all of them, Jake, billions. That means doing terrible things sometimes. I won't let you question me in here, and I won't let you disrespect this office. Don't you dare judge me for what I've done with a crisis you know nothing about."

I couldn't even hear him anymore. My bruises throbbed and in my head a little girl who looked like Carrie called out to me from behind the force-field.

"Do your 'billions' include all those unclass, worthless things that are such an annoyance? Was it your token gesture of benevolence toward them, taking me in? I trusted you. I believed in you. You made me believe you were a good man and that you cared about them, about me. It was a lie, wasn't it? I've been in love with a man that didn't really exist."

He looked ill. "Enough! Not one more word." Turning to Sam, he said, "Take him back to his cell."

I choked back anger that closed my throat and stung in my eyes. "Have I become too much trouble to bother with anymore? Is that it, Pete? Get rid of me so you don't have to face what you've done? So you can pretend this is all my fault? You're a coward!"

"ENOUGH!" he roared. "One more word, Mr. Dawes, just one, and I will have your head, do you understand me? I will not allow you to disrespect the throne. I cannot ignore treason. Stop this immediately or I will have you executed."

"Fuck you."

A collective gasp sucked all the air from the room. Every line of his face hardened.

"Lord Sifer, please schedule Mr. Dawes's execution." The calm in his voice hurt more than anything he'd said. "Three days."

I felt sick and shaky, but I was still filled with adrenaline and rage. He stood there, his face and eyes fixed on me, but I didn't think he could see me.

"I love you too," I spat.

Anger dissolved from his face and a look of unspeakable pain replaced it. I couldn't breathe for the shock of it; not merely the transition, but the stark pain on the face of the man I loved. I gasped for air, as if Sam had punched me in the gut again. I needed to say something, anything, to take that look off his face, but before I could speak I was hauled from the room.

It wasn't a surprise, though it was terribly painful nonetheless, when upon entering the guardroom back in the detention facility, I was beaten again.

It was much the same as the first time. Layered on top of the beating from only five days before, it felt like they were going to kill me, and part of me didn't mind. When I was dragged off, bloody, to my dark, cold cell, I was as grateful to see it as if it had been the emperor's own bed.

That thought brought its own pain. The adrenaline from earlier had been beaten out of me, and I was having a hard time understanding the scene that had passed. With the last look on Pete's face scorched on my brain, I was having a hard time remembering anything at all, or making any sense of it.

Pete, who had been the sun that anchored my wandering satellite, was now a black hole pulling me in, crushing me. Or was it me, wrong about that, and everything else? Again.

Pete was a good person, probably the best I'd ever known. Much better than me. I had always known that about him. I couldn't have been wrong about that for so long. Maybe it was as he said: this was a complex situation, and the best he could do. And if anyone owed him support in public, it was me. No matter what their motivations, everyone else had been loyal. Everyone but me.

Treason. I felt sick. And very afraid. My execution. Three days. Somehow I slept; the prospect haunted my dreams.

A day later when I was brought a meal, I summoned the courage to ask the guard for a tablet so that I could write farewells to my friends. He just looked at me and left. So I was shocked when, a few hours later, the door opened and he entered with a tablet and handed it to me without a word.

It was a text-only unit, and it wasn't in good condition. The battery was more than half dead, and from time to time it would completely shut down for no reason I could discern. Every time it did, I feared it wouldn't come on again. So I kept it off and composed my mails in my head. The morning of my last day, I began to write them.

I wrote to Chuck first. My relationship with Chuck was so uncomplicated. I only told him how much his friendship had always meant to me, how much I admired him. I assured him of my guilt and that the sentence was justified, and told him how sorry I was that I had done this to myself and my friends. That was enough.

The second mail I wrote was to Dr. Okoro. That relationship, too, was simple and straightforward. There were more layers, as he had been both friend and father figure, but I said to him what I'd said to Chuck and little more.

Kirti's was more difficult. I composed and discarded a hundred mails to her in my head. In the end I wrote only:

Kirti,
The others will tell you why this is my last mail to you. I

know you might consider even this unwelcome, but I can't go to my death without telling you that I love you. I have always loved you and I still love you. I'm sorry that I hurt you and that, because of that, I lost you. You meant more to me than anyone for so long. Thank you for all you were for me. I love you.

Pete I saved for last, of course. There were so many things to say to him, and none of them adequate. But I did finally record this:

Pete,

I've taken pains to make sure you don't read this until after it's all over. I don't want you to think I'm asking you for anything, because I'm not. You're doing what you have to do and I know that.

More than anything I need to tell you I'm sorry. I was wrong. It was my fault, and there is no one to blame for any of this but me. I still think you made the wrong decision. But I never should have acted the way I did, and I know that's why I'm in here writing this now.

I can't say why I did it. I don't suppose it matters now.

You're probably beating yourself up about all this. Stop. If you're upset about the end of us, I can't tell you not to be. But don't blame yourself for this. It's not your fault.

All I can seem to think about these past few days is you. Well, really, us. More than anything, I have been remembering the first time we were together, the day I realized I loved you.

You've made me happy, Pete, more than I deserved. Thank you for that. Thank you for everything. Please believe that I deeply regret what I've done to you; how I acted, and that I ended our relationship in such a horrible way. I think even now that you wouldn't want for us to be over. You're ridiculous like that.

I love you. I never stopped loving you. I hope you'll forgive me. Actually, I know you'll forgive me. But move on before long, OK? I want that for you. You deserve it.

Goodbye,
Jake

The mails to Chuck, Dr. Okoro, and Kirti I forwarded immediately to Jonathan. I knew I could trust him to deliver them only after the execution.

Pete's presented difficulties. I could have forwarded it to Jonathan, but I was afraid that, for any number of reasons, it might stop there. But forwarding it to Pete's private mailbox, the one hardly anyone knew of, would have to be done before the actual execution. I was determined that Pete would not to see the mail until after it was all over.

But, with few options, in the end I sent the message as an attachment to a mail. In that I simply told Pete that my final farewells were attached and should he receive this before the execution, to please respect my wishes and not read it until afterward.

I was careful to time my sending. I knew Pete's habits, and waited until an hour when he would be long out of the office and unlikely to return. He rarely checked his messages anywhere else, so with the execution early in the morning, I knew there was a good chance that he wouldn't see my mail until after it was over. Then I lay down on the bed. All I had left to do was done. Of all the ridiculous things to do, I slept.

fg27

It was the light that woke me. My door had been thrown open and light from the hallway flooded the room. I blinked into the brightness, blocking it with my hand up in front of my face. It seemed far too early for them to come and get me. I cringed to think what that meant they had planned for the hours before my execution.

It was Pete standing in the doorway. He stormed into the room and threw a tablet at me. "You love me?" he demanded. "You don't blame me, you don't want me to feel guilty, but you send me *that*?"

I sat up without even looking at the tablet. "You weren't supposed to read it yet."

He glowered at me.

"Look," I said, testily, trying to hide how happy I was to see him, "I did my best to keep it from you until tomorrow. Don't get angry with me that it didn't work out. I don't exactly have a lot of resources here."

His face fell, and I felt sick over the flippant comment.

He was in pain. It was all I could do to keep myself from getting up and closing the distance between us, taking him in my arms, comforting him. Telling him, really telling him, how sorry I was, how much I loved him, and how wrong I'd been. Instead I put my elbows on my knees, clasped my hands together in front of me, and locked my eyes on them.

"I'm sorry, Pete," I said, "I just wanted you to know that. I'm sorry for everything."

I glanced up but he wasn't looking at me, his head was turned to the side, staring off into the distance. "You're making it worse."

"You would prefer I hadn't tried to apologize at all? Or that I'd written you some scathing, heartless mail telling you what a horrible person you were for doing what you had to do? I can't do that, I'm sorry. And anyway, it wouldn't have helped. You're no good at holding grudges. Saying things to make you angry would only work for a little while. And then you'd get over being angry with me no matter what I'd said. It's just the way you are."

He still wouldn't look at me. I could see that he was trying not to cry, and it hurt more than any of the beatings to keep myself on that bed, to not stand and do something.

After a long silence he met my eye. "So what am I supposed to do now?"

"Nothing. You're going to go back to your room and I'm going to sit here, and in a few hours this will all be over with. It's just the way it has to be."

"How can you say that? You want to *die*?"

"No. I'm scared shitless, to be honest. But what other option is there? You have your responsibilities. I did this to myself. I hate what that means for me, for both of us, but I can't go back and undo it."

He was silent for a long time, his face twisted with pain. He stepped forward, put his hand under my chin, and lifted my face, examining me.

"They'll be punished for that," he said, looking at my bruises.

I pulled away from his grip, but not with any force.

"Don't bother," I said. "It doesn't matter."

He didn't answer.

"I can't do it," he said finally. "No matter what you say, I can't have you killed. It's not the only option. Maybe it's what I *should* do, but there are other things I *can* do."

I watched him.

"I'm going to have you Resettled," he said.

The word hit me like a punch in the gut. When I could breathe again I said, "Well that's not so bad, is it?"

He sighed. "There's more. I'm also going to have you publicly flogged."

I shivered.

"I'm sorry," he said quietly. "I don't want to...I wish I didn't have to. You have to understand, they're expecting a public spectacle. And besides, the Resettlement alone can't be justified as a substitute for execution. If there were any other way...But it's better than the alternative, isn't it?"

"Of course. Don't worry about it. I'll be all right."

He moved close again and laid his hand against my cheek. I wanted to lean into it. I wanted him to hold me. Instead I removed his hand, squeezing but quickly releasing it.

"Thank you," I said. "So I guess this is goodbye. It sounds so ridiculous, but I really am sorry. For all of this. It's all my fault, OK? Don't go blaming yourself."

His voice was strangled. "Is that really all you have to say to me?"

It took me a minute to get it out. I put my elbows on my knees again and watched as my knuckles turned white. I couldn't look at him and do what I had to do.

"Yes."

He was quiet for a while. "I love you," he said.

Squeezing my hands together until it hurt, I kept my face down, biting hard on my lip, and nodded. He stood there a long time. I needed him to leave. I couldn't do this much longer.

Before my strength failed, I heard the door open and close, and I was alone again.

I didn't sleep. My head was too full of Pete and the overload of emotions from his visit; the added pain of the happiness at seeing him that had almost overwhelmed me, and the necessity of killing it. I knew Resettlement was preferable by far to a beheading, but that didn't dull the misery over now having to face going on after my life with Pete had ended. And if I managed not to think of that, there was the flogging.

It was a long few hours.

In the morning they came for me. They brought me no breakfast. I wondered if they already knew I was not going to be executed or if the concept of a last meal was simply lost on them. When I was taken out of the building by a different way than before, I decided they must know that someone else was going to beat me up for them. I couldn't imagine them passing up a chance to do it one last time, otherwise.

They led me through the halls and into a part of the palace I'd never been in before. Everywhere we went people stopped and stared as we passed. There were surprisingly few people in the halls, but when we got to the justice square I saw why. The courtyard was teeming, packed with people by the thousands.

The justice square saw little use. It never doubled as a space for any other purpose, only executions and other public punishments, and such events were rare. Only in cases that had come all the way up to Pete himself were punishments meted out at the palace. Cases did not come to Pete often.

My case, of course, the offense against the emperor himself, began and ended with Pete. There was no jury, no appeal; Pete's word was final. I wondered how his reputation of being impartial would be affected after I was sentenced.

I was led to a platform at the head of the crowd, where Pete sat with Aliana beside him, flanked by their guards. Sam smirked at me. Aliana met my eye and gave me a sad little smile. I tried to smile in return but I didn't have it in me. I looked around for Jonathan but I didn't see him. I couldn't blame him for wanting to divorce his name from mine as quickly as possible. Still, I would have liked to have seen him again.

I looked at Pete. His face was set in his neutral, expressionless emperor's mask. The effort he was putting into maintaining it looked painful. He was positioned so that he was facing me, his head turned in the right direction so any spectator would think he was looking at me. But he wasn't. I didn't take my eyes off of him so that when he did look at me I wouldn't miss it.

In my peripheral vision, I saw Lord Sifer move forward.

"Jacob Dawes."

I looked at him as a reflex. He was regarding me as he always did, dispassionate and calm. In all the time I'd known Lord Sifer I'd never gotten the impression that he disapproved of me, but I hadn't gotten the impression that he approved of me either. It wasn't hard to believe that the man held no actual opinions of his own; that every situation was evaluated on the bare facts and circumstances alone. He was the perfect politician.

Lord Sifer continued to address me but I looked back at Pete, waiting for his reaction, or just for him to look at me.

"Mr. Dawes, you have been accused and found guilty of gross disrespect of the person and position of His Excellence, Emperor Rikhart IV, willful defiance of a direct order of Emperor Rikhart IV, and violence against the person of Emperor Rikhart IV. These charges amount to treason. Have you anything to say in your defense?"

Addressing Pete, I said, "I have done what you said. I am guilty of treason. But I beg His Excellence to forgive me and show mercy."

There was a collective boo from around the courtyard. Pete betrayed no reaction at all.

Lord Sifer continued, "The penalty for treason is death by beheading. However, His Excellence has decided to extend mercy and commute the sentence of death." The crowd booed once again, louder this time. I wanted to smirk at them but I felt too miserable to do it. "Instead, Mr. Dawes, you are hereby banished from the person and presence of His Excellence, Emperor Rikhart IV in perpetuity. You will be taken from here to a Resettlement camp, and from there into permanent Resettlement, where you will stay for the rest of your natural life. Any attempt to see, contact, or be in proximity to His Excellence or to leave the area where you are Resettled, will incur the immediate sentence of death."

The crowd was grumbling, by no means mollified. "In addition," Lord Sifer resumed, "you are sentenced to a public judicial flogging, forty strokes of the birch, to be carried out immediately." There was a murmur through the crowd at this that sounded at least somewhat appeased. They wouldn't get their beheading, but this was something; the next best thing.

I shivered.

Still I watched Pete, waiting, hoping. I stared at him, trying to force him to meet my eye, only once. This was the last time I would see him. I'd been so determined the night before to make a clean, swift break, but suddenly I couldn't leave without him looking at me one more time. I needed him to look at me.

He did not, and I was led away.

I was brought to stand before the birching frame and stripped naked. A birching is a nasty version of flogging, designed to humiliate as well as inflict pain. The frame was no more than a bar at a height just above my middle that I was bent over; a thick strap held me in place around my waist. My ankles were shackled together, shackles were put around my wrists and all these attached to loose chains on the ground. The effect was that I was more or less dangling freely with my butt presented for the beating. I could not reach the ground with my hands or feet, or the posts on either side. The chains were long enough that I had a good bit of slack without being able to reach up and free myself. I had no way to brace myself.

Which was the point. It was a psychological trick, to give the victim the illusion of having the ability to escape the torment, and to make it practically impossible not to kick and thrash around in an undignified manner. Though what dignity there was left to me with my naked ass in the air waiting for a very public spanking I couldn't imagine.

The birching stick was a hefty bundle of thick birch switches, soaked in water, bound tightly for most of the length but loose at the end. The proportion, then, of the size of the implement to the total area of the target was appalling. The man who administered the beating was chosen for his strength and trained in techniques to extract the maximum pain possible.

And to top it all off, I'm confident that once I was thus trussed up, there was a deliberate delay of quite a few minutes so that I hung for an agonizing length of time in my humiliating position, in dread of when the beating would start.

But eventually I heard, over the buzz of voices, the sound of footsteps to my left and then, with no other warning, the first blow came crashing down.

I had been under no delusions that I would be able to bear a forty-stroke flogging stoically. Still I had resolved to try, or at least, do as well as I could. That first blow nearly made me cry, and not just because it hurt more than anything I'd ever experienced. Thirty-nine more of such sounded like the end of the world.

And so, after only fifteen blows, all my efforts came to naught and for the balance of the beating I was howling, wailing, and thrashing about in desperation, just as I was intended to. I lost any remaining shred of dignity. Not that dignity was much on my mind at that point. I'd have given away any dignity I had then or would ever have just to spare myself one blow. To make matters worse, I lost count somewhere and experienced the added agony of not knowing how much longer it would go on.

The beating felt interminable, and yet, it did end. I almost didn't realize it was over; I was near delirious with pain. I only became aware of the fact when they began to unshackle me. I was helped down off the frame and two men carried me away. I could barely see but I wanted to try to catch at least a glimpse of Pete one more time, but they never turned me to face him and I was so weak I couldn't even stand on my own. Outside the courtyard, a loose robe was put on me and I was helped down tortuously long hallways until I was brought to an empty lounge just outside the public arrival/departure platform.

It was only when I was being lowered onto a couch that I realized one of the men helping me was Jonathan. He gave me a pained, sympathetic look.

"How are you?"

"I've been better," I croaked. My voice was nearly nonexistent from screaming.

He began to mop my face with a cool, wet towel. Before long I heard Dr. Henriksen's voice.

"Jacob, I'm going to tend to your wounds now. Try to hold still, I'll be as gentle as I can."

It surprised me that it would be Dr. Henriksen who would come. She was Pete's personal physician and saw only the most important people at the palace. She'd been my doctor while I'd been with Pete, but I hadn't expected she'd be the one to see me now.

I reached over and grabbed her arm. "Something for the pain would be nice."

She gave me a sad look. Jonathan's face was similar. "I'm sorry, Jacob, I'm not allowed to do that. It's part of the punishment. No pain medication for seven days."

Seven *days?* I cried as she cleaned and bandaged my rear end. I'm sure she was being gentle, but it hurt like a son of a bitch anyway.

When she had finished she bid me goodbye and left. Jonathan helped me up and into a pair of loose pants and a shirt. I was about to collapse back onto the couch when Pete entered the room.

He stopped in front of me.

"Lie down, Jake, you look terrible."

I just shook my head. His eyes were red and puffy. In spite of myself I reached out and touched his face. A tear rolled down and onto my hand. He put his hand over mine and turned his face to kiss my palm.

"I'm so sorry," he whispered fiercely. "I'm so, so sorry."

"Stop it," I protested, though my voice was weaker than I would have liked. "Stop."

We stood for a time just looking at each other, Jonathan still supporting my weight on one side. Finally Pete removed a ring from his finger.

It was a simple ring with only one black stone in the setting. In all the time I'd known Pete, I'd never seen him dressed and not wearing that ring; even when he wore no other jewelry, even when he didn't wear the Imperial seal. I looked at him but he was looking at the ring.

"It's a true black diamond," he said, still not looking up. "From Earth. One of the last mined here. It was given to Emperor Nathaniel II nearly three hundred years ago as a wedding present from his bride. He was one of the few emperors who ever married for love. He wore the ring every day after that. On his deathbed he gave the ring to his son and heir, and he wore it all his reign."

He held out an empty hand by way of a request. I put mine in it. He slid the ring onto my littlest finger.

"And so the tradition has been, for all this time. My father gave this to me the day before he died. It's actually the only thing he ever gave me himself.

"Over all this time the ring's come to symbolize many things. But I see it as a symbol of family. Because it was originally given in love and worn out of dedication to another. And because of the way I received it, one of the few times in my life my father ever spoke to me as a son. I intended to pass this ring along at the end of a long life filled with family I loved and that loved me."

There was a long silence. "I know how you feel about rings." He looked up, meeting my eye, and gave me a sad smile. "But I want you to have it."

"Pete, I can't—"

"It's fitting it should go with you," he interrupted, looking down again. His voice dropped to almost a whisper. "Another thing I thought I'd never part with."

"Pete..." I started but I couldn't continue. He took my face in his hands and kissed me, a fierce, desperate kiss. As soon as he pulled away, he turned and ran from the room.

"Pete!"

He did not stop or turn around. He was gone.

I sank back down onto the couch and sobbed. Before long, Jonathan told me it was time for me to leave. He helped me up and out onto the public departure platform. I boarded, flanked by guards. All the hustle and bustle of hundreds of people coming and going stopped around me. I made my way onto the windowless, mobile brig in ringing silence.

Jonathan lowered me to the bed in the claustrophobic, muddy-gray cell. He stood over me, silent, his face grim.

"I'm sorry," I said. "For all the trouble I've been. Everything I put you through. But you should be okay, now. Now that you don't have me to screw things up for you."

"I'm glad you're leaving," he said.

The words hit me in the gut and I discovered it was possible to feel worse than I already did.

"Oh." It was weak and pathetic.

"You misunderstand," he said, his voice gentle. "It's better for you. Safer. It's too dangerous for you here. I'm very glad to see you leaving. Alive." He watched me, intensely, emotions I couldn't untangle playing across his face. "And I can't tell you how sorry I am."

"For what?"

"For my part in this."

I was still reeling but that hurt too, that I'd made him feel guilty.

"It wasn't your fault. You tried to warn me about the money and I didn't listen."

He bit off a bitter laugh. "If it were as simple as that—"

A burly guard stepped up behind Jonathan. "Visiting hours are over," he spat.

Jonathan tossed a glare at him but turned back to me without protest. "Goodbye, Jacob Dawes. I'll take care of him for you. Better than I took care of you."

I didn't get a chance to answer that, even if I'd been able. The guard bullied Jonathan out of the cell and snapped the door shut behind him.

We traveled for two days. I never left my cell and saw only the doctor and the guards who brought my meals. I slept most of that time, exhausted in every way. When I couldn't sleep, I thought of Pete. Of us. Of there no longer being an "us," of there never being one again.

After the second night, we stopped at a landing area and boarded a shuttle that took us to the docking station in orbit. I hadn't been told where I was going, and didn't think I would be if I asked, but I hadn't even considered being taken off-planet. Was I going to be Resettled on another world entirely? It was possible that my homeworld was lost to me now and I'd gotten no more of a goodbye than a few polluted breaths between the transport and the shuttle.

I went into space not as a fresh-faced, fascinated scientist this time, but as a trembling, broken criminal. It made the experience quite different.

We boarded a cargo transport apparently chosen for its ability to go only fast enough to avoid being sucked into the gravity of the nearby planets. I was alone in a tiny, windowless cell. My meals were delivered through a slot in the wall, and I began to feel as if I were fading away, as if I'd ceased to exist for anyone but myself. It was a disturbing, twitchy feeling. It also left me a horrific amount of time to think. It took us five days to reach our destination: a dwarf planet or large asteroid on the edge of the solar system. When they came for me at last, I left the cell feeling small and contemptible.

I was handcuffed—though where they thought I was going to run to, I couldn't imagine—and taken from the shuttle into the facility through a long above-ground tunnel. At regular intervals, small windows looked out over the barren surface and the stars beyond.

Two guards waited for us inside the building in a sterile metal-and-poly room. I was handed off like cargo and the new guards led me down a hallway to a small room where I was ordered to strip. After so many days alone, I was desperate for human interaction, but when I talked, they did not respond. Instead, once I was naked, I was thoroughly searched and then handed the standard-issue garb: brown pants, brown shirt, and shoes of an indifferent color. I wasn't given anything of my own back. Including Pete's ring.

"That ring's—"

"You'll get your things back if you leave."

If?

From there I was taken into an office that showed more sign of human habitation than I'd seen so far. There were enough pictures on the walls and the assorted paraphernalia of work that it looked broken-in. The display read "Captain Saubers."

Seated behind the desk was a hard-looking, silver-haired man in an Imperial Security uniform. He nodded once to the guards and they left the room.

He examined me in silence for a minute. "You're a problem for me, boy."

"Yeah, I get that a lot," I grumbled.

His mouth twitched. "Do you even know where you are, son?"

"No, sir."

"This is a Class C Settlement, Designation 14R2. The inmates call it Dead End. It's a good name, because that's what it is for them."

Resettlement is such a ubiquitous, such a normal concept that everyone thinks they know all about it and understand it, the way the concept of prisons made so much sense before society got fed up—and ran out of room, besides.

In reality, we do know about it, and yet we don't. After all, no one can say they have a brother or cousin or aunt who is Resettled, because once someone's Resettled, they're no one's brother or cousin or aunt anymore. I had a father once and then, one day, I didn't—as if I were Jesus himself, son of a virgin, or the Buddha, son of a dream. Meanwhile, some man out there in a Resettlement camp looked like the father I once had. He was getting clean and working hard, or dead because he didn't and wasn't. And he was no one's father or husband or son.

I went off to Resettlement knowing exactly what to expect, and not knowing what to expect at all. I didn't even know who I was anymore.

"You're an oddity here," Captain Saubers said. "Among a campful of oddities. See, what I've got here are lifers. You know what that means?"

"Here for life, I assume."

"You knew that happened before just now?"

I hadn't. Unlike most people, I had been in a position to know things like that. And maybe I should have thought of it then, to find out about all this. How it worked. What to expect once they finally got rid of me. Because, standing there, I realized that part of me always knew they would. Though I'd expected the quick and final boot, the beheading, or the less quick but just as final hanging, the less honorable way to be dispatched for public spectacle. I knew better than to think I'd get the intense but anonymous trip through the incinerator.

Instead I got the dubious mercy of Resettlement.

"So I'm here for good?"

"No, that's the problem. I have lifers here, but now I've got you too, and they tell me, even though they sent you all the way out here, that you're just facing the standard three- to six-month term before they dump you off wherever they're going to put you, like all the other Resets."

"So why am I here?"

"Hell if I know. Though if I had to guess, I'd say you've made some nasty enemies. Hardly a surprise there."

For one horrible moment I wondered if Pete was behind sending me here. But I wouldn't let myself think about it. I couldn't afford to care if he had.

"So in three to six I get out and get Resettled somewhere?"

"I'd expect closer to six than three. They sent you all the way out here, after all. That's a lot of trouble to go to. I don't expect they'll be rushing back to get you at the first opportunity."

No, I didn't expect they would either. And, though I didn't say anything, I wouldn't let myself believe that they really would come back for me at all. It was too easy and convenient for them to "forget" I was there, once they'd gotten me so far away. Or maybe I just wouldn't survive this. Dying in Resettlement camps was common enough that it was considered one of the outcomes anyone could look forward to. Natural means and accidents wouldn't even be blinked at.

"What makes them lifers? Why aren't they Resettled too?"

"Not fit for living in lawful society anymore. They should probably all be executed, but there's got to be a line somewhere, I suppose. And they're not all so bad. Just can't seem to work out how to live with law-abiding people. Some have done no worse than stealing a mouthful of bread, but they do it every time. Reset, then right back again. They only get a couple of chances, at the most. Usually no more than one. But someone somewhere can't see the way to 'cinerating them for petty crimes, even though they'll probably never stop. So they get sent to one of the Settlements. There aren't many. And it's not commonly known that they exist. Wouldn't want people to think there's an option like this. Some might take us up on it rather than stay in whatever shithole they've fallen into."

I agreed with him. So far, from what I'd seen, the place was at least clean, warm, and dry. It had to be significantly unpleasant somehow, but you probably also ate three times a day. For people like those I'd known in Abenez, life was always significantly unpleasant. That plus three squares and a warm place to sleep at night would be like a dream come true.

For a moment I almost wished I'd been one of those Resets who spent a few months in a camp working, detoxing maybe, learning skills to support myself, or getting the treatment I needed for whatever physical or mental health ailments had put me in the position I was in. Then Resettled somewhere, nothing special, but a life. Good honest labor and a clean start. It wasn't a bad thing. For most.

Resettlement would have been the best I'd ever known, a step up for me and not a wicked fall after years of the best the Empire had to offer. All of which paled in comparison to having known Pete...

"So, assuming I get out of here, where do I go after this?"

He shrugged. "Not for me to decide. And frankly, I don't care. They'll work that out and tell you when it suits them." He paused for a minute, considering me. "You're quiet enough. You may do all right. But I'm afraid the general population isn't going to cope so well with the idea that someone can come here and leave again. Not your fault, I suppose. And I can see why they'd put you out here. Still. A termer and a celebrity at that. Not a good situation."

I groaned to myself. Even the blessing of quiet anonymity was denied me. Not just a criminal and a traitor in a hard labor camp as far from Earth as practical, a famous criminal and traitor. My gut twisted with apprehension. Maybe the infamy would be a good thing, something to trade on or a point of pride the others would respect. Somehow I doubted it.

"I don't want to cause trouble, sir. I'll do what I'm told to do and get out of here."

He nodded once. "Then you'll do good to keep in mind what I've said."

"Yes, sir."

His eyebrow quirked. "So you can speak respectfully to an authority figure. You might have tried that with the emperor."

My face was hot. "Thank you, sir. I'll try to remember that next time."

He chuckled. "Keep that sense of humor, son. You'll need it." He looked past me. "Chen! Jones!"

The guards entered the room.

"Take him in," the captain said.

With a hand on each arm they took me into a common area, filled with inmates. They all turned to watch me go by. With everyone in the brown prison-issue jumpers, the effect was like a field full of prairie dogs popping their heads above ground. Grizzled or clean-shaven, mountainous or petite, male or female, they all looked very scary and I began to reconsider my wish for someone to talk to. One woman in particular, standing very near, watched me with a frown that did little to hide the flash of something like hatred or contempt in her eyes. She unnerved me.

The guards brought me to a cell and pushed me inside. It was one of a dozen on the left side of the hallway we'd entered. Every wall was a transparent force-field—even the back wall, where it connected to another cell. Through it I could see another hallway, beyond which was another cell. From where I stood, I could see dozens of cells spread out in all directions.

The guard released my wrists from the cuffs. Then he stepped back and activated the force field that closed off the doorway.

"Consider tonight a holiday, courtesy of the emperor." He recited the line as if it were a stock speech. His lips twisted into a nasty grin as he paused and realized what he'd just said, and to whom. "Tomorrow, you join them," he nodded toward the crowd in the common room, "and you work."

I said nothing, but he didn't wait for a response. The two guards soon disappeared from sight.

With my fingertips I tested the force-field. It was a passive barrier; nothing more than a transparent wall. I sank down onto the cot, noting how familiar such accommodations were becoming. The visually open space and total lack of privacy was new, and eerie.

I heard the sound of footsteps and stood, looking around.

The woman I'd noted in the common room strolled down the hallway, watching me as she approached. She stopped in front of my door and examined me, as if I were an unsatisfactory specimen.

Up close she was very pretty. She had unusual coloring, with hazelnut skin and dirty-blonde hair washed with copper. Even wearing the same shapeless prison-issue as everyone else, her curves were nice. Young too. She looked barely old enough to be in an adult incarceration facility.

"I'm Jake," I offered, to break the silence.

"I know who you are," she said.

"That makes one of us. I don't know who you are."

"I'm K52. My friends call me Kafe. You can call me K52."

"K52?"

"Names are a privilege around here. We don't exist, you see. They took your citID and your name when you were processed. In here, they identify us by the first letter of the name and last two numbers of the citID we used to have."

"K52," I said.

"Yes."

"Well I'm not here to stay," I said. "So, no offense, but I'll stick with Jake."

"Will you?" she smirked. The laughter in her voice was nothing like amusement. "The guards won't care what you're planning to 'stick with.' And they," she jerked her head back toward the common room, "will call you what I tell them to call you. I know it didn't work that way for you in your pretty little life at the palace, but welcome to the asshole of the solar system, Your Highness."

She favored me with one last look of contempt, and then turned and walked away.

As I lay in bed that night, staring up at the dark ceiling, I heard the muted beep and pop of my door opening. I sat up. I could barely make out the figure in the darkness but I heard the door close again and the figure approached. I didn't move, straining into the dark to watch for his first move.

When it came it wasn't anything I'd expected. I saw a knee come up and I raised my arms to block it but instead of coming near my sensitive areas, it landed on the bed beside me. Before I had time to puzzle it out, I was pushed onto my back and the intruder swung over on top of me. Lips, too soft and small to be a man's, pressed against mine. They tasted slightly sterile, like manufactured water.

Suddenly a forearm lay across my windpipe, pressing down with all the weight of the body above me. I tried to cry out but I couldn't get enough air. I grabbed her upper arms but she pushed harder. Her other hand grabbed my balls and squeezed, hard. I sucked in what breath I could draw in a startled gasp.

"Now here's what we're going to do." I recognized Kafe's voice in the harsh whisper. "You're going to lie here, quiet and still, and I'm going to fuck the emperor's piece of ass."

"No, I don't think so," I rasped.

"You don't seem to understand," she said. "Either we do this now, just you and me, or we do it tomorrow, in a quiet corner where the guards don't go, with two of my men holding you down. If you make me do that, I'll let them have you when I'm finished."

"Why are you doing this?"

I heard the rustle of cloth as she shrugged. "Because I don't like you. Because every pretty boy becomes someone's bitch eventually. My reasons don't matter. All you need to worry about is that I have you by the balls." I could hear the smile in her voice as she squeezed harder.

I bit my lips together against the pain. "What did I ever do to you?" I asked. But I didn't fight when her hands went to my waistband.

My head throbbed, filling with white noise and too much not-thinking and the stab of betrayal as my body responded to her.

I turned my head and stared down a long line of dark forms, of inmates sleeping alone one by one in their cells. She moved against me and I closed my eyes.

When it was over she put her mouth to my ear and bit the lobe, hard. "Was I as good as your emperor?"

My throat was tight. "Fuck off."

She chuckled and bit my ear again, this time drawing blood. She stood and put her pants back on and walked out. When she had reactivated the door she said, "Don't forget this, deserter. You're no one again. A nameless, powerless nobody. Get used to it."

I waited for the soft shuffle of her footsteps to recede. Then I buried my face in my pillow and tried to keep from vomiting.

I woke in the morning feeling scared and sick. It was the stress of all the changes, surely. I fought nausea and a crippling anger at myself as flashes of the previous night played through my brain and traveled my body in phantom caresses. Why should it have bothered me? Lucky me. I'd thought I was in for a dry spell.

Then I did throw up. I sat back against the non-wall of my cell, fighting tears that I blamed on the retching and on everything that brought me here. Nothing else. There was nothing else.

As my neighbors began to disgorge from the cells, I joined the line of people filing into the cafeteria. Everyone stared, but no one spoke to me. I took my tray from the dispenser and sat down alone. I ate with a nervous, twitchy feeling, constantly fighting the urge to look behind me.

When a man slid into the seat beside me, I started.

"Whoa, mate, you're a jumpy one."

"Not usually," I mumbled. The man was short and thick. He looked like solid muscle. He had a scruffy, few days growth of beard but was otherwise as almost-too-clean as everything else I'd seen here so far.

"Don't suppose you're usually in places like this."

I smiled a little. "No, I guess I'm not."

"Well, welcome to Dead End. You'll hate it here, but you're just a termer, aren't you? I didn't think they ever sent termers out here."

"I seem to have a talent for being the exception to every rule," I groused. I held out my hand. "I'm...I was going to say I'm Jake but I've been told I'm not anymore."

He grinned. "Had a run in with Kafe, did you?"

"So it's not just me?"

He shrugged. "I don't know. She's nothin' to mess with, and she makes sure everyone learns that lesson pretty fast. But she was waiting for you."

"Waiting for me?"

"Sure. We heard you were comin' a few days ago. She's been stalkin' around lookin' scary ever since."

"Why?"

He shrugged again. "I don't know and I'm not askin'. My name's Enten, by the way."

"Your real name?"

"The only one I got anymore. N10. Enten."

"Ah. I'm J23, I guess."

He grinned around a mouthful of food. "'Fraid not, mate. She's callin' you 'Highness.' That sort of name sticks with a fella."

"Wonderful," I grumbled.

"There are worse things to be called, right?"

"Sure. So, she says and everyone does? Who is she, anyway?"

He shrugged. "Kafe. I don't know any more than that. I do my best to stay away from her. She leads one of the gangs. There were only two, the whole five years I've been here, and then six months ago she strolls in and half the muscle in the place changes loyalties. From both sides too. It was an interesting few months. Things have settled down now. Not much real brawlin' happens. Not worth it. Even the goons are scared of solitary."

"Solitary? That's the punishment for fighting?"

"For everything."

"You manage it," I said with a shrug, but I couldn't suppress a shiver.

He shook his head. "Solitary work detail. One day is bad enough. Fightin' gets you two, and it compounds with each incident."

"What's so bad about it?"

"You haven't been out there yet, have you? At the end of the work detail today, come back and see if you don't already know the answer to that."

A loud alert signaled the end of breakfast and I walked with Enten, joining the crowd to leave the residence facility. The couple-hundred or so inmates divided off into groups filing into smaller rooms where suits and equipment were stored. Enten took my elbow and stopped at a display panel.

"Right. I thought you might be assigned to us," he said, indicating my designation in a column with his. "Our team's been short a man since Fen was spaced."

I didn't ask why Fen was "spaced," or even what "spaced" meant. I figured I had a good idea.

Enten guided me through suiting up, along with the other ten members of his less-than-talkative team. "Here's your air and your backup tank. Here's the emergency sealer, for suit penetrations, though you're probably only going to use it on someone else. If it happens to you, not likely you'll be in a condition to do much about it. You've got isolators here and here, though what good this one would do you I don't know. Hardly seems worth messin' about with survivin' if your balls get frozen off."

He grinned. "Your boots keep you on the surface, but this here will throw out a line that will connect you to the nearest person in a suit. Don't panic and throw one 'cause you think you're flyin' away as soon as you walk out of here. Lots of people do that, mind you, but we'll laugh at you at dinner tonight if you do. Best if you don't."

He pulled my wrist around to show it to me. "Here's your com controls. You're online with your team automatically. It's weird out there, so we keep up a conversation. Don't chatter and drive us all crazy, but if you got something to say, say it. You can talk to someone else by pressin' here and sayin' their designation. Everyone's got it on their helmet. See?"

He held mine up so I could see the "J23" already painted on the side.

"Now, that'll cut off your line to your team, so just use it when you need it. No long lovers' chats."

"Lovers' chats?" A cold sweat washed over me.

"You ain't been here long enough, but you might think of it before you get shipped off again. The rest of us have to make do. It's not a bad selection, all things considerin'. And after a while, even the ugly ones start lookin' nice when you just want someone to scratch the itch."

He chuckled and went back to donning his suit. I stood motionless for long enough that he turned back to me.

"It's not that hard, mate. There's pictures there on the wall." I didn't tell him I hadn't even thought of the suit in my hand, or noticed the diagrams. I was looking around for Kafe and her men.

He resumed suiting up, and I started putting my gear on, as well.

"It's not as bad as it sounds," he said. "In all the time I've been here, only four have died out there. And one of them could have gotten himself killed inside a padded box."

We waited, a suited-and-sealed group, as they cycled us through the airlock and onto the surface. I saw what Enten meant about solitary. It was overwhelming, the feeling of being out there with only millimeters of poly between me and the vacuum. I wanted to grab something, hold on to something. There was a definite appeal in the idea of throwing out a line and being connected to *someone*.

We entered a sloping tunnel leading down into the asteroid's crust, where we worked at glorified rock-moving without a break until the end of the workday was called. Then we shuffled as a tired group back into the facility.

"There are more efficient ways to do that stuff," I said to Enten as we unsuited.

"Of course there are. You think we're out here because they need anythin' off this rock? The work's to keep us busy," he said. "Something to do till we die." He shrugged. "There are worse things."

As I watched him put his gear away, I realized that I agreed.

A week passed in which Kafe did no more than watch me. But after what she'd done to me the first night, and the way one of her lumps of muscle seemed to always be at my elbow, her silence was little comfort.

One evening, as I was walking through the common room, she stepped into my path.

"Have you figured it out yet?" she asked.

I swallowed on nausea and the twist of anger in my gut. "What's that?"

"What you are?"

"What I am? I'm a physicist, or hadn't you heard?"

She leaned close, her breath hot against my cheek. "Not anymore."

I was holding my breath, my fingernails digging into my palms.

"Do you really not remember? You used to know what you were. Before that fancy man came and convinced you they'd let you be one of them. Have you whored yourself out for their approval so long you don't even remember?"

I sucked in a breath. "Fancy man? What do you...what do you mean? What do you know about that?"

She made a sound of disgust and walked away.

"What are you talking about!" I yelled after her.

She stopped, and turned slowly. "Tell me," she said, "did you even bother to find out where Carrie was buried?"

I launched forward and grabbed her shirt, shoving her back against the wall.

"How do you know about Carrie?"

One of her well-muscled shadows grabbed my collar from behind and dragged me off her. I threw an elbow back into his gut and he *umphed* but didn't let go. One of the guards, who never seemed to be nearby otherwise, shoved between us, and the next thing I knew, the goon was gone and my arm was twisted up my back.

"Shoulda known you'd be trouble," the guard said before he hauled me back to my cell and threw me inside, locking the door behind me.

I spent two days on solitary work detail.

I used to dream about the stars, when they were the closest

things I could imagine to the angels and gods of myth and religion. Then I traveled among them, and the experience was as amazing as I'd dreamed it would be. But when I was alone with them—only me, the stars, and an unforgiving amalgam of minerals and ice—they became not just a thing to respect, but a thing to fear. The silence screamed in my ears to the pulse of my heart beating behind my eyes. There was no one. No one to see or hear. I realized what it meant to be completely, utterly alone.

Four days later, a man shoved me to the floor in the food line and he and several others swore it was in self-defense. I spent four days alone on the surface. I tried to hide how I trembled suiting up each morning, but by the fourth day I was shaking so hard I had trouble getting my things on. Enten helped with a silent, grim pity.

Three days later, when I turned in the hall just in time to see and duck a punch, again witnesses swore that I'd been the instigator.

That time, I begged. I could have saved myself the indignity. I served six days of solitary work detail. I cried through the entirety of the fifth day. I tried to distract myself with calculations, but my mind kept going back to calculating the (pitiful) amount of gravity, both natural and artificial, holding me to the asteroid, how far I was likely to drift before I died if I lost contact with the surface (not far, relatively), and the odds of them sending a ship to rescue me (low). The sixth day I kept having hollow, heavy impulses to release the boots and just let it all end, forever.

For the next two days I didn't leave my cell except for work. Enten agreed to bring me my meals. I would lie on the bed, trying not to breathe too loudly so I could hear the echoes of voices from the common room, an indistinct assurance that I wasn't alone.

The next day after work detail, I was summoned to Captain Saubers' office. I didn't allow myself to speculate on what awaited me there. It would be either less or more horrible than what I could imagine. For a strange, confused moment, I wasn't sure which I preferred.

He was sitting behind his desk and he nodded to the guard escorting me to leave his office.

"Not going so well, is it?" he asked.

"No sir." I kept my voice as respectful and neutral as possible.

"Dead End isn't supposed to be pleasant, but you're getting the worst of it. And I'm not stupid enough to believe you're the one doing it."

A warm rush of relief made me weak. I met his eyes, wanting to drink in the sight of human compassion, or at least understanding.

"There's not much I can do, though, if the other prisoners keep swearing you're the one breaking the rules. So I'm going to put surveillance on you, and announce that to the general population. I'll review the data before issuing any punishments and anyone found trying to set you up will get a double sentence. Hopefully that will put an end to it."

"Thank you, sir," I breathed.

"Don't be so quick with that," he said. "It's not a perfect solution and I can't promise it will stop things. There's more going on here than a few disgruntled inmates."

I shivered. "I figured."

He nodded. "Stay out of trouble," he said.

I didn't have an answer sufficient to express how much I wanted to do just that.

The next evening, I sat alone in the middle of the crowded common room. I was too afraid to talk to anyone, but equally unwilling to be alone. Kafe sauntered up and slid into a seat across from me.

"Enjoying yourself yet?" she asked. My whole body tensed.

I didn't answer her. I was too busy trying to stop the trembling in my hands.

She grinned and examined me like a shark planning the first bite.

I just held her eye and said nothing.

"Ask me, then," she said. "And I might answer."

"I don't want to know anything. At first I thought you must know something, since you brought up Carrie. But then I realized it's there in the vid-data for anyone to find. So now I figure you're just a bully, and I really don't care."

She sat back, tucking her legs up under her, and watched me.

"It's not there, actually, information about your sister. Your public file starts with your Selection."

I felt my eyebrows rise, but I didn't want to ask. I wanted her to go away.

"It's just you. The other kids in your year have parents and siblings listed, towns and cities, awards won. But you? They pretend that you didn't exist until they could paint you up to make you look like one of them, and then pretend you'd been there all along."

"So you really knew her?" I couldn't stop myself.

"I knew her. We weren't friends, but I knew her."

I felt a powerful surge of longing, but I didn't want to believe her. "Isn't it a bit of a coincidence, someone who came from my neighborhood at the exact camp I was sent to?"

"Oh yes," she rolled her eyes, "what are the odds of two kids from Abenez ending up on Dead End." She made a noise of disgust. "I knew who you were back then, you know. Before you left. You probably wouldn't remember me. You always thought you were better than us. I saw you that day, when they took you with them. I felt sorry for you. What could they possibly want with one of us? I knew they were just taking you away to do something awful to you. To use you for whatever they wanted. They did, too. You still haven't figured that out, have you? You got to be too much trouble, so they threw you away. See?" She gestured around the room.

"It's not like that," I said, with a sick sense of déjà vu and the sound of my own voice yelling at Pete ringing in my head.

"It's exactly like that. You're just an idiot. Did you really think they cared about you? That you'd ever get whatever it was, fame or fortune or a class-up? Did you really think they'd give one of us anything at all?"

"You don't know anything," I said, my pulse pounding in my ears.

"Do you even remember Abenez? Or were you always so busy trying to get out that you never noticed what you really were?"

"I remember Abenez," I snarled. "I remember being cold, and hungry, and frightened all the time. I wasn't trying to get out. I didn't even know it was possible. But I'm not going to pretend I wasn't happy to go. Whatever you think, I wasn't trying to get out so I could have better things. It's not...you wouldn't understand."

"'Cause I'm not as smart as you?"

My palms were sweating. She smirked. A rush of anger made me sit up straight, suddenly steady and strong. I glared at her.

"You know what I'm afraid of? I'm afraid that when they Settle me somewhere after this, they'll somehow cut me off from science. That I won't even be able to pursue it as a hobby. That I won't have access to research materials, or contact with other scientists. That's what I'm afraid of. Not you. If you hate me because I knew I didn't belong in Abenez, and they gave me the chance to do what I was supposed to be doing and I was glad, then hate me. Even if I could go back and change things, I wouldn't. No matter where I've ended up."

"You'd give up Carrie again, then?"

I sighed, deflating in a rush. "They didn't exactly give me a choice. But, yes, I suppose. She couldn't have come with me, and it wouldn't have done either of us any good for me to have stayed."

"She might have survived. She might not have suffered what she did. You certainly wouldn't have been in a position to give her to that man."

"What?" My breaths were coming in short, panicked gasps. "How do you know about that?"

"Oh I know everything about you, Jacob Dawes. I know things even you don't know."

I shook my head feebly.

She laughed and stood. As she brushed past my chair she leaned down and whispered, her breath hot against my ear.

"And don't you forget it."

I clenched my fists so hard my knuckles creaked, but I didn't feel the urge to hit her. I just felt sick, cold, and empty. I retreated to my cell.

Four more months I kept my head down, and went mechanically through a daily routine of eating, working, and sleeping.

While Enten was an easy enough companion, I wouldn't have called him a friend. I got the idea that friendships weren't common on Dead End and Enten didn't try to forge one with me any more than I did with him.

Then, one day near the end of my six months, Kafe brushed past me in the common room.

"I've got a going away present for you," she said.

The next evening I was backed into a corner and a big, bald goon punched me. I tried to pull away, but he grabbed my hand, which I'd curled instinctively in a fist, and slammed it into the wall. Then he punched himself in the nose and I watched in horror as the slow line of blood trickled into his grinning mouth.

The inmates who "found" us swore we'd been fighting, and my bruised, scraped knuckles, and the fact that we'd been in a corner where the surveillance devices had been disabled, were testimony enough against me.

I served my last eight days of work detail in solitary.

I began to think I was really alone, left adrift in a universe void of any life at all, so that mine too was just a fading nothing. I began to think I was going mad. I began to want to.

The next day, as they processed me for discharge, I couldn't get it out of my head that they were just going to jettison me into space after all.

But they returned to me the things I'd brought with me—none of which, I realized, were mine anyway. Even Pete's ring.

I boarded the ship, trembling with anxiety, choking, paranoid fears, and relief. And I left Dead End.

On the cargo ship back to Earth, I was given crew quarters. Apparently I wasn't a prisoner anymore. But when we docked at the station orbiting Earth, I was escorted to the shuttle by two armed guards. Maybe not a prisoner, but not free either. Not until I got to wherever I was to be Settled. Not ever again, really.

We boarded a shuttle for Earth. I bit down on hope, reminding myself that it didn't matter if it was Earth or elsewhere. Wherever I was going, it would be far from anyone or anything I knew, and I wouldn't be leaving again. There was still a thrill of relief when the greens and blues began to sharpen into the recognizable continents and oceans of my home planet.

Once we landed I was escorted to yet another transport. While it wasn't a mobile brig, it was still an ISS vehicle, with nothing but rows of seating in the areas accessible to me. I was the only inmate aboard so I sat beside the window with my forehead against the poly, watching the countryside slip by, trying not to wonder where I was being taken.

Much of it began to look familiar. It seemed like a particular cruelty to Settle me somewhere that would always make me think of the places I really wanted to be.

At least we weren't moving toward the ocean.

We entered a mountainous area and I closed my eyes, hoping we would pass through quickly. Whatever it was that made me open my eyes just then, I saw the transport crest the last mountain and slide down into a long, level valley.

A flat, glassy lake sat almost dead center, reflecting from its mirror surface the mountains in reverse. And a cluster of buildings, stark white, with no frill or ostentation. Matter efficiently shaped and defined. I caught my breath.

We pulled into one of the IIC's parking hangers. Waiting there was Dr. Okoro, alone. I made it off the transport before my knees gave out. Dr. Okoro pulled me up, pressed my head to his shoulder, and held me tight until the trembling passed.

Are you all right?" he asked, when I finally lifted my head and pulled away.

"Sure," I said wryly. He accepted my attempt to deflect the question and led me into the building. When we entered he turned down one of the service hallways.

"Trying to avoid the welcoming committee?" I asked, with another attempt at sarcasm.

"No one's expecting you," he said, "I just you thought you might want a chance to regroup before you had to see anyone."

"No one knows I'm here?"

"Director Harris received word this morning and he told only me. It was a relief to finally have real news of you." He started to frown in what I recognized as his preferred method of reproof, but wiped it off his face. The simple familiarity of it made me catch my breath.

"I wrote to you," I said. "When I was still at the palace and scheduled for execution. I wasn't going to send it until the last minute. Once I found out I wasn't going to be executed, well, it all happened so fast I didn't think about writing new letters. And then I was taken away and I wasn't allowed to write. Truly. I would have."

"I understand," he said, mollified. We continued on our way in silence.

"Don't you want to ask me?"

"You don't have to tell me anything. If you want to talk, you know I will always be here. But you don't have to talk about anything you don't want to."

"I can only imagine what you've heard. The gossip channels aren't known for accuracy and even the legitimate news isn't much better."

"Yes, of course. But I know better than to believe everything I hear. I know you; you're not a bad person. Whatever happened, happened. You don't have to explain yourself to me."

We didn't talk any more, mostly because I was too overwhelmed to say anything. Before long he turned into one of the hallways of the junior fellows' dormitories. I hadn't thought about it yet, but I realized that was probably what I was now. We didn't encounter anyone; it was the dinner hour and everyone would be in the dining hall. We came to a room, about midway down a hall somewhat central in the building.

"So Chuck doesn't know I'm here?" I asked.

"Not yet."

"Or Kirti?"

"She's made it clear that she finds news of you unwelcome."

I was crushed, even though I should have expected as much.

"Will you tell her?" I asked. He looked uncomfortable. "I know she probably won't want to hear, but will you just tell her I'm here? Tell her I asked for her to know?"

"I will."

I looked around me. The room was small and plain by the standards of the palace, and a mansion compared to a cell on Dead End. Dr. Okoro sank into one of the chairs and talked of general nonsense to catch me up with the goings on at the IIC. On the one hand, I'd been gone three years, but on the other, the IIC was a static environment and little ever changed. What he told me was mostly gossip and minutiae. I loathed every word.

I should have been ecstatic, or at least relieved to be back at the IIC. I'd steeled myself for the worst and instead I was home; with my friends and what I had that resembled family.

Instead, depression descended on me like a blanket and I clung to it, wrapping it around me and hiding my face in it like a child. As if I could make everything go away. Everyone.

I tuned out the actual words and just let the sound of his voice lull me into a stupor. I woke a few hours later, still in the chair and alone.

The sound of a door opening and closing woke me in the morning. I got up and found Chuck in the outer room. I hadn't seen Chuck in more than two years and I felt guilty about that, considering most of that time I'd had more than the means to keep in touch. Chuck, on the other hand—being Chuck—apparently hadn't noticed the lapse.

"Hey!" he exclaimed, "Look at you. I thought those Resettlement places were supposed to be bad news. I was all prepared to find you half dead."

I tried to smile. Everything about him and his manner should have lightened my spirits. I tried to pretend, for him. "They'll just have to try harder next time, I guess."

He grinned at me. "Whatever. Here, breakfast."

He talked as we ate. I let him carry on. I was less and less inclined to talk about anything at all.

After breakfast I went to see Director Harris and was admitted to his office. He stood, and met me halfway into the room, holding out his hand to shake mine. I gave it to him, bewildered.

"Mr. Dawes," he said, "It's good to see you again."

I very nearly asked him why. It seemed such a ridiculous sentiment, no matter who it was coming from.

"Are you well?" he continued.

"Well, enough. But please call me Jacob. If you don't mind," I tacked on, suddenly unsure that he'd even want to. But he smiled in response.

"Thank you. Have a seat. We need to talk about your transition back into the IIC."

"Yes, sir."

"You can take as much time as you need, Jacob. There's no need to rush this."

"I'm fine, sir." I realized I was fiddling with Pete's ring on my finger and snatched my hand away.

"Well, I can understand that. I can't stand being idle, myself. Dr. Bartel will be expecting you when you leave here. He'll be giving you your assignment and what remains of required education for you. Naturally you'll be taking direction from him, as your department head, in all such matters. But I want you to know that my door is always open if you ever have any questions or concerns."

"Thank you, sir. I do have one question: My status here."

He looked puzzled. "Oh," he said, comprehension dawning. "You mean, the circumstances that have returned you to us, how they affect your standing?"

I nodded.

"Ah, well, I do have a list of restrictions, but mostly things I'm to be aware of, not things I need to actively enforce. And I'll make sure you receive a copy, though I imagine you already have." I had. "But beyond what you're aware of, restrictions on your location and on communication outside the IIC, your status here is no different than that of any of your peers. Whatever ignominy brought you here, it does not come within these walls. You face no censure or fallout here. That matter has nothing to do with us."

I must have looked skeptical. In truth, I was reeling inside. Part of my mind was still trying to accept as truth the fact that I'd never be alone on the surface of that asteroid again.

"People, of course, will hold their own opinions," he said. "I know that. But I won't allow you to be discriminated against or harassed in any way. What happened elsewhere is elsewhere."

I wasn't quite sure what to say. He'd always been kind and understanding, but I'd broken the most important of all the unwritten rules of the IIC.

As a group of scientists and scholars, what we did was beyond the understanding of the majority of the citizens of the Empire and even most of those in authority, those who could and did have a say in our future. We lived and died on our reputation.

Being known as a group above reproach, who did great—if mostly incomprehensible—things for the Empire, was essential. And, even when it mattered little in a practical sense, it was a reputation fiercely guarded. Internal scandals or failures were kept quiet whenever possible; a rule understood and obeyed by all. We were prestigious and held in awe based largely on an amorphous concept of acetic devotion to the present and future greatness of the Empire.

I'd transgressed in that area the first time years ago when Director Kagawa had been Resettled; removed publicly and in disgrace. And there were those who judged and condemned me for sullying the reputation of our community with something as vulgar and plebian as a very public love affair. But now I'd been banished to the IIC in infamy. There was no one in the Empire who did not know of my crimes, my fall, and with that, my origins and life story. My ignominy was forever linked to the IIC.

Communities like ours did not countenance such things. And they enforced their own brand of censure. Director Harris, on the other hand, was implying that I'd done nothing like tarnishing the name of the institution and, by extension, everyone in it; that I wasn't to be held to account for my crimes against my colleagues.

He was mad. Generous and kind, but deluded. So I thanked him and excused myself to go and see what would really become of me now.

I reported to Dr. Bartel in his large office near the entrance to the Physics wing. I entered after I knocked, knowing I was expected. He looked up from his desk, frowning. "I don't know the habits at the palace, Mr. Dawes, but here it's customary to wait for an invitation before you enter someone's office."

I'd had my encounters with Dr. Bartel in the years I'd lived at the IIC before. Probably more than with most of the adults.

He was stern and serious but I'd never found him unfair or prejudicial. I was to learn that his fair, even-tempered treatment of me before was a product of lack of interest in me personally, and the lack of any particular opinion of me one way or the other.

He had formed one now.

"I apologize, sir. I was told you were expecting me."

"That makes no difference, Mr. Dawes," he snapped. I bit my tongue and kept my peace, but he waited for a response.

"Forgive me, sir. I misjudged."

He nodded. "I've reviewed your file. You have completed your required education to this point to the satisfaction of the responsible faculty."

"I've also kept up on my continuing education requirements, sir. I am ahead of my classmates in this."

He looked at me with clear disapproval. "Interrupting is also frowned upon here. But you're correct. I have decided to allow the work you completed at the palace to count toward your lab requirements."

I was seething. I had done groundbreaking work over the past few years. He was going to *allow* that to count toward my lab time requirements? I merely nodded acknowledgement, not trusting myself not to say something unfortunate.

"Therefore, it is the consensus of the responsible committee with Director Harris's approval that you be granted the status of junior fellow. If you keep your current pace you will be a Fellow in less than two years. That would be faster than normal which, in spite of your impressive accomplishments, I find surprising."

I didn't answer. I had my hands clasped behind my back to prevent doing anything that I would regret. I realized I was fingering the damn ring again and for a moment I considered taking it off. Only a moment.

He waited, but I remained silent, so he continued. "You'll join your classmates in a proper classroom setting for the remainder of your required instruction. For your lab time, I have assigned you as junior assistant to Dr. Zin."

I had heard Dr. Zin's name before but I knew nothing about him other than that he existed. It wasn't halfway through a day with him that I figured out why. He had to be the most unimaginative man I'd ever met. He was a genius, of course, but he had an absolute focus that excluded the bigger picture and prevented him from seeing what was right in front of his nose. Not only that, but he actually took offense at any of the precious, hallowed rules of physics being questioned. He did not belong in a place dedicated to discovery and advancement. He was the type who could slip through the cracks because of the selection process being based on impersonal numbers and involving such young children.

It would have made sense, to one who knew little of the situation and the personalities involved, that I had been assigned to him as a necessary counter to his stymieing, intractable view of physics. But to Dr. Zin, the rules of seniority and organization were as revered as the accepted laws of the universe. To him I was a capable pair of hands to be directed, not a source of opinions or ideas.

The assignment couldn't have been a more blatant insult. I embraced it. It was exactly what I wanted. Working for Dr. Zin was tedious busywork; purposeless and time consuming. It left me little time to think. It was an unspeakable relief.

Dr. Zin's other assistant, a junior fellow named Sean, was the perfect companion for me at that time. He was quiet, and calm, and spoke little. Not unfriendly, just not a talker. In what conversation passed between us I discovered he had a good sense of humor and a kind, charitable spirit. He was far too valuable a physicist to be assigned to Dr. Zin but he didn't complain. He'd enjoy a wry joke at Dr. Zin's expense or a self-deprecating one from time to time, but he wasn't resentful. It was very restful to work with him. If Dr. Zin was a punishment, Sean and my own mood nullified the effect.

The next morning at breakfast, I joined the others for the first time since my return. It was uncomfortably familiar, this experience of being judged, censured, hated by whatever group I happened to be among at the time. My classmates, with whom I sat, were quiet and subdued. Kirti sat halfway down the table from me and pretended I wasn't there. I'd expected that, but it hurt all the same.

Eventually the shyness or the scruples of my tablemates—one or the other—were conquered. Heather asked, "So you've returned for good then, Jacob?" Kirti glared at her, but I was ready to have this over and done with.

"Yes. For good. I've been Resettled here. I won't be leaving the IIC again." A collective gasp sounded from the table. "But you'd heard that already."

"Of course we've all heard lots of things. But you don't always know what to believe," she replied. I nodded, conceding the point. "Does that mean that you, well, that is, they say that you tried to kill the Emperor."

It wasn't the worst one I'd heard. I noticed Kirti incline her head slightly in my direction, listening.

"No. No, I'm guilty of what I was convicted of, but not quite so bad as that. I said some unacceptable things to His Excellence, and I hit him." My face was hot but I lifted my hands in a shrug. "That's treason. The emperor was merciful and commuted the sentence of death. So I'm here."

It felt like a weight off my chest. More than feeling ashamed of what I was confessing to, I felt relief at being able to assume the blame for what I'd really done, instead of hiding from all the things they imagined.

"Why would you do something like that?" someone else asked from down the table. I flushed.

"It's complicated. But His Excellence is good and just; I was entirely in the wrong, and I deserve what I got."

"Damn right," Sasha said. He was sitting directly across from me.

I looked him in the eye, holding his gaze for a long time before looking away. He was only agreeing with me, I couldn't contradict him.

He chuckled and said under his breath, "His Excellence. Did he make you call him that in bed, too?"

I reached across the table, grabbed a fistful of his collar, twisted to tighten it around his neck, and hauled him to his feet. "You will not speak of your emperor that way," I hissed.

His eyes had gone wide but when I spoke they narrowed. "That's funny, coming from you."

"Well maybe I'll learn from my mistakes," I said, tightening my grip. His face went red, and I shoved him. He fell over his chair and onto the floor. "If you're smart, you'll learn from them, too."

"Is everything all right here, gentlemen?" Director Harris asked from behind my shoulder. Chuck was standing beside me, his eyes fixed on Sasha.

"Fine, sir," I answered. Sasha scrambled to his feet, glaring murderously at me, but when he met the director's eye he just shrugged.

"I'm glad to hear it," the director replied. "Jacob, I'd like a word with you."

"Yes sir," I answered, turning to face him. I wouldn't allow myself to bow my head, though I wanted to. I didn't regret what had passed with Sasha, but I hated that Director Harris had seen it.

We left the room together. Once we were alone in the hallway he put his hand on my shoulder. "Are you all right?"

I turned to him, surprised. "I thought this was discipline?"

He smiled. "I think being required to leave the dining hall with me like a naughty schoolboy is sufficient punishment, don't you?"

I didn't know what to say.

"Jacob, I have no doubt that things are very difficult for you right now, and that Sasha was doing his best to provoke you. But you're spoiling for a fight and I cannot, I will not, tolerate fighting in this institution."

This time I hung my head. "Yes, sir. I am sorry. I'll try to do better."

"You will do better," he said; not as a command but as an expression of confidence in me. "The worst is probably over. After what passed just now, I doubt anyone will be tweaking your nose anytime soon." He grinned. "How did things go with Dr. Bartel yesterday?"

I grimaced but quickly smoothed it off my face. "Fine, sir."

He frowned in disbelief but didn't press the question. "Please come to me with any concerns or anything I can help you with. I mean that."

I searched his face. "Don't you want to know what really happened, if I really did all of those horrible things you've heard? I wouldn't think you'd be eager to help me if some of them were true."

"I don't need to know what happened. I'm sure you made some sort of significant mistake and used poor judgment, maybe let your temper get the best of you like you did just now, but that doesn't make me disinclined to help you. You're too hard on yourself, Jacob. Everyone makes mistakes."

I fought tears and barked a mirthless laugh. "Most people have the sense not to make their mistakes quite so dramatically and publicly."

"You hardly had any other option in that arena, though, did you?"

I didn't contradict him. He was right, of course, but I didn't want to be understanding or forgiving of myself.

"I will be having a conversation with Sasha later today," he continued, "but you're not supposed to know that." He winked. I watched him, bewildered, trying to understand why he would be so kind to me but I could see nothing on his face but genuine sympathy.

The bell rang indicating the end of breakfast. "I imagine you have somewhere you're supposed to be now," he said.

"Yes, sir."

"Then I will see you later. Please don't hesitate to come to me for any reason, all right?"

"Yes, sir." He gave me a parting smile and walked away.

That evening, I tried to block out any thought at all—thinking was dangerous, it lead to feeling, and feeling was horrid—by scanning the offerings on the vid screen.

That was a terrible mistake. I was stopped on one of the documentary channels by the mention of my name. It was a piece on my demise and banishment. The details of the whys and wherefores were complete fabrications, but they did have one thing in complete and perfect detail. There was a full video of my sentencing and the execution of my punishment.

I watched in abject horror as I stood before Pete and heard my sentence read. The camera was on me, then on Pete, then on the crowd. Oddly, I looked less afraid than I remembered being. I heard my little helpless, pathetic speech. I watched myself being led away and stripped naked in front of thousands. I saw myself hoisted onto the frame, shackled. And then I watched, trembling and sweaty, blood pounding in my ears, as I was beaten. Cameras had captured the entirety of the horrific experience. I could hardly breathe when suddenly the playback ceased. Chuck stood in front of the screen. I hadn't even heard him enter.

"Bad idea," he said.

I couldn't talk for a long moment. "You've seen that?"

He gave me a sympathetic look. "Everybody's seen that."

I was shivering now from the adrenaline withdrawal. Chuck cocked his head to the side, examining me.

"You going to throw up?"

I shook my head, afraid of opening my mouth and indeed throwing up.

He gave me a 'do I look that stupid' look. "Sure. By the way, green's not a good color for you. 'S all right." He came over and squeezed my shoulder. "I don't like an audience either. You going to be OK?"

I nodded.

He gave my shoulder one last squeeze and left.

They sent me back to Dead End.

And there, I was sentenced to permanent solitary work detail, until I died.

I screamed. I screamed until there was nothing left to do but die of screaming. But at least then they could never send me out into that heatless, heartless, humanless expanse of darkness and—

I woke alone in a cold sweat.

Somehow it was worse than waking alone on Dead End. At least there, ironically, I still believed there would eventually be an end to the torment. This should have been better. This was home. Though that thought brought an unexpected and vicious twist of pain. Yet here, at least, I wasn't alone anymore.

But I felt alone.

I took the blanket from my bed and slid to the floor in the closet, closing the door behind me. In there, I could touch the wall on every side, the clothes above a false ceiling, only inches from my head. Within my illusion of safety, curled into a ball under the blanket, I could sleep again.

Life went on, or some semblance of such. Each day I got up, I dressed, ate, worked, even played when I was instructed to. But it was all pretense and dissembling. I was no more engaged in life than I would have been asleep. If anything, I lived more in my dreams. On the nights the memories of Dead End didn't drive me to the cocoon of the closet, I dreamed of Pete. Sometimes waking up is the cruelest of life's jokes.

I didn't speak of Pete or my life at the palace at all. As much as possible, I did not even allude to those three years, as if I'd never left the IIC. And not once did I utter Pete's name. If it was absolutely necessary to reference him I did so by title. I hardened myself, drew into myself, shut down. When I was spoken to, I replied. When I was invited somewhere, I went—though that only happened when Dr. Okoro or Chuck manufactured some unusual circumstance. In spite of Director Harris's assurances, the faculty did their best to enforce an unofficial shunning. I couldn't have cared less. I worked when it was time to work, and when my obligations were over I returned to my room, all in a fog of numbness and loss.

I expected it to get easier over time, and in a way it did. The emptiness became familiar. The hollow feeling in my chest never went away, but I learned to operate around it. The world was tainted by my grief; it was a haze in front of my eyes and a film over my heart. I did not live, I existed.

In one of those strange twists that life can sometimes take, in those early months one of the few people I found it bearable to be around was Mr. Kagawa. He sought me out regularly. I suppose there was a sort of understanding of each other now; a shared experience of profound loss.

Months passed. Two, three, four, five. It was approaching half a year since I'd returned to the IIC when, sitting in my room one night, reading, I was interrupted by the sound of the door chime.

"Come in."

It was Kirti. I wasn't sure how long it took me before I remembered myself and shot to my feet.

"Hello. Come in. Sit down." She did. It took me another moment to think of what to say next. "How are you?"

"I'm not here to talk about me."

I waited. "Why are you here?"

"Because someone has to kick your ass, Jacob, and apparently I'm the only one who can do it properly."

"I'm sorry, what?"

"You've been back for six months, and for all that time you've moped around here like your life was over. You're no more living than you would be if you'd actually lost your head. Now some amount of that is fine, and to be expected. But it's been a year, Jake. You're being ridiculous and self-absorbed. You need to talk to someone. I've been asking around and you're not talking to anyone. That's your problem."

"I talk all the time."

She gave me a look that clearly said I was being stupid. "No. You don't. I've talked to Dr. Okoro, and Chuck, and your lab partner, and Director Harris. Oh, you respond when you're spoken to and even carry on conversations. But you're not *talking* to anyone. You can't just hold it all in, you have to get it out, all the hurt and anger and shame. You're just wallowing in it right now, letting it fester. You have to talk to someone. And since no one else is going to force you to do it, I will."

It was almost amusing, after years of not speaking to me, now she came to comfort me; by telling me off.

"I don't have anything to talk about."

She pressed her lips together. "Jacob Dawes, this is our first conversation in years and you're going to insult my intelligence five minutes into it?"

I couldn't help a sad, half-smile. "OK, you're right. I'm sorry." I paused. "There's nothing I *want* to talk about."

She looked at me again as if I was a half-wit. "Obviously," she drawled.

And then she just sat there, waiting. Finally I couldn't help a short laugh. She continued to watch, and wait. I wasn't going to get out of this short of forcibly removing her from my room. And as much as I didn't want to admit it, there were so many horrible things inside of me that were begging for a release. I hadn't mentioned Pete even once in a year. I wanted to talk about him so badly it hurt. Just to say his name and have someone else hear it. I sat back down and looked at the tablet in my hands.

"It's not the same," I said. She said nothing even though I paused for a long time. I looked up at her and waved the tablet. "Reading like this. Pete collects books." His name burned my throat. "There's something about reading that way. It's a total experience, the feel of the pages, the sounds, and smells, the weight of it in your hand. It's almost a misnomer to call this reading when compared to that."

She said nothing, but her face had softened. She was looking at me now, not with impatience, but with sympathy. My eyes were burning and I looked away.

Finally I breathed, "Oh, Kirti. I miss him. I miss him so much sometimes I don't know if I can stand it any longer."

"Yes," she said finally.

I looked at her now, stunned. "Is this what it was like for you?"

She looked thoughtful. "Everyone's different. It hurt a lot, and for a long time. But, well, I don't know. Maybe I didn't have the same burden of guilt. Or maybe it was like something you alluded to, that we were trying to make our relationship something that it wasn't supposed to be. We were good as friends, even as something of a brother and sister. Maybe it really was just that. I don't know. It hurt a lot that you chose him and not me. But I don't think I was ever like this," she gestured to me. "Not a year later, at any rate."

I leaned my head back against the chair and closed my eyes. "What am I going to do?"

"Go on."

"That's impossible."

"Only because you've decided it is."

I looked at her and then away again. "You don't understand."

"I understand perfectly. You've lost what feels like everything. And you've convinced yourself it's all your fault and therefore you have to punish yourself and never let yourself be happy again."

"It *is* all my fault."

"Is that what he would say?"

I froze in shock at the question and the stab of pain in my

chest. "That doesn't matter." I jerked my hands apart when I realized I was twisting the ring.

"Oh? His opinion doesn't matter to you? Is that the way it was?"

"No! I'm sorry, I didn't mean to yell. It's not like that. It's just that Pete's too forgiving."

"Or maybe he's reasonable and you're not. He has a reputation of being intelligent and fair. Are all those people wrong and only you are right?"

"You don't understand."

"No," she said, with only a touch of sarcasm. "I'm sure I don't."

I gave her an apologetic look. Even though I couldn't make myself agree with her, I could still hear myself being stupid.

"Have you asked yourself," she continued after a long silence, "what he would want for you? Would he want you to be miserable like this?"

And that was what did it. I sank down over my knees, buried my face in my hands and sobbed. I cried and cried. At some point I became aware of her on her knees beside me, smoothing back my hair, mumbling quiet, nonsense words of comfort.

I cried until I couldn't cry anymore. At some point, exhausted from the excess of emotion, I realized Kirti was trying to pull me upright, so I let her. She helped me into my bedroom, out of my clothes, and into bed. Then she sat on the edge of the bed, rubbing my back until I cried myself to sleep.

Kirti was the impetus for what changed in my life after that. I made an effort. I didn't cease to feel numb, hollow, in pain, but I learned to live in spite of it.

Besides Kirti, my work was my other savior. While I'd tried to bury myself in mindless pursuits, deny myself the joy of the science and discovery as I denied myself everything else, I did not succeed. I could not make my brain work differently than it did. So it was not a month after Kirti confronted me that I approached Dr. Bartel with an idea for a new project.

It was obvious that he wanted to reject me on principle, but the scientist in him won out over more petty resentments. I was not only allowed to run my own project but to take Sean as my assistant. In my work I found more peace than anywhere else. It was logical and reasonable, never complicated by emotion or circumstance. It was the antithesis, the antidote even, to the miseries and complexities of human relationships.

And so, having committed myself to science again, I buried myself in my work. Dr. Okoro would join me when he could and I spent a great deal of time with Sean of necessity. I tried to do as Kirti had asked. I tried to "live" rather than merely exist. If it was less than what I'd had before, that was as it should be. I couldn't, I shouldn't, have happiness again like I'd had with Pete. I accepted that, and the short straw I'd drawn, and made a new life for myself.

One morning, after a raucous night in my room with Kirti and Chuck, I woke to find Kirti in my bed. I searched my memory frantically, trying to remember how it had happened. It was difficult through the haze of the hangover, but I could conjure up some scenes: Chuck leaving, Kirti still there, talking, laughing, moving closer. Was that her sitting on my lap? And even foggier scenes of nudity, my bed, release.

I was in a panic. One of the very few good things I'd salvaged from the wreck of my life was my relationship with Kirti. To lose it now would be too much to bear. I could only hope she would forgive me; that we could move past this. As I lay there, frozen in horror and indecision, she woke. She smiled at me, wincing, no doubt from a hangover of her own, then leaned over and kissed me. She grinned impishly, retrieved her clothes, and left the room with one last mischievous smile in my direction.

I was completely and totally baffled. I went to breakfast without the slightest idea of what to expect from the day and my future with her. When she sat beside me, grimacing a bit from the noise and an obvious headache, she gave me a sympathetic look. So I tried a smile and she returned to nursing her coffee. But other than those acknowledgements of a shared hangover, she never spoke of or even alluded to the events of the night before. I was more than happy to pretend that it hadn't happened.

But a month or so later, I woke beside her again, this time in her room. There had been alcohol involved that night as well, but not as much as before.

The third time it almost happened, a few weeks after, there was no alcohol at all.

And it didn't happen. Not that we didn't try. I lay there, on my back, staring at the ceiling.

"It happens to—"

"If you say it happens to everyone," I said, "I think I'm going to walk out."

"It's your room."

"I know."

I knew the expression on her face, even without looking. It would have scared me before.

"I don't care, Jake. Next time, then. It's no big deal." She was quiet for a long time. I was about to get up and spare myself the rest of the embarrassing scene.

"Is it because of him?"

"No." The response was so automatic it startled me.

"Because that would be OK. I'd understand. Anyone would."

'That's not it.'

"OK." She didn't need to tell me she didn't believe me. It permeated her tone. I came up on my elbow.

"Whatever it is, no matter what, it's not him. OK? It's not him. Never him."

She nodded once and closed her eyes.

"You tired?" she said.

"No," I whispered as I lay down beside her again.

She made a soft sound of disbelief but was soon breathing the deep, calm cadence of the clean conscience.

I lay awake a long time after that, trying not to think of the last woman I'd been with when I was horribly sober.

The next time, when she made a determined effort to seduce me in the wee hours of the morning, not allowing me to go back to my own room, it happened as we both meant for it to. And she smiled at me. Both satisfaction and relief. And I smiled at her too. Relief and some lessening of the fear that bound my gut.

But not all of the fear. Never that.

We didn't speak of what we were doing. Not that we pretended it wasn't happening, this developing arrangement between us; she simply treated it as if it were something that required no discussion. Everyone breathes, no one pretends otherwise, but who talks about it in depth, or analyzes the whys and wherefores, or plans for the future of the activity? This was something born, not of passion or eternal devotion, but of normal desires, and trust. In the absence of any emotional partnering for either of us, we had this; each other. She knew my heart belonged to another. But he was lost to me. And we were both still young, vital, and human. This was a way to help each other, and ourselves, and avoid all the messy complications of casual affairs in such a closed community. Any confusion or resentments over the nature of our relationship had passed. And this was the reward for that.

It was good being with Kirti. We weren't a couple in any real sense of the word. I would simply find myself in her bed, or her in mine, every few weeks or so. When it happened, it happened; when it didn't, it didn't. And usually, on those mornings, we would enjoy a quiet, companionable breakfast together, talking; being friends.

It was on one such morning, two full years after my return to the IIC, that I saw it. When I read it in the morning announcements the blood drained from my face; I was cold and ill. I set down the tablet and stared into space, too full of conflicting emotions to name any one or two now. Kirti looked up at me and gasped.

"Jake! What's wrong?"

I looked down at the tablet, meaning to give her an explanation but no words would come. She picked it up and scanned the page.

"Oh," she said quietly. "Did you think he wouldn't come? He said last time that he would."

I shook my head. "I...I don't know. I guess so. I...It's a year overdue, I thought maybe he'd decided..." I put my face in my hands. "I was trying not to think about it at all." I tried to smile but from her grimace, I guessed I hadn't succeeded.

"I'm so sorry, Jake. You know, you probably don't have to participate in the ceremonies if you don't want to. I'm sure Director Harris will excuse you."

"Well, he'll have to do something. Taken literally, the terms of my Resettlement both forbid me leaving and forbid me to be here when Pete comes." Somehow it was still difficult to say his name. "So my feelings on the matter may be the least of my worries."

She looked concerned now. "Surely someone would have thought of that and made some arrangements."

"No doubt," I agreed. "They're nothing if not thorough at the palace." I stood and kissed her forehead. "I'm going to talk to Director Harris. I'm sure he's got all the answers."

I entered the lobby outside the director's office full of foreboding. No matter what he said now, this was going to be very bad in one way or the other. The functionary, Jason, told me to go right in, that the director was expecting me. I knocked and entered the office.

He looked up at me from his seat at the desk and smiled, "Jacob, thank you for coming. You saved me the trouble of sending for you. I told Jason that you'd probably be here this morning. I owe you an apology." He stood and approached me. "I intended to tell you of the emperor's visit myself, but Mr. Gorkachev put it in the announcements sooner than I expected. I'm sorry you had to find out that way."

Here in this room, so layered with memories of antagonistic encounters with Director Kagawa, Director Harris's perpetual kindness was always shocking, no matter how much I should have expected it. "You don't owe me an apology, sir."

"Nevertheless, I do feel badly that I didn't make the time to tell you myself. I suppose you're here now to find out what accommodations have been made for you?" He returned to the desk and picked up a tablet.

"Yes, sir. I imagine I've been instructed to leave campus for the day?"

He grimaced, re-taking his seat behind the desk.

"No," he said, examining the tablet. "No, in fact, this specifies that there is no waiver of that restriction and reiterates the penalty for violation."

"Oh," I said. I wasn't surprised. What I'd said had been purely wishful thinking. Of course I wouldn't be allowed to leave.

"I'll just read the relevant portion of this," he continued. "With regard to Jacob Dawes, currently Resettled at your facility, the following provisions have been made:

"Mr. Dawes is permitted to participate in the ceremonies as any other resident of the facility. He is, under no circumstances, to attempt to draw attention to himself in any way either verbally, physically, or by any specific action on his own part or conducted for him by another person. He must not come within fifty feet of Emperor Rikhart IV at any time unless His Excellence puts himself in such proximity to Mr. Dawes and an attempt on Mr. Dawes's part to maintain the acceptable distance would draw attention to himself.

"No exception has been made to any other terms of Mr. Dawes's Resettlement. Restrictions on contacting or communicating with His Excellence in any manner remain in place. The planned visit of Emperor Rikhart IV in no way lifts the requirement that Mr. Dawes remain, for the rest of his natural life, on the campus of the Imperial Intellectual Complex.

"Any infractions on Mr. Dawes's part will result in immediate removal from the facility and reinstatement of the original sentence of death by beheading."

He looked up at me, seeming embarrassed, or expecting I felt that way. "It gives a contact at the palace for any questions we have about any of the arrangements. If you have any questions or concerns, I will most certainly take them up for you. I know this will be unpleasant for you, Jacob. We'll just do our best to make it no more unpleasant than necessary."

I nodded, too conflicted to know what to say. On the one had there was relief, even a surge of excitement in knowing that Pete was coming and that I would see him, hear him. But at the same time, my stomach was in knots that multiplied with each restriction placed on me.

It wasn't embarrassment, as Director Harris seemed to expect. No, it was anger at the insult of being more than marginalized, of being made to disappear. They were making me a nameless, faceless part of the crowd that would watch Pete come and would watch him go as any of hundreds of crowds had and hundreds more would. He'd be *right there* but every attempt was being made to make it so that I *wasn't*. Not physically, no that was the insult in it. I would be required to be there physically. I'd simply be disregarded, of no consequence, immaterial.

"Jacob," he continued tentatively, as if reluctant to pull me from my thoughts, "it has occurred to me that there was no specific *requirement* for you to be in the group, simply that you're permitted to be, and you mustn't distinguish yourself from the crowd in any way. You could hardly be accused of doing that if you didn't join the group at all. If you were to keep to your room or a lab for the day, you could avoid the whole matter without having to leave the grounds."

I watched his expressive, kind face for a long moment. I wasn't considering his offer at all. It was impossible to think that Pete would be here, with the restriction of being near him lifted, and that I would avoid seeing him. If the price of that was that I had to accept the humiliating position of being made invisible, so be it. To see him in person, to hear his voice, to watch him for hours, the play of his expressions, his quirks of movement and habit... even the thought filled me with helpless longing. No, I wouldn't stay away.

I delayed answering the director because I knew that the decision I'd already made was the wrong one; that I should decide to hide away because it was safer for both of us. But I couldn't bring myself to even consider doing what I knew was the right thing to do.

"Thank you, sir. I appreciate the offer, but I don't think that's necessary. You're right, this will be uncomfortable, but I'll be fine."

He nodded soberly. "I understand. It's up to you, of course. I want to help in any way I can. You just let me know what you need and we'll work this out, OK?"

I couldn't begin to express my gratitude to this man. How could I ever say how much his empathy meant to me in that moment? "Thank you, sir. Truly, thank you for everything." I reached out and shook his hand and I think, from my manner and my expression, the pressure of my hand on his, I think he heard what I couldn't say. He smiled and squeezed my hand before letting go.

"Anytime, Jacob. Anytime."

I left the room calmer than I had entered it and didn't even stop myself when I realized I was rubbing the ring again. There was still a horrible jumble of emotions knotting up my gut, but I felt stronger and the stirrings of hope that this was, in fact, not going to be the death of me in one way or another.

I was on my way to the lab when a servant passing in the hall informed me of a mandatory meeting of the entire physics department that had started ten minutes earlier. I hadn't read past the first announcement in the morning bulletin and had missed the part about the meeting. I hurried to the main physics hall. Unfortunately the doors into the room were opposite where Dr. Bartel stood addressing the assembled scientists. When I entered, he turned and waited, watching me as I found a seat. Sean had saved one for me and I slid into it.

"So good of you to join us, Mr. Dawes," Dr. Bartel intoned dryly. "Now," turning back to the group, he continued, "there are some projects that the senior fellows and I have determined will be a part of the exhibit. After I list these we will entertain your ideas as to which projects will fill the remaining slots. The selections are as follows: Dr. Smith's work on micro-gravity, Dr. Natanail's theorem on relative viscosity, Dr. Kor's ongoing work with heavy matter, Mr. Dawes's project on refined matter as well as his project on macro-gravity—"

"No, sir," I interrupted, "I don't think I should include my projects in this exhibit."

Everyone turned to look at me. "Mr. Dawes," Dr. Bartel said, his face hard and his voice cold, "I imagine that you find this experience distasteful, but your personal feelings, sir, have no bearing whatsoever on the decisions I will make for this department. We have decided your projects will be included in the exhibit and therefore you will prepare displays of your projects for the exhibit. Whether you want to or not."

I stood. "Sir, if my personal feelings were the sole motivation behind my objection then you'd be right. But there are more important matters involved here than either my feelings or yours. No doubt you are unfamiliar with all of the particulars of my current residence at the IIC. The very fact of the emperor's visit puts me in violation of the terms of my Resettlement and under penalty of death. I've just come from a meeting about the special provisions that are necessary so that his visit doesn't cost me my life. One of those provisions is that I am forbidden to draw attention to myself in any way. Forgive me sir, but if it's all the same to you, I'd rather not put my name prominently before His Excellence and take the chance that he might consider it a violation."

Dr. Bartel's lips were drawn together in a thin, angry line. "Well. I see. As you said, I was not aware of the complexities of the situation. Of course, we are not going to ask you to risk your life, Mr. Dawes." I got the impression he wouldn't have minded, though. "However, I believe we can check with someone at the palace and get a definite answer as to whether including your projects is permissible or not. I recommend you begin working up displays for both projects right away, in the hopes that we get approval from the palace."

"Sir," I objected.

"Mr. Dawes," his voice was a warning now, "you have explained your position and I have given you your answer. I will not discuss the matter further in this forum. If you have additional questions or objections you will present them to me in a more appropriate time and place."

He turned away and went back to his list. I sank into my seat. Sean leaned over and whispered, "I can start working on them. You don't have to worry about it yet. And if he gets approval then we'll finish them up together."

"He'll get his approval," I mumbled.

"You're sure?"

"Very," I muttered.

He shot me a sympathetic look before returning his attention to the meeting. I sat, silent and impatient. When the meeting was over, I was the first out the door.

But halfway to the director's office, I stopped. If I did go to the director, he would take my side; I had no doubt of that. He would be able to see the whole picture without Dr. Bartel's myopic focus on the department. Director Harris would realize how small an impact overall it would be for two, even excellent, projects to be left out. He'd see why it would be prudent to exclude my work in particular. He had promised to try to make this easier on me.

The entire prospect of this visit overwhelmed me with such conflicting emotions. The urgent need to stay and not only see, but be seen. The knowledge that it was best for everyone if I didn't.

I knew I should go to the director. It was the right thing to do, and not just to thwart Dr. Bartel. Pete shouldn't be putting either of us in this situation. He had made the wrong choice. It was my responsibility to blunt the impact, to protect him from the fallout of his error of judgment. I owed him that. I should do it.

But I knew I wouldn't. I needed to see him. I knew this was going to hurt, a lot. Even happiness at seeing him again would only become pain later. But I welcomed that. I hated that I was healing, that I'd begun to find myself feeling more and more. Less numbing pain, more of the mix of good and bad that life brings. I didn't want that. I wanted Pete, and barring that, I wanted to retain whatever I could of him; the pain of not having him if nothing else. The prospect of Pete's visit opening old wounds was ridiculously welcome.

Except that the visit would hurt Pete. Guilt gnawed at me, and it was ludicrous that it did. I'd been given no choice in the matter; the situation was entirely of Pete's making. But I couldn't help it. The whole thing had been my fault from the start.

But as much as I wanted to protect Pete from himself, he had decided to make this trip and I wasn't strong enough to stay away from him when I should. My decision made, for all the wrong reasons, I returned to the lab where Sean was already working on the design of one of the displays. I tried not to think about how I'd looked the right and the wrong in the face, and chosen the wrong.

fg33

In the end, I avoided Director Harris for the following two weeks. I respectfully addressed and answered everyone who sought me out during that time with questions or for advice. And they all sought me out, each department head as well as the Head Chef and the Head Steward. Dr. Warvrinosossi, the head of the chemistry department was the first; not the bravest, simply the most oblivious.

"Mr. Dawes," he called out to me one day as I was leaving the dining hall, "may I have a word with you?"

"Yes, sir."

"I'd like to ask your opinion on a particular display we're putting together for the emperor's visit. As you know him so well, I'm sure you can give me some insight on how to proceed."

I was shocked speechless. I hadn't expected this, but it seemed so obvious now, how they would all approach me for my insights into the mind, tastes, and preferences of the emperor. The thought flitted through my head that I could make a polite escape and seek out the director, putting a stop to these requests. But I didn't.

"Sir, the emperor has far more than a layman's knowledge of chemistry. He won't appreciate the full scope of the discovery but he'll understand the underlying principles and the advancements the project has brought to the study of chemistry. I think it's safe to assume that with His Excellence, too much detail is better than not enough."

His eyes lit up with excitement at the prospect of another who could understand and appreciate fascinating nuances of his science. And so I couldn't feel sorry about the decision. Even though my stomach was tied in knots again, as it always was when I spoke of Pete. There was an almost illicit thrill in speaking of him aloud, of allowing myself to acknowledge things I'd been hiding from for two years. I managed a convincing smile and excused myself.

They came with predictable regularity after that. Even Dr. Bartel approached me as I was working in the lab, for my insights on a project Dr. Teague was working up. His manner was gruff and almost confrontational, as if daring me to object. I didn't.

When Dr. Avaya, later that day, changed the subject of our conversation just as Director Harris walked by, I realized that the director had anticipated this and had tried to nip it in the bud. I felt the now familiar swell of gratitude for him, even though his attempt hadn't succeeded.

I answered each and every applicant, and more than one night I went back to my room and vomited from the sheer buildup of stress.

I was distant and, honestly, rude to nearly everyone else. Dr. Okoro I saw often, as he helped Sean and me work up my displays. I talked as little as possible and only of the work at hand. They both tried to engage me in other conversations but I avoided talking to them with determination. I felt guilty about that but not guilty enough to stop.

After a few attempts to treat me as he always did, invitations to games and such, Chuck registered the obvious rebuffs and left me alone. The nice thing was that Chuck wouldn't take offense or hold it against me. I didn't have to feel guilty about the way I was treating him.

The worst was Kirti. I put her off and turned her down again and again and finally, one night when she came to my room and tried to seduce me to no avail, she too backed off.

Even then I realized the irony in my actions, that I would be polite to those who were tormenting me and rude to those who wanted to help. It didn't stop me, though.

I often found my mind drifting, during my enforced silences, to imagined ways that Pete might say something to me, do something to acknowledge me, during the visit.

There were so many subtle ways, so many things to be said or done that would have meaning for the two of us alone. There was far too much history over three and a half years together for there not to be a dozen ways to do so.

After all, my work would be up there. His interest in physics was well established, his interest in my work went without saying. What would be more natural than him calling me up and talking to me about it just as he had on the last visit?

Perhaps natural was stretching it, considering the vast difference between the situation now and before, and my very particular status. But while I was prohibited from even sneezing too loudly and causing him to look at me, he was under no restrictions. Should he decide to talk to me, there was nothing anyone could or would say or do to prevent it.

I was jittery and nervous with anticipation just from imagining seeing him up close, having him say something, anything, to me and me alone. I knew he shouldn't. I also knew he would.

In any case, I kept to myself and my thoughts as much as possible those two weeks and wished for the dreaded, longed-for day to come and just be over with.

It did come, of course. I crawled out of bed that morning having spent a sleepless night trying not to think of Pete at all and failing miserably. Pete's transport arrived sometime in the wee hours of the morning. I thought again and again as I lay there of getting up and going to see if he had arrived yet; just peeking out a window or sticking my head out the front door, just to know. I cursed myself for a pathetic idiot and stayed in bed.

So it was hard, as I got ready that morning, not to think of Pete just outside, wonder if he was showering when I was, or sitting down to breakfast at the same time I did.

As for breakfast, my stomach was a gnarled, twisted thing inside me and I only downed several cups of coffee and ate nothing. I wondered if Pete was eating anything.

I couldn't have done anything special with my appearance even if I'd been able to get past my disgust at the thought. I put on my dress uniform, just like everyone else.

I was wearing his ring, but I always did that. I hadn't removed it voluntarily since Pete had put it on my finger. What a sentimental sap I was turning out to be.

When I left my room for the Great Hall, I felt like a man approaching his own gallows—and I did know something about what that feels like.

Most everyone was already assembled, arranged in loose groupings where they would soon stand in rows to receive the emperor. I made my way over to where Kirti and Chuck waited for me.

As before, we had been organized into five rows of seventy-five people each, ranked according to age and seniority. This arrangement left me squarely in the middle of the third row. I couldn't have been in a more anonymous, unimportant position. I didn't even have the distinction of being made to go to the back. I was simply hidden away in the middle of the crowd.

I had not been standing there long, brooding while Kirti and Chuck exchanged worried glances, when a palace functionary entered from the lobby area and spoke with Director Harris. We were called to order. Chuck fell in beside me on my left, Kirti on my right. According to the protocol, Chuck's positioning beside me could—with a loose interpretation of the instructions to group according to specialty—be justified, in that we were both in the sciences. Kirti's position, not at all. No one said anything to her about it. I wondered if Director Harris had anything to do with that.

It seemed we stood there much longer than normal waiting for the emperor to enter. I had to remind myself that I'd been on this side of things only once and for the several dozen times I was basing my estimation of "normal" on, I'd been with Pete. My anxious dread probably didn't help.

But eventually there was a small but perceptible change in the group of dignitaries waiting to meet the emperor. They all stood a bit straighter, smoothed hair or clothes. I noted with amusement that in a ripple effect, the entire crowd mimicked the greeting committee's unconscious preparations. I caught myself doing it, as well.

A figure appeared in the doorway and Pete was announced.

And he was there.

His hair was longer. I'd forgotten how intensely blue his eyes were. He was different, and the same, and *right there*. My heart passed through my throat and soared, took a sickening drop, and clenched painfully in my chest. He took a few steps into the room and turned to face the crowd. His eyes found mine like magnets drawn together. I felt the blood drain from my face and then flood it again in an excess of incompatible emotions. My view of him was cut off as I was jerked halfway into a bow by

Chuck's hand on my sleeve. I finished the bow out of reflex and ahead of the others. I sought Pete again but he had turned away.

He began greeting and accepting the greetings of the director and heads of departments. After completing the well-choreographed scene, Pete turned to address the spectators. I couldn't breathe from anticipation. These opening words were where he would say something to me. It would be so simple for him to say something that would sound completely benign, but would have meaning for him and me alone.

He began to speak, to say what he'd said hundreds of times and would say again hundreds more: thanks and praise and some few words specific to the day's crowd or occasion. He delivered it as if he were saying this for the first time.

That was one of the things I loved about Pete. Under and among the layers of ceremony and formalities and repetitious audiences, he cared about these people. And while the words may have been the same as they were the day before, it wasn't the same for Pete. He meant them today as he'd meant them every time he'd spoken them.

The thoughts were fleeting, though, and intrusive because I couldn't allow myself to miss whatever he would say, however small, to me alone.

The stock speech concluded, he turned to the director and began to chat with him as he approached the first display.

Nothing. He'd said nothing to me. It would have been so easy. There had been no risk. Nothing.

I felt sick.

I didn't realize I was trembling until Kirti reached over and took my hand. She gave me a worried look. Of course, she couldn't have known exactly what I was reacting to, but they'd all been expecting me to react badly in some way. Did the exact reason matter?

I was lost in pain and confusion as I watched him tour the exhibit. More than an hour into the morning he came to my first display. I was confident, now, that he would find some opportunity to acknowledge me here.

Both the experiments I had put on display had been born of work he and I had done together aboard ship. He wouldn't fail to notice. I had referenced that in the timeline, and included him in the list of contributors. Now he would say something to me, do something to send me a message, even just look in my direction.

I watched in breathless anticipation as he began to examine the display. After a couple of minutes he turned to Dr. Bartel and began to talk with him. My heart clenched. Wouldn't this have been a perfect opportunity for him to send for me, to discuss the work with me? They spoke, examining the display, for several minutes.

And then he moved on.

I couldn't breathe.

I lost sense of time or where I was for so long that I was still awash in brutal emotions when I realized that the next display in the exhibit was also mine.

He approached the display and began to examine it, chatting with Dr. Bartel as he did. A full five minutes had passed. More. I was going to be sick, I was sure of it.

Mr. Dawes." I nearly jumped out of my skin.

I didn't turn. I knew the voice, and I wasn't prepared for how to respond to Jonathan.

"Mr. Dawes," he began again, "His Excellence commands you to attend him immediately."

Commands? *Immediately*? As Pete-protocol went, he couldn't have summoned me in a way that was any more insulting and belittling unless he'd sent guards to drag me over without even asking. All the nausea and hurt swimming in my gut boiled into a slow, hot anger.

I turned to Jonathan. He looked like he was in pain.

I was afraid that if I opened my mouth I'd scream, or cry, or throw up, or maybe all three. So I said nothing, only gestured for him to lead the way. He gave me one long, meaningful look before he returned to Pete and I followed.

Jonathan waited until Pete finished what he was saying to Dr. Bartel, then whispered his announcement of me. Pete nodded his head in distracted acknowledgement and returned to his conversation with my department head. Dr. Bartel cast a glance in my direction before answering.

With an exaggerated, casual air, Pete finally turned to me.

"Mr. Dawes," he said.

I bowed low, nearly prostrating myself. "Your Excellence." He wilted a little, and I bit back a sudden urge to apologize.

He recovered quickly. "I recognize this experiment," he said, gesturing toward the display.

"Of course. This one was your idea. I began the initial work on it at the palace." The pained expression was just a flicker on his face, a tightening of his eyes, but I knew those eyes too well to miss it.

Sam shifted at the emperor's side; the same guard captain with whom I had a very unfortunate acquaintance. He glowered at me, but I turned back to Pete.

"Of course, I remember," Pete answered. "I also remember that, because it was my idea and my request, you assured me that you wouldn't work on this project unless I was able to join you. I see you decided not to honor that."

I stared at him, dumbfounded. He was going to make an issue about *that*? Was it just that he just wanted something, anything, to pick a fight with me about? After all my hope, my daydreams about the subtle ways he could have acknowledged me, this was how he'd chosen to break his silence? The faltering burn in my chest flared in a rush of anger. "If you mean I decided not to abandon the project entirely then, yes," I snapped.

Pete hesitated only a moment. "Strange that I never realized your word meant so little," he said.

I sucked in a loud, angry breath. "And I never realized you were so petty!"

He took two quick steps toward me, his eyes flashing. He was so close that I felt the harsh rush of his breath against my cheek. "Take care, Mr. Dawes," he said, his voice low. "I have my limits." He stepped back, his face hard. I watched him deliberately relax hands that had clenched into fists. He took a deep breath and turned his back on me, wandering back over to the display.

"This is the second of your displays I've seen, Mr. Dawes, in as many hours. Is this to be like it was the last time I came? The entire physics section a tribute to the *genius* of Jacob Dawes?"

"You needn't worry about that, Your Excellence. You may remember, I spent most of the last five years away from the IIC." He turned away and I didn't see his reaction to that.

"Of course," he replied, still angled away. Then, waving his hand in my direction he said, "You may go."

I stiffened. Pete didn't dismiss the lowest servant so rudely. My hands balled into fists. The entire group was still, watching, breathless when I didn't do as he'd commanded.

"You know," I snapped, my voice loud and hard, "most cowards have to run away from their problems. Aren't you fortunate that you can make your problems run away from you?"

Pete turned on his heel and was in my face before I could blink. "You never learn, do you?" he hissed. "Have you forgotten all the trouble your mouth gets you into? What I am? What I can do to you?"

"I haven't forgotten anything," I said, half choking on the many meanings of that. "But I'm not afraid of you."

"Oh, I know you're not." He coughed a rude laugh. "You're not as bright as people give you credit for. So let me help you." He lowered his voice and spoke with exaggerated slowness. "Go away, as you were told, and save yourself the embarrassment of being dragged out of here." He turned his back on me, returning to the display and those waiting for him there.

I quivered with rage, and grief, and the overwhelming need to punch something. "You can kiss my ass, Peter Killearn!"

He rounded on me, but checked himself a couple of feet away. "Sam," he said, finishing his sentence with a gesture in my direction. Two guards flanked me. Their hands clamped down on my arms. He held my gaze. "It never occurred to me that I'd need a brig on my personal transport."

To the guard captain he said, "Confine him in one of the unused servants' quarters."

"Yes, Your Excellence."

Pete turned away. As if an afterthought he added, "Sam, I won't overlook you doing him any harm...yet."

Sam's smile was his only answer. He led the way out through the lobby and to the transport. The guards followed behind, hauling me with jerks and thrusts so that I stumbled along between them. They steered me aboard and down a small corridor to a nondescript door. Sam pushed me inside the small bedroom with so much force that I landed on the floor in front of the bed. I got to my feet. Sam was still in the doorway, examining me.

He was struggling with something—apparently, his self-control. He drew in a breath and, closing on me, threw his fist into my stomach. My knees buckled.

I gasped, struggling for air. Breathing like a fish on land, I stood in a rush of fury. "You've only got that one trick, don't you?" I croaked.

His face screwed up in confusion.

"The punch in the stomach. It seems like every time I see you, that's how you greet me."

I saw his fist spasm, but he held himself back. "You going to tattle on me again?" he growled.

"I didn't tattle on you last time."

"Oh yeah?"

"Yeah, sorry, I forgot you have the IQ of my little toe. I was covered in bruises and you brought me to the emperor yourself. He's not as dumb as you. When he saw them, he actually figured out what happened all by himself."

He stepped closer and loomed over me. "If you're lucky," he said, "when the emperor gives me my head with you, I'll beat you with only the few men I have here, rather than waiting until we're back at the palace with my entire squad."

"Generous of you," I quipped. He smiled.

"But you're not really a lucky one, are you?"

I just held his gaze, not answering. He made a disgusted noise and stormed out.

I slumped down to sit on the bed, cradling my aching gut and drooping over my knees, cursing Sam, myself, Pete; myself, mostly.

I couldn't stay still. I paced around the small room, taking the opportunity every now and then to bang my stupid head against the wall, only to sink back down to the bed for a time, cradling my stupid head in my hands, before I'd be back up again, pacing. Anger didn't wane but I layered guilt and fear and self-loathing on top of it.

More than an hour passed before the door opened. Pete entered and the door closed behind him. I froze like a startled rabbit. We stood, him just inside the doorway, me motionless where I'd been pacing, staring at each other. His face was unreadable, passing too quickly through the barely perceptible emotions behind his emperor's mask. The silence became unbearable.

"Look—" I said.

But he was there, pressing against me. He grabbed my head and kissed me. I melted into him, pulling him closer, moaning. He only kissed harder. I tangled a hand in his hair.

He pushed me backward and we fell onto the bed together. There was a tearing of clothes in a desperate rush. Somewhere in the feel of his skin on my fingertips, his long body beneath me, and the smell that was overwhelmingly *him*, I forgot who I was, where, or why this was such a bad idea. We were together, and for the first time in two years I felt whole.

We lay together afterward, panting, saying nothing. I was on my stomach with my face away from him. I felt him move against me and kiss my shoulder, my neck.

"I love you," he whispered.

I jumped up and got off the bed, searching for my pants. "We shouldn't have done this," I muttered at the floor, choking on a wave of contempt for my ridiculous lack of self-control.

"What?" he said, with a look on his face that made me ache. I cast a quick, bitter look at him as I snatched up my shirt. He stood, grabbing my arm. "What do you mean?"

I jerked my arm away. "Why are you here?"

He flinched. "You know I said I would come, last time I was here."

"You've gotten out of more important things for less."

"You wish I hadn't come?"

"Yes. You shouldn't have come. If you were dead set on it, you could at least have let me leave. You shouldn't have done this to either of us."

I was nearly dressed again. My shirt was missing too many

buttons and it hung open. I grabbed for my shoes. He jerked me by the arm. "How can you say that? You listen to me, Jacob Dawes—"

"NO!" I yelled, jerking away again, "You listen to *me!*" Righteous anger rushed through me, anger at myself for allowing this. The pain in his eyes was a vicious condemnation. "Stop doing this, Pete. You're not stupid. Think! You knew better than to see me. You're being sentimental and emotional. You're being ridiculous." I turned my back on him, sick with necessity, hating the one person who had put us in this position: me. "Get the hell out of here."

He grabbed for my arm again but, batting it aside, I punched him. He fell to the floor, hands cupping his nose.

For a brief eternity I couldn't move. I stood there gaping at the sight of him several steps away holding his nose, a line of crimson blood trickling between his fingers, my head swam and my heart thundered as I tried to convince myself I was at the IIC, that this wasn't the throne room, it wasn't two years ago, and I wasn't going to Dead End again.

I hadn't even noticed he'd moved before his fist slammed into my mouth.

We fought.

I'd been in far, far more fights than Pete, who'd been in exactly none, but I took as many punishing blows as I delivered. My head was ringing and throbbing when I finally thought to drive my fist into his stomach. He doubled over, all his breath going out in a whoosh. I shoved him away and he staggered back into the wall.

I started to walk out, but stopped. After a long moment I turned back, bent down and took his face in my hands, put my forehead to his. "I'm sorry I hurt you," I whispered, kissing him lightly again and again. "I'm sorry, I'm sorry, I'm so, so sorry." He didn't meet my eye; there were tears in his as he shook his head. I wiped a stray tear away with my thumb.

Ripping myself away from him, I slipped on my shoes and grabbed my jacket off the floor. "Do me a favor, Pete," I said.

With an arm around his stomach, he pushed himself up with

the other and looked at me.

"Tell them when you leave tonight that you're not coming back in five years. That you're not coming back ever."

He dropped his head, but I still saw the twist of pain in his features. "Jake..." He stopped. He looked up at me, and for a moment I thought he was going to say no, that he wasn't going to give in. My heart twisted in a tempest of fear and elation. Then, as I watched, the slow spread of resignation crossed his face and he dropped his head again. "If that's what you want," he said.

"Yes," I choked.

He nodded. I opened the door and started to exit but two burly guards blocked my way. "Where do you think you're going?" the bigger one demanded.

I looked back over my shoulder without turning.

"Let him go," Pete said from behind me. They moved aside, looking ready to spit nails. I stepped past them quickly, trying not to run from what I'd just done.

As I exited the transport and barreled through the lobby I realized that I'd have to pass through the main hall on the way to my room. I tried to figure out how long I'd been on the transport, what time it was at the moment. I only hoped that it was still the lunch hour and everyone was in the dining hall.

I wasn't so lucky. I entered the main hall to find the whole of the faculty and student body standing about, waiting for the emperor's return to be announced. There was a significant stir when I walked into the room instead. I had the attention of all as I made my way the entire length of the head of the room in order to get back to my own. I was painfully aware that my shirt hung open, that there was probably still blood on my chin from where Pete had split my lip.

As fast as I walked, I couldn't go fast enough. And I could hear their comments, loud enough that I knew they meant for me to hear.

"That's what happens to people like him."

"If there was any justice he'd have gotten worse."

"Too bad they didn't execute him two years ago."

"I can't believe they let him go. They should get rid of him this time. Did you hear what he said to the *emperor*?"

When I made it back to my room, I sank to the floor, wishing I were anyone but who I was, where I was. The first thing I did, when I realized I'd have to get up eventually, was get into a cold shower.

Not for the obvious reasons. I needed the shower because I could smell him on my skin and clothes. I washed away, as best I could, what lingered of his scent. I could still smell him afterward, even over the soap and starch but most, if not all, of that was probably traitorous memory.

As much as I wanted to crawl into my bed and never get out again, I had an obligation. To Pete. If I hid away, if I ran from all the pain of seeing him again, of rejecting him, of watching him leave, it would only be that much harder for him. He needed me to be there, to see me accept the situation we had to accept. He needed to see that I chose to watch him go, that I wouldn't ask for or even allow another lapse. I had to be firm, and strong. For him.

As soon as I could, I left my room to rejoin the group. Of course, I had no way of knowing what had happened after I'd fled the room, but I guessed that Pete was doing the same as I was, putting himself back together to return to the ceremonies. If I hurried, there was a chance I'd rejoin the group ahead of his entrance; and I could already be there when he entered, as if nothing at all had happened.

Entering the room I registered, with relief, the director and department heads all standing at the head of the room, waiting. Pete hadn't returned yet. I hurried toward my place in the crowd. Not many people were watching my progress. It didn't take me long to figure out why.

Only a few steps into the room I heard the rustle of voices preceding and the actual announcement of Pete's entrance. I froze. I briefly considered hurrying back to my place but I knew I wouldn't make it before Pete arrived. There was still a wide space of empty room between me and the first row of spectators, let alone my place in the middle. So I stopped where I was and waited.

As he walked into the room he looked over and saw me and froze as well. Knowing I had to act, I bowed and then, without a pause, returned to my place in the crowd. The weight of Pete's gaze accompanied me, somehow heavier than all the other eyes in the room.

When I stopped in my place and looked forward, I could see out of the corner of my eye that Pete was still watching me. I didn't acknowledge his gaze. Eventually he moved on.

The rest of the afternoon was an escalation of agonies. Pete had a black eye and a fat lip. That much could be seen even where I stood. And I wasn't seeing it only because I knew to look for it. I could hear the scandalized whispers around me.

The conversation behind me was intended for me and hard to miss. Sasha stage-whispered to Joshua, beside him.

"Do you see what that son of a bitch did? I always said he was an arrogant piece of shit. Don't think anyone will doubt me now." Joshua muttered agreement. "You know," Sasha continued, "I don't know why the emperor's guards didn't have to balls to give him the beating he deserved. But that can be fixed."

Sasha, who so easily insulted the emperor as a way to provoke me, was now adamant about defending him. I hadn't thought it was possible to hate him more than I already did. Chuck turned his head and glared at Sasha.

"You think you're going to stop me this time?" Sasha said to him. "Every guy in this building will be lined up ready to beat the shit out of this piece of garbage before the emperor's transport is even off the grounds. You get in the way, you're going to get yourself hurt."

Chuck sucked in a breath to reply, but I stopped him with a hand on his shoulder and turned to face Sasha. "Be patient. You'll get your chance."

Beside me, Chuck muttered, "Like hell you will."

I sighed. I'd do what I could to keep him out of it. There was doubtless someone who would hold him down, if necessary. If not for me, then for Chuck.

Neither my worries about Chuck nor the dread of a beating could hold my attention. I couldn't think of anything but Pete. It didn't take someone who knew him well, or even someone aware of the scene that morning, to see that Pete was agitated and distracted.

He walked, mostly unseeing, through the displays. He spoke not at all unless addressed, and not always then. Before long, no one made any further attempt at conversation. I tried not to watch. I kept my eyes on Jonathan instead.

That was almost as bad. The tightening around his eyes, the shadowed glances, the ill-suppressed winces at new signs of distress in his emperor tormented me. But I watched. I had to.

So I saw when, more than an hour into the afternoon, Pete startled at the sight of the next display. I looked at what he'd seen and groaned. It was a sculpture by an artist that Pete had favored even before he and I were together.

Senzio did incredible human subjects, and was a decent guy besides. I'd had some contact with him in my time at the IIC before going away. So when I'd heard of a troupe of famous contortionists coming to the palace, I had suggested we invite Senzio. He'd sat in the Imperial box with us and Pete had been delighted by his absolute concentration throughout. Several very good pieces had joined works at the palace since then. This was one of his latest, and one of the best of that collection in my opinion.

I had avoided Senzio since returning to the IIC; he reminded me of being with Pete.

Obviously it was the same for Pete.

So it wasn't a surprise when he looked at me. I met his eye. I couldn't help it. There was a pleading look on his face. I dropped my head to make myself break the eye contact. When I raised it again I didn't look at him. I could see in my peripheral vision that he was still looking at me. Eventually he turned away and resumed the tour.

And so I stood in the crowd and watched him view the exhibit. I sat in the dining room and watched him at the head table, though I turned away every time he looked for me. I stood in the crowd as he thanked and praised us. He didn't say explicitly that he'd never come again, but he implied it. In spite of the fact that I had asked him to, it still made my eyes fill with tears.

And I held myself in place when he left.

The moment he was out of sight I turned, without waiting for a dismissal, and tried to make my way out in the opposite direction. I wasn't out of the room before I fell to my knees, retching. I was dimly aware of my friends at my side trying to help me, but the moment I was able, I scrambled to my feet and retreated.

When I got to my room I locked the door and buried my head under my pillow. There was more than one knock on my door, but I ignored them all. Eventually, I was left alone with my misery.

fg37

In the morning I got up, dressed, and went to breakfast. I felt dead inside, but what alternative did I have? I'd feel no better or worse alone in my room. I entered just before the occupants of the head table and took my place between Kirti and Chuck. Sasha slid in front of me. I hadn't forgotten he'd promised me a beating.

We sat for the meal and I didn't bother taking any food. I nursed my coffee cup instead. I was deaf and blind to what was going on around me, so it was only dimly that I registered a sudden excited murmuring, people coming to their feet all around me. Kirti smacked my arm. "Jake!" she hissed. I looked up at her; she wasn't looking at me but across the room. Out of reflex more than curiosity I did as well.

And saw Pete coming toward me. I shot to my feet, felt the blood drain from my face. He wore casual, everyday clothes, he wore no jewelry but the Imperial seal, and he was unaccompanied. It made the scene that much worse because it wasn't the emperor approaching me, it was Pete. He stopped in front of me.

"May I speak to you?"

I couldn't breathe from the pain of seeing and hearing my Pete, so I had no words to answer him. I just nodded once and walked away, trusting that he'd follow.

He caught up and walked beside me. He was a physical heat against my side. I was panicky. I knew I didn't have the strength to be alone with him.

As we approached one of the exits I angled and stopped in the corner of the room, turned to face him and waited. He gave me a look of disbelief.

"Could we go somewhere more private?" he asked, gesturing toward the doorway.

"No."

He looked at me, incredulous for a long moment, then made a soft sound of amusement.

"OK, Jake," he said, a smile playing at his lips, "have it your way." He took one of my hands and dropped to a knee in front of me. "Jacob Dawes," he said, "will you marry me?"

The room started to spin. I looked up, horrified, to confirm that there was indeed a crowd of people watching us with a variety of astonished expressions on their faces. I looked back at Pete, still on one knee in front of me. I grabbed him by the upper arm, hauled him to his feet, and dragged him from the room. He didn't resist.

"Where are we going?" he asked, as if he was just making conversation.

"Somewhere more private," I growled. He chuckled.

I pulled him with me into the nearest lounge and slammed the door behind us. I released him.

"What the hell was that!"

He stared. "A proposal of marriage," he said slowly.

I huffed in disgust. "You know what, Pete? You win. OK? You win. That hurt like hell. I wasn't trying to hurt you yesterday. I was just doing what I had to do. I'm sorry that hurt you, but that's just the way it is. But you've gotten me back. You sure have. So could you please, please just go now and leave me alone?" I said, turning away and pressing the heels of my hands into my eyes. "Please?"

He grabbed my arm and pulled me around to face him. "What the hell are you talking about?"

"I don't buy it, OK? I admit, for one horrible fucking minute I hoped, but then I remembered reality. It's over. I'm not buying it, so you can give up the fucking pretense."

"Pretense? I'm proposing marriage! You think I'm making a

joke? You think I'm trying to hurt you?"

"What the fuck else could it be!" I yelled. "Three years ago it was all you could do to spare me execution by having me sent away for life. You can't tell me now that I can come back and marry the fucking emperor himself and expect me to believe it."

"Would you please stop saying 'fuck' every other word?"

"No."

He made a wry face but took a step closer, reaching for me.

"I can make this happen, Jake, you know I can."

A wash of nausea and fury crashed into me with such force that I couldn't breathe.

"You selfish, manipulative, fucking *son of a bitch.*"

All the blood drained from Pete's face. My first reflex—to grab him because he looked like he was going to faint—was checked by the anger gripping me.

"What?" he breathed.

"You're unbelievable." My voice was shaking. *I* was shaking. "You can make it happen? You want this bad enough now, so now nothing can stop it? What about three years ago when I was beaten and fucking Resettled? You couldn't make it happen then?"

"I—"

"It's so easy for you, isn't it? You want something to happen and it happens. I was probably, what, a minor inconvenience? Someone actually thwarted you and took away your favorite toy. But you're going get it back. Because you can."

"Jake—"

"Fuck you. Fuck you and what you want. You can't make *this* happen, Your Excellence."

He reached back with one hand but still fell ungracefully into the chair behind him. He clasped his hands together in his lap, but I could still see them shaking.

"Go ahead and stick me wherever you want to put me next." My voice sounded weaker than the protest felt. "You can *make it happen*. But I'm not participating anymore. I'm done."

He buried his face in his hands. He was shaking all over.

The silence stretched.

"I'm sorry," he rasped. He looked up at me, his eyes so bleak that some of my anger receded. "I didn't—" He clenched his hands into fists twice, watching them as if he didn't know who they belonged to. "I didn't realize." He met my eye again. "I didn't know."

All the strength went out of me and I collapsed into a chair. I thunked my head back and closed my eyes.

"No, you probably didn't. But that doesn't change what you did. Or what you do. I can't do it, anymore, Pete. I just can't."

"No," he whispered. "No."

I cracked my eyes open and watched as he stood. He stumbled the first step and had to reach out to catch himself.

"I'll go now," he said.

My stomach tightened watching him.

"I'm sorry, I didn't mean—"

"No, you're right. I'm sorry."

I closed my eyes. I couldn't watch him leave again.

His voice came from the direction of the door.

"You're right, but I want you to know I didn't mean to hurt you. I thought—I'm not sure what I thought anymore. You do that to me. I feel so competent when I'm dealing with all of them, but when it's you, when it matters to *me*, it's like I know nothing, like I don't even speak the language."

My throat was closing and my eyes were burning. I squeezed them tight.

"Maybe this *was* all about me. I feel like I'm falling apart, like someone's pulled out the supports and there's nothing left to hold me up. I tried to leave yesterday but I didn't even make it back to the palace. I can't do this without you, but I don't know how to make it right for you." He drew in a shuddering breath. "I'll figure it out. I owe you that much. I'm sorry I came back. I'm sorry about everything."

The door opened.

"Wait."

My eyes were still closed. I wasn't sure about this. I wasn't sure about anything. But I felt like if he left, there would be nothing left of me.

"Don't go."

I got up and went to stand in front of him. He pressed his back against the wall, as if he needed the support. I had this sudden urge to just brush my finger down his cheek, maybe shake him first, or collapse in his arms and cry. The planet spun beneath my feet and I could feel it turning, rolling over me, this, us.

"I don't know what to say to you," he said, with a shaky laugh. "I'm scared anything I say will be the wrong thing."

I shrugged. I didn't know either.

"I do want to marry you," he said. "I want to spend every day of the rest of my life with you. I'm not asking you for anything now. Just, maybe you'll consider it? You can teach me, how to do it right."

"Do what right?"

He gave me a lopsided smile. "Everything."

I looked down at our feet. At his feet, actually. He had big feet. It was a stupid thing to remember, to notice now, but it was suddenly the most important thing in the world.

I raised my head and found him looking at me, his eyes devouring my face.

"I'll marry you."

He didn't say anything for a moment, as if he hadn't heard me. Then he went pale again.

"You will?"

I nodded. "Yes. Just don't tell anyone, OK?"

He spluttered a laugh and grabbed me, crushing me to him like he meant to discover a new kind of fusion.

I closed my eyes and lost time and perception of everything but Pete in my arms and in my life again. Everything was right and everything was wrong and it was all OK because I loved him and I'd never done anything else. And he had come back for me.

We were very shy with each other. We sat on a couch and talked in halting bursts, of nothing at all that was important to either of us. But we'd been unconsciously shifting toward each other and I realized all of a sudden how close he was. I reached out and laid my palm against his cheek. He stopped what he was saying mid-word and sucked in a breath.

I kissed him; an awkward, chaste kiss. He was still, as if he didn't know what to do.

I snorted a laugh and sat back.

"We just agreed to get married and we're sitting here acting like a couple of scared virgins. We've done this before, you know."

He laughed and reached for me.

"We have, haven't we?"

When he kissed me it was a real kiss. We lay down on the couch, tangled together, breathing each other's breaths. One person rather than two. And in a haze of silence and sensation, we started to become us again.

We walked hand in hand through the halls to my lab.

Stares and whispers followed us everywhere. More than anything else, that made it real for me. The familiar feeling of us vs. them, Pete and Jake against the world.

In the lab, I worked with Sean on extricating myself from our ongoing projects. Sean, at first, could barely speak with Pete sitting there, commenting from time to time or joking with me. But eventually Pete's relaxed manner overcame the worst of Sean's fear. The other team in the lab did little more than stare at us.

Later we left to find Kirti, Chuck, and Dr. Okoro. The only negative feelings I had about leaving the IIC behind without warning were that I'd have no time to say a proper goodbye to my friends. Pete solved that problem by suggesting they accompany us to the palace for a visit. Kirti and Dr. Okoro looked intimidated, but Chuck was excited.

By the time we sat down to dinner, Pete's announcement of our engagement was superfluous but greeted with loud applause. I figured, just like the last time, they were happy about being rid of me more than anything else. After dinner, and the champagne and congratulations that followed, my friends accompanied us as Pete and I boarded the transport to return home together.

We didn't retire to our room right away, but sat in the main lounge with Kirti and Chuck and Dr. Okoro. Pete insisted they drop all titles and call him Peter, which they tried to do with varying degrees of success. They all managed it in the end, but never looked comfortable about it.

Still, they did relax in his presence with time. Pete was good at encouraging that. Here with them he was as he'd always been with me, just a man and nothing more. It's hard to continue to treat a man as something more, something other, when he refuses to be such.

It was good, so very good to see Pete and my friends laughing and talking together like old friends. I wanted for them to see and know this side of Pete, the man I was in love with and not the emperor. In spite of the fact that I did really want to be alone with him, that evening with my friends was so enjoyable I was almost sorry to see it end. Almost.

Later that night, as we lay together in the big bed on his transport, I circled the discoloration around his eye with a fingertip. "I'm sorry about this," I said.

He grinned. "I think it makes me look tough, don't you?"

I frowned, "Yes, well, that ought to make my homecoming at the palace go smoothly. I'm sure everyone will love it."

He smiled. "Homecoming. I like that."

"Will you be serious for a minute?"

"I am."

I rolled onto my back with an exasperated sigh. He came up on his elbow so that now he was looking down at me. He traced his finger over my split lip. "I think this needs a couple of stitches."

I shrugged. As happy as I was, as happy as I should have been, I couldn't shake the sense of foreboding about my return to the palace. That wouldn't have gone well anyway. Pete's black eye promised to make it a doozy.

"Can't we just run away?" I asked. "We'll go where no one can find us. Just you and me."

He kissed me once, twice. "Why are you so worried?"

"Why aren't *you* worried? It's going to be bad enough that I'm coming back at all. I don't see how you can be so calm about that. And with this?" I pointed at his eye.

He leaned down and kissed me, a long, lingering kiss. My lip stung but I didn't care. Several minutes later we broke apart.

"You're trying to distract me," I said.

"Did it work?"

I laughed, but it was only halfhearted.

"You let me worry about that, all right?" he said. "Whatever complications there are because I'm emperor aren't yours to worry about. That's my business and I'll handle it. And believe me," he kissed me, "whatever there is to deal with, is worth it. A thousand times over."

I pulled his face back to mine. He was right. I had Pete again. What could there be to worry about?

fg**38**

In the morning, when we got off the transport at the palace, Pete tried to send guards to accompany me. I refused.

"Jake, no one knows you're here with my permission. You don't want to cause unnecessary trouble. Just take the guards with you this one day while we get everything sorted out."

"No thank you," I said. An armed escort, no matter that it was now for my protection, was too much like being in custody for my comfort. "It'll just make me conspicuous."

He looked at me with his eyebrows raised in disbelief. "You think you're going to walk through the palace and *not* be conspicuous just because you don't have guards? You need an escort Jake, I'm sorry."

"So let Jonathan come with me. If he's with me, everyone will know that I'm here with your authorization. And then it won't look like a military parade."

"You know," he said, "when we're married you'll have guards with you all the time. It's part of being a member of the Imperial family."

"All the more reason for me to enjoy my freedom now."

He frowned at me but said, "Fine. Take Jonathan. But try to avoid crowds as much as possible, please."

"You know I do that anyway," I answered, dropping a light kiss on his cheek. "Thank you."

He smiled, kissed me purposefully, and made his way to his office.

I led my friends into the palace and through the less populated areas by choice; I would have done so without Pete's exhortations.

Unfortunately, while my chosen area was less populated, it was also the haunt of some of my least favorite people.

We were walking down a main hallway, talking and laughing, so we were almost upon Duke Blaine before I noticed him. He was talking to another man and when he caught sight of me he stopped mid-sentence. Both of them stared at me in astonishment. Duke Blaine turned red and barreled toward me.

"How dare you! How you're even here, I can't understand. How dare you thrust yourself into the presence of decent, loyal citizens? You have more gall than even I gave you credit for. You loathsome little toad. I'll see you beheaded for this."

I stared him down. "Do you really think I just wandered in here on a whim?"

"How am I to know what your traitorous mind could cook up, or what treasons you'd sink to?" He turned to his companion. "Call the guard."

"Knock yourself out, Blaine. Make a fool of yourself. Makes no difference to me."

He stepped even closer, putting his face in mine. "Even should you somehow have permission to be here, let me be clear. You won't come between me and the emperor again."

I couldn't help but laugh. "You say that as if you think there was ever anything for me to have ruined. You're such a fool. You know, Blaine, no one can stand you. No one."

"You think you know anything at all about your betters? The emperor may have allowed you a glimpse of those so far above you, but you're nothing. You know nothing. You can't possibly understand the complexities of my world. His Excellence understands my worth. He and I have gotten quite close of late."

I laughed again. "Really? Impossible. Wait, maybe you tried a new angle? After all, with me gone..."

It really was too easy. Duke Blaine was one of those Neanderthals who managed to perceive homosexuality as insufficiently masculine.

"Do you mean you're willing to bend over and take it?"

His fist crashed into my mouth, reopening my split lip. I felt warm blood trickling down my chin.

"What is it with me and this shit, lately?" I muttered.

I put my hand out to stop Chuck, who was already advancing on Duke Blaine.

"Don't," I insisted. "Please, just trust me on this one." The setting seemed to be enough to convince him. He stepped back.

I rounded on Blaine and punched him full in the face. A sickening crack was followed by a pained howl from Blaine as he fell to the ground, cradling his broken nose in his hands.

"You disgusting little fucker!" he screeched.

His companion had returned trailed by four guards. They all stopped and surveyed the scene with confusion. When two of them made the obvious conclusion and advanced on me, Jonathan stopped them and spoke to them quietly. They looked up at me, stunned, but then, at Jonathan's direction, assisted Duke Blaine. As they helped him up and started to help him away, he turned to me.

"The emperor will hear about this!"

"Of course he will." I laughed, gesturing at our growing audience. "But I'll tell you what. No need to hurry yourself; I'll let you do all the tattling. I won't try to beat you to it."

He glared murderously at me, but I just turned and walked away.

I stormed through the nobles' area and into the emperor's wing with my friends on my tail. I was halfway into the sitting room before I realized they had stopped in the doorway of Pete's rooms in astonishment. I turned back, embarrassed.

"So, this is the emperor's suite," I said, "Make yourselves at home. I'm going to clean up." Jonathan had already sent for Dr. Henriksen, and she wasn't long in coming. She greeted me with no reserve or reluctance. As I sat and accepted her ministrations, I watched her, puzzled.

"Aren't you surprised to see me?"

She smiled, though she was watching her work and didn't meet my eye.

"I was prepared by the nice young man who came to get me."

"You don't seem...unhappy."

"Why should I be?" She looked at me, her expression kind. "Believe it or not, Jacob, not everyone was happy to see you go."

She knitted my lip with an instrument that fit over her fingertips, numbing me as it went along. I tried to watch what she was doing, but her fingers flashed too fast and too close for me to see. It itched.

"You know," she said, "before we had the micro-sutures, a gash like this might have left a scar. You know what we use to get rid of scars?"

"Lasers?"

She grinned at my sarcastic tone and her own cleverness.

"Now," she said, as she slipped the pads off her fingers, "try not to get yourself in another fight anytime soon."

I offered a wry smile. "That's the plan."

I had just finished changing my clothes when a steward came to summon me to the emperor. "That didn't take long," I commented dryly. I apologized to my friends and asked Jonathan to take them to see something interesting.

I went to Pete's office and was shown right in. I found what I expected: Pete at his desk and Duke Blaine standing before him. Blaine's nose was set in a brace. It occurred to me that Dr. Henriksen, who saw the upper nobility as well, had been tending to me, so Blaine would have been forced to settle for someone else. I hoped he knew that.

Just the sight of Blaine raised my ire again. I strolled over to take a place beside him, inclining my head at Pete.

"I hadn't expected to see you again so soon," I said.

Pete betrayed no reaction to my flippant manner. Blaine raised his eyebrows, looking to Pete, no doubt waiting for the reprimand for my overly casual manner with the emperor. It didn't come.

"Duke Blaine tells me there was an incident this morning," Pete said.

I shrugged. "Incident? I wouldn't say that. A misunderstanding."

Blaine glared at me.

"Duke Blaine's nose is broken, Jake. I think that's a bit more than a misunderstanding." Blaine looked shocked that Pete had addressed me by name.

"True."

Pete gave me an exasperated look. "Why don't you tell me what happened?"

"Why? Didn't he tell you?"

"Yes, but I'd like to hear your version."

"Oh, I'm sure Blaine did fine, and I'm no storyteller. What did he say?"

Pete held my eyes for a long moment before turning to Blaine, waiting for him to recount his story. Blaine was clearly flabbergasted at the way this was playing out.

"Well," he said, "as I said before, Excellence, I saw this criminal in the palace and I was concerned for your safety. I sent for the guard to apprehend him, and Mr. Dawes struck me."

Pete turned to me. Blaine, of course, did not.

"Bullshit," I said. "Complete and utter bullshit."

I could see Pete was suppressing a smile. "It would be helpful if you would elaborate on that."

"We had words, that's all. He did send for the guard, but I said something he didn't like and he punched me. I only hit him in self-defense."

"And what was it you said?"

I could feel my face heating. "Oh, nothing important."

Pete gave me a warning look. "Humor me."

"Well, he said something about trying to get in good with you, and I might have asked if he was talking about sexual positions..."

Now Pete glared at me. He held my gaze for a long, uncomfortable moment. He turned to Blaine. "It's true that you hit him first?"

"Yes, Excellence," he answered. "I do remember that now."

"Well, Jake obviously provoked you, but it seems you decided to handle the matter yourself. That you didn't win the altercation isn't my concern. You both behaved badly, but it was between the two of you. Unless you're asking me to punish you both."

"No, Your Excellence, I didn't mean to trouble you with something trivial. I was only concerned for your safety and your reputation. I didn't want to take the risk of assuming you were aware of Mr. Dawes's presence. I can see you are, and I apologize for wasting your time."

"Thank you for your concern, Duke Blaine. Your loyalty is appreciated." Hearing his dismissal, Blaine bowed and left.

I smirked at his retreating back, but the smile melted away when I turned to face Pete again. He was not smiling.

"I'm sorry?"

His expression didn't change.

"I am, really, I'm sorry. I shouldn't have said that, I know."

"How could you do that? I mean, really, Jake, there are a million different ways you could have insulted him. *That* was appalling. I don't appreciate it at all. At all, Jake."

"I know. It was stupid. I'm sorry. Truly. Blaine brings out the worst in me."

"You can't always use Blaine as an excuse. And aren't you even the slightest bit motivated to be cautious, coming back here?"

"I know, I know. I don't know how many more ways to say I'm sorry, though. I can't take it back. But I swear I'll be on my very best behavior from now on."

He still didn't look appeased.

I gave him a sly grin and approached him, coming around the desk and pulling his chair around so that he was facing me.

"Well, come to think of it, there's more than one way to apologize." I slid down onto his lap, one knee on each side of him.

He was trying not to smile. "You can't buy your way out of trouble, Jake."

"I'm not trying to buy my way out of trouble. I just want to make it up to you." I kissed him until we had to come up for air.

"You know it's a crime to try to bribe the emperor."

"Have I asked you for anything?" I kissed him again. This time I let my hands wander.

Finally he pulled away, grinning at me. "You're incorrigible."

"I know," I chuckled. "I think you only put up with me because I'm good at that."

"Nonsense," he said. "I love you."

"I know that, too," I said, laying my hand against his face. He nuzzled his cheek into my palm.

"By the way," Pete said, "you'll be happy to know that your pardon has been recorded. I'll announce it unofficially tonight at dinner. All the official notifications will go out tomorrow. And the same for your patent of nobility."

"My *what*?"

"Patent of nobility. You know what that is, don't you?"

"Of course I know what that is," I said, getting up. "But why? I don't want that. I didn't ask you to do that. Are you saying I'm not good enough the way I am?"

"Calm down, Jake," he said, standing. "It's more a technicality than anything else. And, frankly, it makes it easier for me to accomplish all this."

"That makes no sense."

"Class matters. You know that. And it provides its own protections. The people who will be the least happy to see you again will also be the ones mollified once you up-class or outrank them. Besides, you could use the practice. Once we're married you won't just be nobility, you'll be royalty."

That threw me for a loop. "Royalty?"

"Of course, what did you expect?"

"I don't know. I hadn't thought about it." I groaned. "Ugh, Pete, what are you doing to me?"

Taking my face in his hands he kissed me. "Deep breaths, Jake, you'll be all right," he said, a twinkle in his eye. Then he lost control and laughed. "Do you realize how many people would kill for a chance to be the most minor noble? You're amazing, Jake, really you are."

I gave him a wry look. "Yeah, yeah. Once again, we're both reminded of how I don't belong here."

"No. You do belong here. You belong with me."

I pulled him close. "You're right," I said against his ear. "You're right, this is where I belong."

That evening, when I returned to our rooms to dress for dinner, Pete was already there. It was then that I realized that Jonathan was Pete's head servant now. I pulled Jonathan aside and asked in a whisper, "Where's Davin?"

Jonathan gave me a long look. "Davin has been gone a year and a half now."

Davin had been Pete's head servant since before I met him. He wasn't much older than we were and before me, he had been the closest thing Pete had to a friend.

"Gone? Where?"

Jonathan looked reluctant to talk about it. He sighed. "Once you were gone, the emperor began to show a decided preference for me over Davin. We tried to work it out between us, I kept insisting that it would only be temporary, but when it persisted, he retired. He lives in Imperial City now. I see him from time to time, but I don't go often. He's bitter."

Pete never said anything about Davin's absence, or the fact that some young man I'd never met before was acting as my personal servant. I decided not to broach the subject just yet, but I wasn't going to drop it either.

As we made our way to the pre-dinner lounge, Pete took my hand and held it as we walked along.

"You're really going to do this?" I asked, looking down at our clasped hands and then around us at the few people still in the hall.

He shrugged. "Do you mind?"

"No, of course not. I'm just surprised."

"You weren't the least bit formal yourself this morning when you and Blaine were in my office."

I couldn't help grinning. "Well, that's because I was trying to piss him off. But this is good. I like this."

Pete chuckled. "I knew you were just goading him. I almost said something. But he's been such an ass that I let you do it."

We entered the lounge and the first face I saw was Aliana's. She met us halfway into the room and, taking my face in her hands, she kissed me on each cheek.

"Jacob Dawes," she said, "I am very angry with you."

"Forgive me, Your Grace, if I've offended you. I would never want to do that."

"I think you have been here all day, and you did not come to see me."

"I apologize, Your Grace. My status here today was complicated. I didn't think it was appropriate to pay my respects just yet."

She frowned. "Paying respects? Is this what you call saying hello to a friend after years apart? And what is this you call me?"

I smiled. "I'm sorry, Aliana, I'm out of practice, and honestly, a bit discombobulated."

She laughed. "You will come and see me tomorrow, yes? And you will bring your friends from the IIC with you?"

"I'd be very happy to."

She leaned closer now and whispered, "I hear rumors, Jacob, but Peter tells me nothing. They are true?"

"I don't know what you're talking about," I said with feigned innocence.

"You are just as bad as he is. I am hurt, Jacob. Peter does not surprise me, but how can you do this to me?"

"Maybe he's not as afraid of you as I am," I said. She laughed. "But..." I continued in a dramatic whisper and smiled. She beamed at me and squeezed my arm.

Before anyone else had a chance to approach me, which I'm sure was deliberate on Pete's part, he led us into the dining room.

Other than having the eyes of the room on me, dinner was oddly normal. Pete and I talked, including others at times just as if there had been no treason, no Resettlement, no absence at all. No one said a word about any of what had passed, not even asking Pete about his visit to the IIC the day before.

Before the dessert course was served, Lord Sifer stood and commanded the room's attention. When he had it, Pete stood and Lord Sifer yielded the floor. The room was unnaturally quiet, even for an announcement by the emperor.

"No doubt you've all noticed that Jacob Dawes is once again at my side," he began. "As you must have guessed, this means that he has been granted a full pardon. His past crimes are forgiven and to be forgotten. He has my full trust that the Empire as a whole, and I personally, can count on him to be a staunch defender of the Empire and an exemplary citizen.

"In addition to this, today I have granted him the duchy of Mexico."

The silence in the room exploded into a collective gasp that reminded me to breathe.

"There is no one who appreciates something more than one who has lost it. Having regained his good standing in the Empire, I have no doubt that Duke Jacob will be diligent in executing his duties and fiercely loyal to both his people and to all of the Empire. I'm sure you will all want to find an opportunity to welcome and congratulate Duke Jacob in the days to come."

He gestured for me to stand and the diners produced the expected applause. It sounded wan and grudging to me.

"*Duke?*" I demanded. I wasn't ready to even acknowledge the other part yet. "You didn't tell me that."

He was grinning. "You didn't ask."

I made an exasperated noise. "Really Pete, you might have prepared me."

"I told you I'd granted you a title of nobility. If they're all disagreeable to you, does the specific one really matter?"

"Less is more," I grumbled, but he just grinned at me and turned back to the room.

"But the real news of the evening," he continued, "certainly the most important to me, is that yesterday I asked Jacob to marry me and he graciously agreed."

He turned to me and his look held so much emotion a lump formed in my throat.

The applause was much more genuine. I suppose it was for Pete and his happiness rather than his specific choice.

A swarm of servants flooded the room distributing glasses of champagne. Aliana stood and toasted us. We ate delicate desserts, little works of art crafted in sugar.

Pete stood again. "Things such as engagement celebrations take time to arrange. But I'm not willing to wait so long when I'm in such a mood to celebrate. So tonight, at the conclusion of dinner, we'll have an impromptu ball." The applause was enthusiastic.

The palace loved a ball, even one they weren't given an opportunity to prepare ostentatiously for. I'd never been one for balls. A long party where I was unwelcome wasn't exactly my idea of fun. Even when I was promoted from being an insulting degradation of their lofty personages to unimportant background noise, I avoided the functions as often as possible. But I wouldn't be allowed to get out of this one.

The orchestra began to play the first waltz. Pete always led the first dance with Aliana. So when he came over to me I didn't understand what he was doing.

"You want us to dance together?" I sputtered, when he explained.

"Of course."

"Pete, we've never danced together before. I barely know how to dance at all. How are we supposed to work that out when we're both used to leading?"

"I don't always lead when I dance with other men. I know how to follow."

"Pete I'm no good at this. I can't do it in front of all these people. You're crazy."

"I know," he grinned, "but we're celebrating our engagement and that means we're going to dance together," he concluded in his not-to-be-dissuaded voice.

So we danced. It went better than I expected. I didn't fall on my face. I had to admit it was nice, dancing together.

The dance ended and we parted to make our separate ways to the next partner. I was angling toward Kirti, since Pete was already claiming Aliana, when Duchess Xian intercepted me.

Duchess Xian held a distinction no other could claim. In spite of having been at the palace and in Pete's inner circle through the entirety of my previous residence there, I was certain she had never spoken to me at all.

"Your Grace," she greeted me.

"Duchess," I replied in return. I knew I was supposed to ask her to call me by name, the use of titles simply a necessary first step that would be dispensed with among equals. I didn't. She waited but when I said nothing more, she moved on without any noticeable loss of poise.

"Next to the emperor you are doubtless the most sought after dance partner this evening, and a lady must seize an opportunity when she sees it, lest she lose out. In other words, Your Grace, I'm not going to wait, as I should, for you to ask me to dance. I have come to claim you."

I knew exactly what I wanted to say to her. And I knew that I couldn't. Well, that I shouldn't. I looked for Pete, hoping that he would see and rescue me but he was already leading Aliana to the floor. Short of faking an injury or an illness, there was no way for me to extricate myself without creating problems that I didn't need and that Pete wouldn't be happy about. I only nodded in a slight bow of acceptance and led her to the floor.

She was an elegant dancer. Her manners were perfect, her conversation smooth and flowing. Her voice and inflection, even her laugh were expertly crafted. She was a professional. She'd spent her whole life training in the art of social politics. I had to acknowledge grudging admiration for her skill even as it galled me.

As we moved around the floor I could already discern the vultures circling. All of the most important women in the room, and the men who were so inclined, were maneuvering themselves so as to have the best opportunity to pounce on me next. I looked around for Kirti but couldn't see her. When the song wound to its end I excused myself from Duchess Xian as quickly as could be argued to be polite and approached the first likely young lady.

She was hovering near two of the least impressive looking men in the room, but from the way she was positioned and her complete lack of participation in the conversation, she was essentially alone. She stood by Lord Edwards, a very minor noble from Faln. I only knew him because I'd had a few encounters with him in his official capacity in procurement. From the resemblance I assumed she was a relative, probably a daughter, and I didn't think I'd met her before. Though it was possible I just didn't remember her. She was unremarkable and forgettable in every way.

Lord Edwards was in animated conversation with another man I didn't know. He was turned with his back to the room but his conversation partner saw me and, with a jerk, straightened up and watched me approach. Lord Edwards turned to see what had made the other man react. He actually jumped a little when he saw me standing there waiting to talk to him.

"Your Grace!" he exclaimed.

"Lord Edwards," I greeted him. "Will you do me the honor of introducing me to this young lady? I'd like to ask her to dance."

He gaped at me, glancing at the girl, as if he was checking to see if she had changed since he'd last seen her. The young lady was watching me, wide-eyed, as white as a sheet.

"Your Grace, this is my daughter, Elizabeth."

"I'm pleased to meet you, Elizabeth. Would you do me the honor of dancing with me?"

She reddened from her collar to her hairline. For a moment she said nothing and then she dropped into a shaky bow and mouthed, "Yes, Your Grace."

It was obvious she had attempted to speak the words but no sound had come out. I took what I could get. I held out my hand to her and she placed hers in mine. She was trembling so much that I tucked her arm around mine so I would have a better hold on her in case she fainted.

Thankfully she didn't and we made our way into the crowd of dancers. She danced nicely, not the stumbling, nervous manner I'd expected. She said nothing at all, however, so I did my best to carry on light conversation. She did occasionally nod or mouth "Yes, Your Grace," but as for actual spoken words, there were none. That is, until I mentioned the subject of my current work.

"We're studying that in school," she whispered.

It was quiet but audible. Once she got started, she managed to relax just enough that the rest of the conversation was, if not stimulating, at least pleasant. She seemed sensible and bright. When the dance ended I found that I hadn't been watching for it, as I had with Duchess Xian.

I thanked her for the dance once I led her back to her father. She blushed as she bowed again.

I was too far away from any other desirable target to avoid the next two ladies who attempted to snap me up, but I told them that I had promised the next dance to Aliana. I hadn't, but from where I stood, she didn't appear to be in danger of taking to the floor with someone else and I hoped that I could catch her in time to claim her.

I did. She told me, once we were safely alone among the other spinning couples, that I'd looked desperate.

I told her how things were going so far and she laughed with me at the foolishness and snobbery of others. She helped me position myself so that I claimed Kirti for the next dance before anyone else intercepted me.

I hadn't been alone with Kirti since Pete had appeared at breakfast that morning and the wait hadn't helped me figure out what to say to her. But she saved me.

"He really loves you, doesn't he?" she asked.

"He seems to."

"Good," she said, and the matter of how she and I stood with each other seemed to be closed.

I made an effort to alternate every dance that evening with a partner of high rank followed by a partner of low rank. Though, privately, I thought the distinction was all in their heads—as everyone in the room who wasn't a servant belonged to one of the highest classes. They noticed the pattern before long. The most important among them began to look frustrated and insulted. Which was the point.

Later that night, when we were alone, Pete asked me about my unorthodox pattern of partners and I explained it all to him. He laughed, and after that night, he regularly chose dance partners of low rank, too. Of course, I liked it best when he danced with me.

39

It took me two days to work up the courage to speak to Pete about his grant.

"Why Mexico?" I said as we ate breakfast.

He looked up at me. "I'd think that would be obvious."

"I'd think it would have been nice for you to ask me what I thought of that. Pete, that's..."

He waited. But when I didn't continue he said. "I thought you'd like it. You're the one who would understand its poverty issues. It certainly seemed important to you two years ago."

"And what am I supposed to do about that? I'm a physicist, not a politician. We've all seen what happens when I get anywhere near political issues."

"It's just a symbolic position, Jake. The governor's still in place. You can ignore them if you really want."

I glared at him.

"See? It obviously matters to you what happens to them. Why not be a symbol of hope for them? You can speak up for them and maybe even help improve their lives. Clearly we're not doing it right without you. Just pay a visit, shake the governor's hand and smile at the pretty girls. It'll mean a lot to them. And then you can worry about the rest of it when you come back."

I bit my lip and looked down at my plate. "I'm not sure I can handle this. I think you're asking too much of me."

"And I think you're underestimating yourself."

So I went, and Kirti and Chuck and Dr. Okoro went with me.

We never went near Mexico City, much less Abenez. A fact that made me feel both guilty and lightheaded with relief.

But as our parade wound through the capital city of Puerto Vallarta, we came upon part of the crowd markedly different from the rest; their poverty made even more obvious by the glittering buildings of the financial district they stood in.

"I took the liberty," Jonathan said, "of making sure the unclass had access to the parade route. Though, as you can see, they were restricted to this one section."

The injustice of it burned in my gut.

But as I looked at them, it hit me like a punch in the face that I'd never cared about them at all. Everything I'd ever said or done in defense of the unclass was for myself, not them. They scared me too. It wasn't that I was a defender of my people, I was just too proud to be marginalized and prejudged. I hadn't been trying to help them. I'd been trying to fix them, to pretty up a shameful part of my past.

I closed my eyes tight against that condemning realization.

"Your Grace?" Jonathan said.

I glared at him, privately thankful he'd done one of the things guaranteed to distract me: call me that title. He knew I hated it and I'd asked him at least three times not to use it.

He stared me down. I dropped my eyes first.

"I think I'm an asshole," I said.

"It's not an incurable condition."

That got a huff of amusement out of me.

"We need to do something about it, Jonathan."

"We will."

My friends stayed at the palace through the full week of celebration of the engagement. Every night's dinner was a feast, with the chefs attempting to outdo their spectacular creations of the night before. Each night there was a ball, more grand and splendid than the last. There was something going on at all times throughout the whole of the palace. Plays and exhibitions and concerts were in constant rotation.

I proposed a soccer game between the best of the amateur players at the palace, with Pete and me the captains of the opposing teams. The players voted for their all-stars and Pete and I divided them up—with plenty of good-natured bickering—into two teams. Out of consideration for myself and also the others playing with us, I positioned myself opposite Pete. Everyone loved that.

It was a good game and my team won. Pete challenged me to the best two of three. His team won the next two games. So I challenged him to the best three of five. After two more, hard-fought games, my team won our third by one goal. The crowd was wild with excitement.

We returned to our rooms, hot, sweaty, and high on adrenaline and goodwill.

We were in the bathroom stripping for the shower. "You know, you may be better at this politics thing than you think you are," Pete said.

"Huh?"

"The games, that was a brilliant strategy. I don't think you could have done anything that would have worked better to sway public opinion in your favor."

"That's not why I did it."

He grinned. "I know. That's why it worked so well. Something so basic and universal as sports and competition is an equalizer of sorts. You saw them today, screaming and cheering, for your team, for you. They forgot who you were or weren't. And the fact that your team won? All those who were rooting for your team rode out of there on a wave of high spirits and victory and they know that you were part of what gave that to them. This is going to change things, you'll see."

"Are you saying you let us win?"

"Of course not. Imagine how excited they'd have been if I'd beaten you." He grinned.

"You couldn't beat me if your life depended on it," I said, stepping into the shower.

"Oh yeah?" he said, following me in and backing me against the wall. "We'll see about that, Mr. Dawes."

He was right. There was a distinct change in the general treatment I received after that. People stopped me in the hallway to enthuse about the win. Servants, functionaries, and other palace employees and residents would wave as I passed in the hallway. It was odd and gratifying. It had always galled to be judged for something I had no control over; the approval I found now at least had a basis in something I had achieved myself.

There was a parade midweek, Pete and I rode in all pomp and circumstance through Imperial City; which I hated.

Not long into the procession, as I was surveying the crowd, I was stopped by the face of one man. There was nothing particularly strange about the man himself, only his manner. Lost among a sea of people loud in their happiness, his face was very serious, his gaze, when locked with mine, intense, almost grieving.

There was nothing about him that was overtly frightening, he didn't strike me as some mad discontent who would assassinate the emperor or his intended for his own twisted ends. And yet my gut knotted. Something about him was familiar in a way that made my palms sweat. I couldn't place him, though. I couldn't even decide from which section of my life I imagined he belonged to. My first thought, from the way he made me feel, was Dead End. But I had vivid memories of my time there and I knew that wasn't why he bothered me. If he'd been a servant, a functionary, a visitor, or anything like at either the IIC or the palace, I couldn't conjure the memory. I wondered if he was from Abenez, but the idea was far-fetched, and anyway, I couldn't picture who he would have been there, either.

It was odd and unsettling, but my glimpse of him was brief and then he was gone. I couldn't find any part of my past to connect him to, so I dismissed him as one of those people who simply looks familiar for no good reason and I forgot him.

The last night of the week was the culmination of all the celebration. There was a ceremony planned for that night, an official pledging of our intention to marry. It was a long standing tradition born of the fact that most Imperial marriages were political alliances; a pledging of faith and intentions that was necessary for the furtherance of political ends, especially when the marriage, for any number of reasons, might be a long time off.

Though I tried to get out of it, the ceremony was simple and painless. Oh, I was stuffed into ostentatious, uncomfortable clothes; Pete wore the official Imperial crown, I was forced into more jewelry than I was happy about. But in the end I only had to stand before the assembled and promise to marry Pete. That promise was easy to give.

The preparations for the emperor's wedding didn't take very long, in spite of the fact that such weddings are always, without a doubt, the most ornate, ostentatious, involved, and expensive. There were armies of servants and administrators who saw to arranging every detail. I had little to do with any of it. Beyond showing up where I was told I was needed and sometimes providing an opinion when it was asked of me, the preparations intruded little into my life.

But now I was someone of importance. As a duke I had responsibilities, ceremonial and unimportant to my mind, but Pete insisted that I take them seriously. As Prince Consort I would have even more. Pete felt the transition would be easier if I worked into it gradually. I studied the formalities, the traditions, the unwritten rules of society at that level, and the expectations and responsibilities. I had very little time for the lab in the months before the wedding.

One project I took upon myself, though, was restoring Davin to his position. I hated for Pete to lose what had been a relationship much like I'd had with Jonathan because of what I'd done. And also, I wanted Jonathan back.

I consulted Jonathan first. He was the emperor's head servant now, and there was no more prestigious posting for any servant in the Empire. An assignment to the Prince Consort was the next best thing, but it was still a demotion.

I was nervous. I was afraid Jonathan would feel obligated to agree with me even if he didn't want to. He'd always been too humble in my opinion; I wouldn't put it past him to simply accept my suggestion as an order in spite of his own feelings on the matter.

So I spent an excessive amount of time explaining to him what I wanted to do and why, and telling him over and over again it was up to him, that if he asked me not to pursue this, I wouldn't. "Your Grace," he said, "I do understand how these things work. And, you'll forgive me, but you don't seem to remember that it was my idea for Davin to be persuaded back into his position."

I blinked. Now that I thought about it, maybe he had been the one to bring it up.

"Oh, well, you may be right," I said. "You know, you work so hard at fading into the background that you make me think the things I hear you say were my own thoughts. You should quit doing that."

He gave me a long, bland look. "Yes, I'm sure I'm the reason you imagine things."

I laughed. "You're glad to have me back, aren't you, Jonathan?"

His expression suddenly became serious. "Things are rarely so simple, Your Grace."

I stared at him, stunned. But then he gave me an apologetic smile.

"But I am glad you're back."

The next step was to talk to Pete. When I told him all that I knew from Jonathan, he was appalled. It took no persuasion. The next day he visited Davin at his apartment in Imperial City and asked him to come back. Davin did. I congratulated myself on a good deed done, and on having Jonathan for myself again.

Several weeks later, we lay together one night, sweaty and

spent, his head on my chest. There was no moon and it was much darker than usual. His arm had fallen over my neck, a little too close, a little too heavy.

For a moment I felt, heard, *smelled* Kafe as if I was in that cell again, and every muscle in my body tensed.

"Mmmm?" Pete's half-asleep question shattered the memory. I came back to the present in the shaky, cold aftermath of adrenaline. He lifted his head when I didn't answer. "You OK?"

"Yeah," I said, my voice shaking. I bit down hard on my tongue and managed to steady myself. "Just a dream."

He accepted without question and laid his head back on my chest. Under the guise of finding a more comfortable position, I moved his arm well away from my neck. He shifted with me.

I lay there, my heart racing. "Pete, you know the Resettlement camp I went to?"

He didn't answer for a moment and when he did his voice was thick with sleep. "No, actually," he said, stirring as if he was trying to wake up enough for a conversation. His voice cleared. "I don't know. I wouldn't let myself find out where you were. I was afraid I'd... No. I don't know. Why? What about it?"

I fought an overwhelming urge to cry, and I wasn't even sure why. "Nothing. Just wondering."

He was quiet for several minutes but I could tell from his breathing and the tension in his body that he wasn't sleeping. Finally, as if he didn't want to know but couldn't help asking, he said, "Was it bad?"

"No. No, it wasn't. That's why I wondered."

I felt the sigh through his whole body as he relaxed atop me again. "You don't know how glad I am to hear that. I was afraid... Anyway, I'm so glad. I worried about it a lot."

I kissed his cheek and pulled him closer. "I'm sorry I woke you. Go back to sleep. I love you."

"You didn't wake me," he protested, even as he was drifting off again.

It was several hours later before exhaustion dragged me into sleep.

Time flew by until the day of our wedding arrived; less than six months after Pete had proposed.

It was a colorful, overwhelming, elaborate affair. The ceremony was long and involved. And there was the necessity of a portion to be dedicated to installing me as a prince of the Empire, a member of the Imperial family, and for me to take the required vows and make the necessary promises required of those positions.

But, in the midst of all of it, when everything was said and done, all that really mattered was that I pledged my life to the man I loved. He put a ring on my finger and I did the same for him. I made the promises and took the vows that were the real reason I stood there. And at the end, he was mine and I was his. Forever.

The feast that followed outshone all others, which was a feat indeed. When we were announced upon entering the room, I was announced as Jacob Dawes-Killearn as had been decided. But I didn't even notice because Pete was announced first. As Rikhart James Talved Peter Evan Dawes-Killearn. I gaped at him.

"You didn't tell me you were going to take my name."

"You took mine," he replied.

"Well, yes, but...can you even do that?"

"It's already done."

It took me quite a while to recover from the shock of that, though I was enormously pleased. It was a while longer before I became convinced it was really going to happen. And there were those who tried to prevent it, tried to find some rule or precedent. They didn't find what they needed. He became Dawes-Killearn, and so he stayed.

At the dinner there were gifts and well wishes, and toasts from Kirti and Aliana.

When that was done, I stood. There'd been no plan for me to offer a toast but in the moment it just happened. Pete looked at me but didn't say anything.

"I have something I would like to toast to. My husband. You know him as a good emperor and a good man. But you can't know what a truly great man he is, and how much he deserves from life in the way of happiness and love. It wasn't very smart of him to decide to find that in me," I grinned at him, "but I'm terribly grateful that he did. And as some small repayment of all that he has given me, I pledge today to spend the rest of my life attempting to be worthy of him."

Pete stood and took my hand. "Why did you say that?" he asked, tenderness in his voice.

"Because it's true."

"You're crazy," he replied. "But I love you that way."

I sat back down, but Pete did not. Instead he too raised his glass to signal an impending toast.

"I shouldn't have married Jake." My heart stopped. "At least, that's what many, probably most of you have thought at some point. I have been told that many times by advisors and those who no doubt had good intentions. But you're all wrong.

"Jake makes me a better man and thus a better emperor. He's a good person, in spite of his flaws—and we all have flaws. He's one of the best men I've ever known. I love him more than I can possibly express." He looked at me now. "Thank you."

I stood and slid my hand into his. He interlaced his fingers with mine, holding my gaze. There were tears in his eyes, but he laughed.

"Did I scare you?"

"A little," I admitted.

He grinned. "You should have known better."

"You're right."

fg41

At the wedding ball, I stayed close to my husband, basking in what he was, and what we were now. I wanted to be this happy for the rest of my life.

As I stood by Pete's side, while he talked with people I cared nothing about, I saw Duke Blaine and, in a sudden rush of charitable feeling in the aftermath of my wedding, I approached him. He bowed but it was stiff, almost as if it was painful.

I held out my hand. "Your Grace, we've been at odds from the very first, and I know I've done my part to make it so. Perhaps we can set aside past offenses and have a more amicable relationship in the future?"

He looked at my hand before he met my eye again. "No, Your Highness," he said. "I don't think we can."

I lowered my hand, letting the slow wash of anger calm before I said, "I'm sorry to hear that. It seems to me, though, that you're only making your life unnecessarily difficult, since you can't get rid of me again."

"You think not?"

When my voice came it was quiet and hard. "I think we've had this conversation before, Duke Blaine. Do you really mean to threaten me again?"

"Of course not, Your Highness. Forgive me a clumsy choice of words." But he was holding my gaze and the flash in his eyes and the slight curl of his lip gave the lie to that. "Congratulations on your marriage." He bowed again and started to leave but stopped and turned back to me.

"I nearly forgot," he said. "I thought you might like to know I've had word that your former lover is doing as well as can be expected in her circumstances."

"My former lover?" I asked, baffled. I turned, looking for Kirti.

"I believe you knew her as Kafe."

My head snapped back around as if of its own accord. "What did you say?"

"I'm sorry, does the news not please you? It seems I've misspoken again. I may have had more champagne than is advisable. I should excuse myself." He bowed. "Your Highness," he said before he walked away.

I was shaking, suddenly cold and sick.

I let him go. I probably shouldn't have. I probably should have done something, said something. Instead, I looked across the room and saw my husband talking to a small group of nobles, resplendent in his wedding suit, his face flushed with happiness. I clenched my fists, closed my eyes, and willed myself to stop trembling, forced my breathing to return to normal. When I opened my eyes again Pete was just turning his head, looking for me, the smile he'd worn all day still brightening his face.

I couldn't ruin this day for him.

He met my eye. His smile didn't exactly change, but something in the quality of it, the intimacy in his eyes, transformed it into something entirely for me. I crossed the room to him and he took my hand. When the others had excused themselves he turned to me.

"I'm happy, Jake," he said, smiling as if he couldn't possibly do anything else.

"I know," I said, squeezing his hand, swallowing Blaine's words and the memories he had dredged up. "I'm glad."

"I feel like I could fly," he said, his voice lower, but excited. "I feel like I could do anything. *We* could do anything."

"We can," I said, smiling back at him. "We will. I've got you now, and I won't let anything happen to you," I said.

A brief, puzzled frown creased his brow for a moment, and I

realized it was a bit of an odd answer to what he was saying. But Blaine's words still gripped my stomach.

"I just mean we're together now," I said, "and everything's going to be great."

He hugged me. "Yes, it will."

I hugged him back, hard; holding on to him maybe a bit longer, with something more than he knew, in the way I clung to him. "Everything's going to be great."

www.ingramcontent.com/pod-product-compliance
Lightning Source LLC
Chambersburg PA
CBHW030344020726
47493CB00003B/683